D1501658

ROUTE
1

ROUTE

AGNES

1

SANFORD

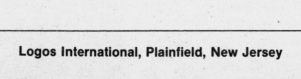

Logos International, Plainfield, New Jersey

Chapter One

The mountains were dark even in the morning of this pre-Easter day, their rocky crags, usually high-shining in the gentle sun of southern California, covered with a solid mass of sullen clouds.

Rain will come, thought Gideon Bruce, as he parked behind the church in the place reserved for the rector, and entered the building. Rain for Easter! He pictured his festal choir, lined up outside the church door, drenched with sudden showers. The hills would rejoice and be glad, and all the desert plants—stiff grass, wild lupine, and golden poppies—would stir into new life. Gideon knew that he, also, should rejoice in the healing of long-withered vegetation, but for reasons he did not understand, there was a shadow upon his heart.

"Father Bruce?" The sharp sting of Angela Pritchard's voice forced its way into his brooding mind before he could reach his office. "Don't you think the altar is too untidy, too unrestrained? After all, at Easter there should be dignity, and all that asparagus fern, even touching the candlesticks—"

"But it's pretty," faltered Doris Panella, gazing pleadingly at the president of the altar guild as that grim female stood, arms akimbo, surveying the lilies and greenery on the Trinity Church altar.

"It's too much! Besides, it's not reverent—all that green stuff trailing over the white cloth. Don't you agree, Father Bruce?"

Gideon stood by the altar, shoulders hunched, knuckles whitening. He must not lose control!

There was a moment of silence. Then his nerves snapped. "You can take the damned things and put them on the *roof* for all I care!" He flung his arm toward the altar, and one of the silver vases crashed to the floor, its lilies lying disconsolately on their faces and water seeping into the crimson rug.

Gideon hardly remembered how he had escaped from that holy place, which had suddenly become intolerable. There were muttered apologies, much scrambling on the floor, and the lilies were rescued. The inappropriately named Angela stalked in from the sacristy with a cloth and wiped up the water, muttering between clenched teeth, "I'll do it," while, "Oh, dear," and "Never mind," issued from Doris, standing helplessly by.

Then somehow Gideon was at home, walking heavily up the rectory steps while his wife, Susan, waited anxious-eyed at the door.

"What happened?" she cried, and he knew that she already knew. "Angela says you ought to see a doctor!"

"I ought to see less of Angela, that's all." Gideon let his tall form sink into the sofa and closed his eyes, resting his head upon the cushions.

"You need a vacation," Susan said, patting his arm gently when he had finished his story, as one might soothe a child. She was strong and vital, yet motherly, with dark eyes and a wide, gentle mouth.

"Fat chance!" sighed Gideon, nonetheless feeling vaguely comforted as he glanced about the homey living room with its shabby, comfortable chairs and restful pictures—a path through autumn woods, a bit of quiet sea, mountains far away and dim. Beyond the living room was a small dining room, kitchen, and den, and the other wing comprised three bedrooms strung out in level California style. It was a pleasant house, with roses and lilies already blooming in front, and a comfortable backyard where bicycles and forgotten playthings reposed among trampled flower beds.

The rectory was not near the church, but on a side street which sloped toward the San Gabriel mountains, wild, rugged and at the moment draped in darkening clouds. From the kitchen window, Susan could look at the mountains beyond the small plants on the windowsill—carrot tops putting forth feathery leaves, an African violet far from home, and an avocado seed pinned to the top of a jar, wondering whether to live or die.

"Why can't you take some time off after Easter?" Susan persisted. "We could drive into the desert, and camp somewhere."

"I wish I could!" sighed Gideon, for the desert was to him a place of peace, "but I've got to go to the bishop's Quiet Day."

"Quiet Day!" said Susan, tightening her lips. "That means that the bishop will talk all day, and the rest of you will try to stay awake."

"Very likely," said Gideon grimly.

3

The clouds lifted from the mountains for Easter, and the choir was not drenched. Communion was served from an altar innocent of asparagus fern, and the lilies serenely lifted their shining heads. If there was no outburst of holy joy, at least neither was there discernible gloom on the people's faces as they came to partake of the Lord's Supper and returned complacently to their pews.

Perhaps after all, thought Gideon, the two altar guild ladies had not relayed the disgraceful story of the rector's inexplicable burst of anger on the very eve of the holy day. Or perhaps they had told, and were telling, and he would hear of it sooner or later.

As Gideon drove home the Tuesday after Easter from the bishop's retreat, replete with other men's smoke and wise words, he was thinking about this, but did not really care. If he were not a minister, he reflected, possibly his own son Bob would not have found life so hard that he ran away from it. A kid in a jalopy, looking a bit like Bob as he roared by, started Gideon on this train of thought. Bob, their firstborn, such an unspeakable joy to Gideon and Susan during all the early years! Gideon's mind flooded with pictures: Bob riding his tricycle, clamoring for a story at bedtime, coming home from camp, serving at the altar . . . Then the kaleidoscope of happy pictures began to turn dark in Gideon's mind as he rolled along the freeway, his mind on his family more than on the car.

What had gone wrong? Where did Bob's secretiveness, sullenness begin? He had wanted to learn to drive, and Gideon would not teach him until he was of proper age. Even on vacation trips off the road, Gideon would not venture to teach him. Vividly he now remembered times he had refused. Young men began wearing long hair. Bob's high school friends grew sideburns, and hair hanging over their collars. Bob refused to go to the barber, and in the end, even to comb his tousled locks. Gideon shuddered, remembering the ultimatum he had issued one Sunday morning to his teenage son: "Comb your hair, and put on clean clothes, or don't come to church!" Bob did not come. Never again did he come.

After that, various issues came between them, blotting out the old closeness, as though it had never been. Who would mow the lawn, take out the trash, stay with the younger children, Josie and David, on the few occasions when Gideon and Susan wanted to go out together? Who, if not Bob? But Bob was always roaring about the countryside in some friend's noisy car, and could seldom be persuaded to take any share of family responsibility. There were harsh words between son and father about friends, habits, school grades. Once when Gideon was giving Bob a lecture, the boy seemed to look right through him with an expression of disdain, as though he were looking not at a loving, wise father but at a—a hypocrite. Bob had used that word once—hypocrite!—just before he ran away.

Traffic on the freeway was light, needing little of Gideon's attention, and he began to wonder uneasily about Josie, now fifteen. Would she also leave home, in rebellion, against—against what? "No, she won't," Susan had said firmly, once when they talked about it before going to sleep. "I'm sure she won't."

But day after day, Josie came home, giggling outside the door with some boy or other, and talking of things that in Gideon's day were not discussed. More and more, Gideon's fears veered away from Bob and settled upon Josie, his little daughter, now so frighteningly grown up.

Gideon drove through the pass and into the coastal valley, where the air lost its desert clearness and grew thick with the mixture of fog and city fumes. The highway wound past an area of wild land, low hills covered with rocks and cactus. The smog increased, and depression settled more heavily upon Gideon as he swept around the hills on the fast road to Pasadena.

The swift nightmare of his outrageous behavior in church the day before Easter flickered into his mind and out again. Why did I ever go into the ministry? he asked himself. With a slight twist to one corner of his firm, well-shaped lips, he thought, and said aloud, "Figured it would be becoming to me, maybe—vestments and all that." But Gideon knew that it was not vanity that led him to seminary, even though he was aware of his own handsome features and penetrating blue eyes, deep-set beneath shaggy gold-brown eyebrows. Even as a boy, he had liked to play church with his younger brothers, setting them in unsteady rows while he draped his small form in a towel and shawl and solemnly stood before them, intoning out of any book at hand.

His was more than a desire to play minister, however. Gideon remembered uneasily the time when he was fourteen years old, and he seemed to see a strange light shining from the elm tree in his father's yard, and a voice said within him, "I want you for My work."

Such things did not really happen. He knew that after three years in seminary, and there had never been anything like it since. Besides, it was incumbent on him to set aside childish fancies and busy himself at making a better world by leading the church in the familiar avenues of social action. But now, after some years of his ministry, the world did not seem better. I should be named Ichabod, he thought bitterly. "The glory has departed."

6

Gideon's father was not a minister, but he was a lay reader in the small church near his ranch. His children were required to attend services there every Sunday. Gideon had muttered token objections to this discipline, but actually, at times, he rather enjoyed it. He ceased hearing the words of the service, and a dim sense of peace came into him, like a light that one could not quite see. As he helped his father water the stock, or cleaned out the sheds, he had thought about that not quite visible light, and wondered.

Raising a few uncooperative cattle and fewer stringy horses had not proved financially profitable. The elder Bruce had come from the east, and his background was scholastic, not earthy. He had attended his own father's elegant alma mater, solemn and beautiful in red brick and ivy, its wide corridors embellished with statues and its far-spreading grounds close-clipped as green velvet, but somehow those corridors became too circumscribed for him, and the ivy-covered walls too confining. On graduating, he had gone west and sought a bit of land that he could make his own.

The pull of tradition, however, was still strong within him. While his spirit rejoiced in the wide places and towering mountains of the west, his mind could not accommodate itself to the company of animals, and by the time Gideon himself had graduated from college, his father turned the ranch over to him and his brothers and went back to teaching.

Thus ruminating, Gideon glanced to his right across the lanes of traffic boiling along at the speed limit, and his eye caught some sort of chase beyond the freeway fence—a young girl running, apparently screaming, judging by the glimpse he had of her small, terrified face, and behind her a man, reaching out, almost catching her.

Somebody should do something! thought Gideon. What was she screaming? It must have been for help, but of course he could not hear her above the traffic. He swung his car over into the middle lane, without conscious plan except that someone should help, someone should stop this. But the right-hand lane was impenetrable as he flashed past the next exit, and Gideon had no way of slowing down or turning off.

Nobody was stopping, he thought. Nobody. But the people traveling in the slow lane could have seen much better than he, if there really was anything wrong. Perhaps it was some game that the man and child were playing on the grassy hillside. But no—he could not believe this. It was no game. Maybe it was the child's father, running to warn her of danger—a mad dog or bull—he had vaguely glimpsed a small cattle farm as the cars swept by. It must be something like that, he thought.

He found an opening and edged over into the slow outside lane. Should he park and put up the hood to indicate trouble? There was no hope of climbing the fence, and anyway he had gone more than a mile beyond the man and child now. Maybe the father had caught up with the girl and taken her safely home, or—anyway, there was nothing he could do.

"Don't be a fool," he muttered to himself, knowing his tendency to be just that. He had been a fool to leave his father's ranch and go to seminary, intending thus to save a world that obtusely refused to be saved. If he had stayed on the land, he might now be dividing it into building lots and becoming a millionaire instead of spending his time coping with domineering women who demanded that the altar

8

flowers be placed this way and that. And he stepped on the gas and moved back out into the fast lane.

Gideon winced inwardly as he imagined Reginald Crabtree, the church's senior warden, listening with gimlet eyes and lowering brows to Angela's report of a distraught rector hurling flower vases from the altar. That just might be the end of his ministry at Trinity Church, he thought, trying to forget the picture of the little girl running for her life—or was she? Right in view of the freeway, she couldn't have been! And what if he did wave down the next highway patrol car and tell his tale of possible violence while hundreds of other cars roared past? "They'd haul me in for stopping traffic and disturbing the peace," he muttered aloud, "and if Crabtree should hear of that—!"

Gideon's vestry did not approve of some of his ideas, which they termed "modern" and "un-churchly." The few black faces in the congregation disturbed them. The sessions promoted by Gideon's assistant perturbed them even more. Leslie Ainsworth, recently out of seminary, thought that the world could be saved by people coming together in groups for eyeball-to-eyeball sessions in which they stared into each other's optics and then poked into their souls. Gideon himself was a trifle uneasy about these groups, but he was even more uneasy about obstinate church people clinging to rituals crystallized two thousand years ago into forms devoid of meaning to today's young people.

"We must be open to innovation," he said aloud as he drove toward the darkening city, forcing himself to think about matters of program and policy in order to forget the little girl running in the field. If someone should have stopped, he argued, putting it in the past tense because whatever it was would have happened by now, it would have had to be someone in the outside lane. There I was, all the way in the center . . .

By the time Gideon reached home, the smog had thickened, and clouds hung low over the mountaintops. There stood Susan on the front steps, smiling with relief at seeing him home, but with something else behind the relief. This he knew without words or signs.

"How was the Quiet Day?" she asked.

"Oh, all right, all right," replied Gideon, who had totally forgotten the Quiet Day. "The bishop had some good ideas about uniting with another diocese—Nebraska, I think," he added, searching his memory for something that had been discussed. "And he wants to subdivide the Committee on Social Action, and—"

"What's wrong?" asked Susan, for she also knew many things without words.

"Well," he murmured, as he came to rest on the sofa and waited for a reviving cup of coffee, "I wonder whether Angela has talked to the senior warden about my—"

"Tantrum," said Susan, pulling down her mouth humorously and supplying the right word. "Angela is very understanding and forgiving," she added with her sharp gift of irony. "She said so. She thinks you should see a psychiatrist."

Gideon choked slightly over his coffee. "You know what would happen then," he said. "Crabtree would decide that a rector in therapy should not run a parish, and I'd be shipped off to some little mission while he put everything here back where it's been since the year one."

"Oh, now," said Susan, patting him briskly on the shoulder as she rose to look at a roast in the oven. "He doesn't have that much power; you know that."

Gideon did not know it at all, but before he pondered further on the matter his younger son bounced into the room. "Hi, Dad!" said David, pointing his popgun toward the window and squinting, to take aim.

"Don't do that!" exclaimed his father.

"Gee, Dad, I wasn't going to, not really. Say, Dad, can I go to Disneyland tomorrow with the kids? It's Easter vacation, and—"

"Were you in Sunday school this week—and church?" his father inquired sternly, changing the subject.

"Yeah, sure, but say, Dad—do I have to keep on going to Sunday school and hear all that stuff? I don't mind church so much, except it's kind of long, but Sunday school—!"

"What are they teaching you now?" Gideon had turned the church school over to his assistant, and had some doubts about the direction it might be taking.

"Oh, how to be good, and stuff like that," David said. "Last Sunday they said something about Jesus coming out of the grave, but nobody can believe that kind of thing, not nowadays," said the ten-year-old, world-weary.

Gideon's heart sank. "Can't *you* believe it?" he asked in low tones.

"Aw, come on, Dad, come on! Did you ever see anybody come out of a grave?"

"No, but—"

"Did you even see any lame guy get up and walk?"

Gideon shook his head.

"Okay then, I don't have to believe things like that. What's more, Mr. Ainsworth doesn't."

"How do you know?"

"I asked him, and he said what it really meant was that God is our friend, or some such junk."

11

Gideon's heart sank even further.

"No use trying to believe something you never saw in your life," propounded his youngest. Then, at Susan's firm suggestion from the kitchen, David went to wash for supper.

"Where's Josie?" asked Gideon, wandering to the kitchen door. It was lonely in the living room all by himself, and that scene he did not want to see floated up from his memory.

"Out somewhere with a boy," answered his wife. "She'll be along pretty soon."

"What boy?"

"He had a red beard and long hair. I think it's that Leroy," answered Susan, darting a quick glance at Gideon's face.

"Anybody who'd call a boy Leroy—" muttered Gideon. "Did you say she could go out with him?"

"She just went. They go off to a park or hamburger joint, and sort of hang around—I don't think there's any harm to it."

"Come suppertime, they ought—" began Gideon belligerently, but at that moment the front door banged and Josie erupted into the kitchen, her eyes dancing.

"Bye!" she called to someone slouching in a heap of a car by the front walk. Then she cried, "Hey, wait!" and darted down the three front steps and out to the car, to speak again of a forgotten matter of importance.

Gideon thought wistfully of the old days when a young man would bring a girl to her front door, but he said nothing.

"Josie's practically an adulteress, isn't she?" David remarked innocently as he pulled up to the table.

"David!" cried Susan, alarmed for a moment out of her usual calm.

"I mean, she's almost grown up, isn't she?"

"Adult," murmured Gideon with relief.

"That's what I said. Only she's a girl, so—"

"Adult is still the right word," said Gideon, while Susan, recovering rapidly, added in a choked voice that "adulteress" meant something different.

"What?" demanded David.

At that moment Josie again burst into the room and plunged into conversation. "Some of us kids want to go to Laguna Beach tomorrow, Mom," she said. "Could you pack us some lunch?"

"Who's going? And how many?" Susan asked.

"Oh, I don't know. Leroy's going to take us, and he'll probably pack the car full."

"What would you do there?" asked Gideon, for he knew that beach as a hippie haven.

"Oh, Dad, we'll have a swell time. The boys will go surfing, and we'll wade, and build a campfire, and sing, and a couple of the guys have guitars. We don't want to drive back after dark because—you know Leroy's car—so we'll just roll up in blankets and sleep on the beach, and watch the sun rise, and—"

"You will *not!*" Gideon exploded, glaring at her.

"Now Dad, don't be archaic," urged Josie. "We're not going to do *any*thing—just sleep, and—"

"Josie!" cried Gideon, flinging down his napkin and rising to his feet. "You are not going to drive to the beach in a car that might die at any moment, and spend the night with that—that—" Gideon paused for lack of an adequate word.

"What's the matter with Leroy?" demanded Josie, her eyes sparkling angrily. Those eyes were greenish-brown, and when Josie was very angry, as at this moment, they seemed to spark with green fire.

The telephone shrilled loudly from the living room. "Answer the phone," said Susan, "I'll handle this."

13

When Gideon returned to the dining room, Josie, apparently vanquished, rushed from the table and into her bedroom, whence issued lamentable sobs.

"She'll get over it," said Susan, comforting and practical as always. Then, seeing Gideon's grim expression, she inquired, "Mr. Crabtree?"

Gideon nodded. "He wants to meet me in my office in half an hour. There are certain matters he must talk over."

Susan nodded sympathetically. "Don't worry about Josie," she said, accompanying him to the front door. "I'll think up something fun for her to do tomorrow. Perhaps we could go to that new Magic Mountain."

But it was not Josie that Gideon was concerned about as he drove the five blocks to the church, parked, and walked around that solid Spanish-style building to the parish house, which was of no particular architecture but simply a parish house. In his mind was another girl, smaller and younger than Josie, running.

"You look a bit seedy," rumbled Mr. Crabtree, heavily sympathetic as he sat in the leather armchair opposite the rector's desk. Gideon always sat behind that desk, like a soldier behind a parapet.

"The festival seasons are always tiring," Gideon admitted, pushing back his tawny hair as though to brush away a load of weariness.

"I'm afraid we have a bit of trouble on our hands," said Mr. Crabtree. "The altar guild is threatening to resign—the whole lot of 'em."

Gideon choked down the exclamation, "Good!" which sprang unbidden to his lips. He had often dreamed of having an altar guild of young girls, teaching them the holy mysteries of cross and candles, bread and wine. However, he knew that actually, Angela would not think of resigning, and if she were forced to make good her threat and do so, bedlam would break loose in the congregation. "I'm sorry," he said, looking up at Mr. Crabtree from under heavy brows. "Once in a while the 'Church Mothers' just get to me."

A tiny flicker of what might be a smile touched Mr. Crabtree's mouth. "Just the same—bad idea," he said. "You must talk 'em out of resigning, or you'll have the whole parish on your neck."

"I'll try," murmured Gideon, visions of angry women floating through his mind, but he thought at the same time how trivial it all was! Move the candle here; move it there; iron that wrinkle out of the surplice; count the wafers—as though such things mattered! Here was the world about to blow up, and he must spend his time placating touchy women quarreling over asparagus fern. I'd like to ram it down their throats and choke 'em, he thought pettishly. Then he noticed the senior warden's eyes upon him.

"Under a bit of strain," said Mr. Crabtree, clearly indicating that the rector, not himself, was thus afflicted. "Need a vacation, maybe. Or—"

Gideon answered hastily. "No, I don't think a vacation would help. I still have a heavy burden on my mind—my boy Bob, you know."

"No word from him?"

"Not a word." Gideon leaned forward, elbows on the desk, and rested his chin in his hands.

"Ran away from school, didn't he?"

Gideon nodded. "He always hated it," he said.

"Always? I thought he was quite a scholar."

"Well, not quite always," admitted Gideon, picturing a sullen-faced youth banging into the house and shutting himself into his room. This was on the first day of being bussed to a school all the way across town.

"They don't want us there!" he had said, on being questioned at the supper table. "They hate it! They hate us! You can't even go to the john without a gang of friends with you. They'd nail you to the wall!"

Gideon had lectured Bob severely on equality, liberty, love, and other virtues, with the result that the boy had stopped talking to him.

"How are your grades?" he had asked Bob near the end of the term.

The boy had asked, "What grades?"

"We don't give grades," the teacher had replied when Gideon inquired at the school. "It is effort that counts, and interest, not the grade."

Mr. Crabtree, studying Gideon in silence, seemed to be reading his mind. "Nothing to work for," he said shortly. "Good students mustn't get better grades than poor students or they'll feel badly, the poor ones will. Everybody's got to pass, even if they can't read. My sister's been a teacher all her life, and a darn good one. She's resigning. Says you can't teach any more."

"Don't you believe in equality?" Gideon asked the senior warden.

"I do," said Reginald. "I believe in every child's equal right to exert his full brain power and receive the best possible education."

"Some day it may work out," said Gideon wistfully. "It's got to, but meantime, my boy—"

"Oh, I expect he'll come back," announced Mr. Crabtree. Then he tightened his lips; this was not the subject under discussion. "A few decisions to make at vestry meeting this

16

week," he said. "Whether you need a vacation, or . . . some kind of professional help—"

Gideon froze at the ominous words. "No!" he cried.

"And, if so," Mr. Crabtree went on, quickly, "whether Leslie Ainsworth can take your place for a while."

"Certainly he could keep things going for a week or so, if necessary," said Gideon, "but—"

"Not for long," declared Reginald Crabtree, his mouth drawn down as at an unpleasant taste. "A couple of weeks ago, I got up and went to early communion—needed a quiet service, you know—and Leslie hardly waited to get through the opening prayers before telling us about a 'marathon' he'd just held. Disgraceful affair! Began with cocktails. Then they all dived into the pool more or less drunk, I take it, and then they sat up all night and probed each others' souls, or some such darn foolishness."

"Some of them came out new creatures I was told," interrupted Gideon. "It shook them up and transformed them, as years of going to church and receiving communion hadn't. However," he added, noting the sour look on the senior warden's face, "it may have gone too far, and it won't happen again—not in that way," he said, reflecting that something must be done to awaken people, lest they go to sleep in their pews and remain there until judgment day.

"Between now and the vestry meeting," said Mr. Crabtree, cutting through Gideon's meditations, "let us consider whether you need, say, a month's vacation—or something else. It may be necessary to ask the bishop for an interim rector, because the parish can't be entrusted to the curate for any extended period."

"Some of the young people think Leslie's great," said Gideon, a slow flush rising in his face.

17

To this, Mr. Crabtree merely replied, "No doubt," and rose and left the room.

Chapter Two

Gideon was late to breakfast the next morning. He had not slept, thought Susan, glancing out the kitchen window to the high mountains towering in the distance. The clouds had lifted, and early morning sunlight outlined their deep folds and illumined their high, piercing crags. But the clouds had not lifted from Gideon. The night before, he had turned and twisted in the bed beside her, muttered jerkily in moments of uneasy sleep, and again wakened.

"What's the matter, Gideon?"

"Oh, I don't know. I get this way sometimes. I'll go and read awhile."

She had crept into the living room behind him, brought him warm milk as a gentle soporific, and left him glumly reading in the big shabby chair.

"Where's Dad?" asked David, banging into the kitchen and flopping down in the breakfast nook.

"He's still asleep," Susan lied. "Cheerios or cornflakes?"

"Well, I hope he is," said David. "I heard him charging around all night."

By this time Josie had wandered in, and after she had slumped down at the table, Susan asked from habit, "Have you got your homework done?" Then, remembering that it was vacation week, she added, "I mean, whatever reading you had to do over the holiday?"

"Heck, no!" replied Josie. "What's the use of reading and homework? Nobody does it!"

Susan put down the frying pan with a bang. "What do you mean, nobody does it? Don't you have to do homework?"

"We used to," said Josie. "Just juice, Mom. I don't want an egg this morning."

"Don't the teachers ask if you've done your lessons?" persisted Susan, who was the persistent type. As she asked, she remembered her own childhood in this great country, so different from the bleak and frozen plains of Russia whence her Jewish grandparents came, bringing her father as a small child, and landing with a huddle of other steerage passengers in New York. Once freed from immigration authorities, her grandfather set about earning his living in the new land, and from the time Susan could remember him, he had worked from dawn to dark in a little tailor shop making gentlemen's clothing, repairing ladies' coats, doing all odd jobs that came his way. Somewhere along the way, Susan's father learned that it was unwise to proclaim his heritage. He had a lonely boyhood in New York City, and eventually married a rosy-cheeked girl whose parents were also immigrants, but not from Russia.

Thus, when Susan, the daughter of this couple, grew up and married a Gentile, Gideon Bruce, she was separated about as completely as one could be from the ties of the past. Gideon vaguely knew that somewhere in her ancestry there was Semitic blood, but he never thought of her as Jewish, and indeed she was not. Susan was most completely American, small and dark, with great brown eyes and her mother's straight nose. She had seized on every advantage of this country and had studied with all her heart.

Now here was her daughter Josie, flopping down at the breakfast table, refusing to eat anything except orange juice, not caring about her school work, frittering away her time in what Susan considered complete idleness and foolishness.

"What are you going to do today, since you're not going to the beach?" Susan asked her pointedly.

"I don't know. Just kind of be with the kids, I guess. There's a movie that's not too bad. Most of them are lousy, but maybe we'll go."

"With that same boy with all the hair?"

"Oh, probably," said Josie, knowing perfectly well what boy her mother meant, "him and some of the other kids. I guess they won't go to the beach after all. We'll kind of mill around."

"I suppose so," answered Susan. What could she say? In her day, one came home from school, helped with the housework, studied, and possibly on Friday night asked permission to go to a movie. Life nowadays was so different that she had no idea how to cope with it. Even the Christian church to which she had allied herself seemed to have little to say to these young people.

Susan went faithfully to her husband's church, and had worked on the altar guild until more or less pushed aside by Angela Pritchard and Doris Panella. She washed dishes at church suppers, attended meetings of the women's guild, and even taught Sunday school, or church school as it was more often called. Vaguely she felt that there should be

21

something there, some source of strength and power, even some bubbling fountain of light and joy. But, she thought, sighing as she gathered up the breakfast dishes, nothing like that had appeared.

At last, after the children had eaten and departed, with a quick heartbeat of joy she heard Gideon's footsteps. He came in, formal in black clericals and white collar, for his day bristled with committee meetings and counseling appointments. How beautiful he was, thought Susan, and did not laugh at herself for thinking it. She loved the way his gold-brown hair waved away from his broad forehead. She loved his brilliant blue eyes, set beneath eyebrows too heavy perhaps for conventional good looks, but to Susan, adding a touch of distinction to his appearance. His nose was straight and rather long, his chin square, his mouth firm yet gentle. Yes, he was beautiful.

She had first seen him at a football weekend at Harvard. They met on a dance floor, and both of them had paused involuntarily, looking at each other, not just with the eyes of the body, but with the eyes of that inner wisdom that we call the soul. From then on, neither of them had any interest in anyone else.

Sometimes Susan wondered a little sadly whether Gideon perceived anything more in her than the long dark hair which he would not permit her to cut, and her great dark eyes. Certainly there was much in her past which he never could see.

"Another day," sighed Gideon, looking out at the faraway mountains as he pulled up to the breakfast table.

"It's going to be all right," said Susan, quite as if she knew the burdens on his heart. Indeed she did know, for the incident at the altar the day before Easter had again been recounted to her by Angela. "It's too bad," she had said at last, "but you know he was very tired."

"Yes, my dear," Angela said with unctuous sweetness, "yes, I quite understand. Sometimes a person is laboring under strain, and nobody guesses it until all of a sudden the nerves just crack— Now a rest will be good for him, perhaps even—a real vacation?"

"What did Mr. Crabtree say last night?" Susan asked her husband as she put his breakfast before him.

"Oh, just what you'd expect—probably I was overtired, and all that. He didn't quite say that maybe the church needed a new rector, but—"

Susan came around the breakfast table, coffeepot in hand, and patted Gideon on the shoulder. "Every minister wonders that after Easter," she said. "It's such a difficult time, I don't know why."

"I don't either," said Gideon. "One feels as if he were just holding the church and parish and all the people in his arms. Of course it's ridiculous; there is no reason to get so tied up." He did not tell Susan that it was not weariness that had caused him to explode and sweep the treasured decorations from the altar. The feeling that had suddenly erupted had been growing for months. He was living a role, putting on a kind of show.

What did it all mean? Did Jesus Christ really rise from the tomb? If so, what in heaven's name was He doing now?

But Gideon only smiled halfheartedly at his wife, and lifted his coffee cup in a hand that trembled a little. Susan sat down opposite him and glanced at the daily paper. "Oh dear!" she said.

"What's that?" asked Gideon, his throat tightening.

"Poor little girl," said Susan slowly, regretfully, for she

wished that she had not said anything, that she had hidden the paper from Gideon. "Right by the freeway, too."

"What happened?" Gideon's voice shook.

"Raped and killed—by a crazy man," Susan said, as he took the paper from her. "At least it's not anyone we know," she went on hastily.

Gideon pushed the paper aside and rose unsteadily to his feet.

"Aren't you going to finish your breakfast?" asked Susan.

"I'm not hungry," he said, turning away. Then she knew! The time mentioned in the paper would have been just when Gideon was on that stretch of freeway. He could have seen the girl running, the man pursuing. Susan did not say it aloud. She would have been glad to pretend that she did not know, but there was no use pretending with Gideon.

"I couldn't stop," he said hoarsely. "I saw it, but I couldn't do anything. I was on the inside lane, with two lanes of traffic between me and the edge of the freeway, all going like blazes. I—couldn't—stop!"

Susan went and stood beside him, reaching up to put one arm around his shoulders. "Of course you couldn't," she said. "And after all, there must have been hundreds of other people who saw it, too."

"Yes," choked Gideon, "hundreds saw it, and—nobody—stopped!"

"Oh Gideon, don't grieve!" said his wife. "It was impossible. It was just one of those things."

Gideon whirled about, almost fiercely, but she knew that the fierceness was directed not at her but himself. "I could have done something," he said. "I could have taken the next exit and gone back."

"You'd never have found her."

"I think I would," said Gideon. "I saw the lay of the land. She must have run beyond that little hill covered with cactus and rocks, almost in sight of the freeway, almost in sight."

Gently Susan pushed him into a chair. He rested his elbows on the table and dropped his head into them, trembling all over. "But Gideon," said Susan, stroking his thick hair, "hundreds of people were on the freeway, hundreds. Why do you take this as meant for you alone?"

"Because," said Gideon, speaking low from beneath his hands, "God was trying to tell me to take care of His child. For several days I had felt a heaviness. You know that feeling. I didn't know what it was. I thought of Bob, of course, but it wasn't he. Looking back, it was as if God were giving me a specific premonition, a warning . . . "

Inevitably, knowledge of the freeway incident percolated through the congregation. One day his assistant, Leslie, came to Gideon with solemn words of advice. "Look," he said, "you're letting things eat on you—this freeway thing, for instance. Sure, I heard about it; nothing to it! Everybody in southern California saw it and breezed by, so why should you get the wind up?"

Gideon tightened his lips and replied, "Everybody ought to get the wind up. Things like that are—unbearable!"

"Where do you think we are—the kingdom of heaven?" demanded Leslie. "Well, we're not! We're in California, and the law is that on the freeway, you've got to keep going, no matter what. Tell you what—you know the encounter groups I organize? They really are good. You get things out of your system. You find out what you really are, and you're not afraid any more, because everybody is like that—some more, some less, but everybody. So why don't you come to one? It would do you a lot of good."

Therefore, late in May when the Holy Spirit had been duly ushered into the church with a few doleful Whitsuntide hymns, and the church colors changed to green for the season of Trinity, Gideon went to an encounter group.

Susan saw him into Leslie's car with a little sigh of relief. This would be an excellent time for her to do some extra housecleaning. She betook herself, therefore, to the children's rooms, where she straightened bureau drawers, discarded worn-out shoes, hung clothes neatly on closet hooks, and tidied everything.

Susan's feelings of joy and thanksgiving for the children did not last, however, when she got to Josie's bureau drawers. In the top left-hand drawer, tucked away under some knee socks, her eyes fell upon a small bottle of pills, at the sight of which she nearly fainted. "Contraceptives, that's what they are!" she said to herself, and then, with resounding horror—"The pill!" Josie, their little daughter, not yet sixteen—the pill!

Susan waited with sick and shifting heart until Josie came home from school. Minutes stretched into hours, hours into eternity. Finally, Josie appeared, as usual with a boy who waited in his old car while she racketed in the front door, yelling behind her, "Okay, I won't be a minute. Hold it!"

"You *will* be a minute—and more," Susan said, meeting her at the door and holding out the bottle of pills.

Josie turned white. "Where did you get that?" she demanded.

"In your bureau drawer."

"What were you doing in my bureau? You've got no business snooping around in my room!"

26

"I was not snooping around. I was doing my usual spring cleaning. Josie, are you taking these things?"

"Well," Josie said, tightening her lips, "I'm not. But I might."

"Sit down," said Susan. "Tell that boy to go away, and sit down."

Josie hesitated. "Oh, all right," she said, going to the door and once more calling to the waiting boy. "Can't come now—catch up with you later!" She banged the door again, sat heavily on the sofa, elevated her jean-clad legs, and flung her head against the cushions.

Her mother, gazing at her, did not know how to ask the question on her mind. "Josie," she said, "did you—have you—?" She choked and could say no more.

"Oh, Mom," said Josie, "don't be antique. You know things are different nowadays."

"I am asking you, Josie, have you—" Again she paused, unable to say the words.

"Well, not yet," said Josie. "No, I haven't. But the kids say it's fun. And our psych teacher, you know, he said if anybody doesn't follow their impulses when they're in love, they're just copping out. That's what he said."

Susan froze to the marrow of her bones, determined to speak to Gideon, and to take the matter to the school board. "Josie, I don't care what the teacher said. This is wrong! You know the ten commandments. Dad reads them in church. 'Thou shalt not commit adultery.' "

"Well, this isn't adultery; it's just fornication," said Josie, with a worldly assurance that her mother could not follow. "Look it up in the dictionary," she added airily.

"I am not looking up anything," Susan said. "The meaning of the commandment is perfectly clear: keep yourself clean and pure. Then when you marry you'll—you'll be a good wife. I'm going to throw these things out—" she indicated the pills— "and you're not getting any more."

"What do you want, Mom?" said Josie. "Want me to have a baby?"

At this Susan turned pale and, being unable to speak, burst into furious tears.

"I'm sorry, Mom," said Josie, temporarily repentant. "Tell you what— Okay, I won't. Not for a while anyway. But you'd better let me keep the pills—just in case."

Chapter Three

Leslie Ainsworth was exuberant when he and Gideon returned from the encounter group. With a flourish he drove up to the rectory, accompanying Gideon inside to report on the great work that had been done. Leslie actually entered the house first, prancing ahead of Gideon's slower, meditative walk.

"It was great!" Leslie burbled, "absolutely great! Wait until Gideon tells you. All kinds of things came out. It was marvelous!"

At this Gideon smiled wanly and murmured, "Yes, it was really pretty good."

"You can hardly imagine," Leslie prattled on, "what freedom it is to get to understand yourself, to recognize yourself for what you really are—rather a louse, actually—and not to mind; just to know that's the truth, that's it, and on we go from here! It's great!"

Leslie at last departed. As he slammed the car door and sailed off, Susan said gently to Gideon, "Sit down now, dear, and tell me what it was really like."

Gideon sank down on the sofa, looking about the room as though he had never seen it before, while his wife bustled into the kitchen to pour his coffee.

"Was it really as good as Leslie said?" she demanded, returning with the coffee and sitting in the rocker across from him.

Gideon grinned ruefully. "I can't say I enjoyed it as much as he did," he admitted. "They do get the truth out of you."

"How?" asked his wife.

"Oh, they pounce on you with all kinds of questions, call you names, needle you, bother you, pick at you, until finally, in sheer exasperation, you blurt out what's on your mind. It is supposed to make you feel better."

"Does it?"

"No," said Gideon shortly. "First, of course, they got me to tell them about the little girl killed beside the freeway. They laughed me to scorn. They laughed; they really laughed! 'Worrying about that?' they said. 'You're an idiot!'—only they used stronger words, the dirtiest ones they could think of. 'Of course you're like that,' they said. 'Everybody is! Face what you are! You're a coward. You're selfish. You're an utterly no good human being. So what? Accept it. Don't fight it! Then you'll be free!' "

"Are you?" asked Susan.

"Well no," said Gideon. "It just made me wonder all the more."

"Wonder what?"

"Wonder why I'm in the ministry. I mean, what was I looking for? What was I trying to do?" Gideon thought of the empty sacraments in which no power flowed. He thought of his congregation, little cantankerous, dissatisfied, quarrelsome groups who sat through church and went out, relieved

30

at having done their duty for one more week. The next Sunday they came again, just as cantankerous, cross, smug, and self-satisfied, and again warmed the same pews—again, and again, and again.

"For years I've wondered what was the use," Gideon blurted out. "Maybe in the long run it will do me good to say it aloud to other people. What *is* the use?"

The days passed, and Gideon stumbled through his work, trying to keep busy while, in fact, interior darkness hung upon him ever more heavily. He could not forget the death by the freeway—nor that he was there, and might have stopped it—nor what the encounter group had sought to show him about himself, which was that he, like everybody else, was utterly no good. If this were really so, he would have to resign from the ministry. He knew he should, but being a coward, as the group had shown him he was, he could not persuade himself to take the step.

What would he say, Gideon wondered, to one of his congregation who might come to him for counsel, suffering the kind of agony he was now suffering? "You should see a minister." But *he* was a minister, and there was no point whatsoever in anybody seeing him. What then should he say? "You should see a psychiatrist?" In effect, this was exactly what the senior warden had said to him.

They had had another talk after the recent vestry meeting. "Gideon, you're not in very good shape," Mr. Crabtree had said. "No doubt, you're overworked." Gideon thought he detected a sly twist to the senior warden's mouth. He knew that he was not overworked, because after the encounter group it had been very difficult to force himself to work at all. He would sit idly at his desk, his thoughts running away as he tried to congeal them into a sermon. He would rise and walk back and forth, seeking to gather his wandering wits into some sort of cohesive whole—but they would sink out of sight, just as he dreamed of himself sinking, sinking—into some sort of quagmire.

"You know," Mr. Crabtree went on, "if you need professional help, you shouldn't put it off. I know a very good man—"

"A doctor?" Gideon broke in.

"Yes, a splendid fellow, a doctor of the mind—as a matter of fact, a psychiatrist. Seems to me it would be good for you to go and talk with him."

"I'll think about it," Gideon had replied vaguely, but he did not want to talk to a psychiatrist. No, that was the last thing he would do, because— He paused, hardly wanting to finish the thought even in his mind. Suppose he should be put in a mental hospital. Maybe that was where he belonged, but he would rather die. As he meditated on this, there grew in him the feeling that there was no reason why he shouldn't die. His life was his own. If it was no good to him, why should he continue to live? However, he had not only himself to worry about. There were his wife and children, particularly his beloved son, Bob, wherever he was.

"Don't worry about him," Susan often said. "Bob is old enough to take care of himself."

"Why doesn't he come home?"

"He will," Susan answered confidently, adding, "even the prodigal son finally came home."

There was also their daughter Josie. Gideon knew that Susan had something on her mind about the girl, and finally she had confessed it. He, too, had tried to reason with Josie and elicited only a halfhearted promise not to do anything that would require the pill—for a while.

32

Pondering these things, Gideon drove his car down the main street of the little foothill town to the neighborhood gas station. As he drove in, he deliberately pushed his dark wonderings into his unconscious mind, and shut the door on them. The garage owner came rambling forth, wiping his hands on a rag, and said with a broad grin, "Hi, Rev! What's the trouble now?"

"Seems like the transmission," Gideon said. "Sometimes it'll go; sometimes it won't. When it quits in the middle of traffic, it really bugs me. I never did like a car to stall—but who does?" He threw up a barrage of casual words about cars, while Tom, the garage owner, peered beneath the hood. "I'm certainly no mechanic," said Gideon with forced cheerfulness. "I never could understand how the darned things work."

"I don't always understand either," said Tom. "This is Stan's job anyway. I'll call him."

Gideon always enjoyed talking with Stan—tall, blue-eyed, direct, with a rough, carefree manner. "Hi, Stan!" he said, "How're you doing?"

To his surprise, Stan answered not a word, but only bent over the engine, examining it with expert fingers.

"He'll take care of it," said Tom. "Come on in here," and he motioned Gideon into his little office. Tom jerked one thumb in the direction of the mechanic. "Don't try talking to him," he said. "He won't answer."

"What's the matter?" asked Gideon.

"Lost his kid," Tom replied. "Didn't you see it in the paper? Kid attacked and killed right by the freeway, and nobody bothered to stop."

Gideon sat down suddenly on a stool. Everything seemed to whirl before him.

"Hit him hard," Tom went on, not noticing. "She was all he had, you know. Wife died a few years ago."

"How could he manage?" asked Gideon, wildly reaching into the air for words, any words, to cover the darkness engulfing him. "How could he take care of a kid all by himself?"

"Oh, his sister lives with him. The day it happened she and the kid were visiting relatives at a little ranch near the freeway—you know, the one among those first hills? Yeah, well some nut was loose around there, and that's where it happened." Tom sighed. "I don't know what to do about Stan."

"Yeah, he muddles through, doesn't say anything. But every time I look at him, I feel kind of sick inside. Well, life's like that, isn't it?"

"It seems to be," murmured Gideon.

Tom nodded sagely. "Just like in the Bible. The priest and the Pharisee passing by—only this time there wasn't any good Samaritan."

"I'm sorry," Gideon said to Stan, as he climbed back into his car.

Stan made no reply, but only looked at him out of somber blue eyes.

Now Gideon knew what he must do. He had not yet planned how he would carry out the sentence passed on himself, but he knew it had been passed. He could not go on living with this burden of guilt.

He drove back to the parish house, looked at his engagement calendar, spoke to the secretary, and went on with his day, part of his mind functioning with comparative smoothness. That night he dreamed that he was sliding down a very steep, very smooth mud bank, with no way to stop. At the bottom was a pool—a deep pool glaring with unwinking eye, ready to suck him in and drag him into the very depths of the earth, there to bury him forever.

Gideon woke heavy-eyed and toyed with his breakfast, while Susan looked at him anxiously. She did not ask what was the matter, because she knew. This darkness had been growing on him ever since the fateful day on the freeway. What should she do? she wondered. Was there anyone to whom she could talk?

There was, and he came to her that very day. "May I come around?" asked Reginald Crabtree's voice on the telephone.

"Gideon's away," she answered. "He's at the young people's retreat."

"Yes, I know," said Mr. Crabtree, "that's why I want to drop in. Or, if you'd rather, come to the parish house—?"

No, Susan preferred to talk in her own house, and so Mr. Crabtree came, closing the front door carefully behind him, as Susan had already closed the other doors into the living room, lest their conversation be overheard.

"I am greatly concerned about your husband," said Mr. Crabtree.

Susan nodded, her eyes heavy with the tears that could not be shed. "So am I," she said.

"Is he still worrying about that child killed beside the freeway?" Mr. Crabtree blurted out.

Susan nodded. "He just can't get it off his mind."

"Hmm," said Mr. Crabtree. "I told Gideon he ought to see a psychiatrist, but—"

"He has always had a fear of psychiatrists," said Susan, and she laughed uncertainly. "He has a perfect horror of mental institutions," she went on. "There was one quite near the ranch where they lived when he was a child. Sometimes when there was a full moon he thought he could hear the patients crying. They seemed to get more excited then, I don't know why. I think Gideon is afraid of being sent to a hospital."

"That's about what I figured," said Mr. Crabtree, "but he needs treatment. He's getting thinner every day, and more absentminded. He's not doing a good job."

"Isn't he?" faltered Susan. "He tries so hard."

Mr. Crabtree shook his head, his face set in somber lines. "I know he does," he said, "and I like the boy. I'm sorry for him, but—he can't go on this way. I have wondered if a vacation, maybe a month off, would help. Do you think so?"

"I don't know," said Susan. She remembered the old days when Gideon loved to go on vacations into the desert, camping beneath the stars. Then he entered into it with real, deep joy, but could he do so now? She tried to imagine it, and could not.

"If he *would* go," she asked, "could you get along at the church? Could Leslie manage?"

Mr. Crabtree snorted inelegantly. "I'd hate to think of it," he said. "As a matter of fact, well—"

"I know," said Susan, swiftly reading his thoughts. "If Gideon should have to—leave, you wouldn't keep Leslie."

"Not more than five minutes," agreed Mr. Crabtree. "Silly boy, his head always full of foolishness. What does he think he's after?"

"What does he say he's after?" asked Susan.

Mr. Crabtree shrugged his thick shoulders. "Oh, reality," he said, "he's searching for reality, of all the darn foolishness. What *is* reality anyway?"

No answer was expected, and Susan made none.

"Well, I've made up my mind," went on Mr. Crabtree. "Gideon's got to see a psychiatrist whether he wants to or not."

"Do you mean," asked Susan, "if he doesn't, he's out?"

"That's about it."

"But how will you persuade him?" asked Susan fearfully.

"I'm not going to persuade him," answered the senior warden. "I am the business head of this outfit, and this is business. The congregation is falling off. They get uneasy in church. Just to look at him, just to listen to him, trying so hard, pretending so hard—it makes everybody uneasy. Can't have it! This is business. I'm going to make an appointment for Gideon with Dr. Bayle. Good chap! Known him for years. And I'm going to tell Gideon, either he goes to Dr. Bayle, or we go to the bishop."

"To do what?" asked Susan.

"Well, to see about getting a new man," said Mr. Crabtree. "That's what it'll boil down to, unless Gideon will get proper help, which God knows he needs."

God did know, and Susan knew it, too, but when the matter was broached to Gideon it was like the sentence of an old-time judge, placing a black hat on his head. He would not go through psychiatry, Gideon decided. The death sentence had been pronounced, to be sure, but he would carry it out in his own way, his own time.

This, of course, he did not tell Mr. Crabtree. He only looked at him and said, "A week from Friday at two o'clock; is that when I see the doctor? Okay." He wrote it on his engagement calendar, but within himself Gideon decided that next Friday at two o'clock the sentence would already have been carried out.

Chapter Four

The following Thursday afternoon, Susan stood at the kitchen sink peeling potatoes and scraping carrots for a pot roast. She lifted up her eyes to the tall mountains, dim and hazy on this spring day, but they gave her no peace. All morning, there was heaviness within her—a nameless, wandering dread—and it settled around the picture of her husband. Gideon was on his way to Los Angeles to talk things over with the bishop, and as she thought of him driving on the freeway, her heart sank heavily, like a weight, and the very mountains seemed to darken before her eyes.

Was the church so unhappy with Gideon, Susan wondered, that both he and his assistant would soon be leaving? Leslie himself was less buoyant than usual, and his wife Lisa, when she had come to call recently, with one baby under her arm and another in a stroller, sat wearily on the sofa and uttered no word of cheer. "I don't know," she sighed. "Kids don't want to come to Sunday school anymore. And Leslie's getting up another youth retreat. They're supposed to go to the mountains for a week, and learn to know themselves—but not many want to go. We don't understand. We thought it would be just the thing for them."

It was not long before the front door banged, and with a reassuring, "Hi, Mom!" David bounced in, slingshot in hand. Spinning it toward the window, he exclaimed, "Look, Mom! I bet I can hit that bird out on the fence! What'll you bet, Mom?"

"Put that thing down, David," said Susan shortly. "You know you'd break the window. Let's have no more such nonsense. Why can't you just be quiet for a while?"

David became quieter, muttering, "Anything to eat?" He went to the refrigerator and presently returned with a jar of peanut butter and some bread.

"You're always hungry!" Susan half-smiled as she said it. "Don't I give you enough at meals?"

"Sure," said David, "but it's a long time to supper, and a guy's got to live, you know." He sat down at the kitchen table and suddenly inquired, "Mom, what's a kike?"

Susan turned sharply. "Where did you hear that word?" she asked, remembering it bitterly from the streets of New York, but not expecting it here in her own kitchen.

"Oh, the kids at school. You know what they said, Mom? They said I'm a kike. What's a kike, Mom?"

Susan turned back to the sink so that David would not see her face. "Kike is a stupid, ugly word for a Jew." She reached for a carrot and pared it with a hand that shook a bit.

"Am I a Jew, Mom?" asked David.

"Of course not," said Susan. "Look at your father, as fair and Anglo-Saxon as anyone could be."

"Yeah, but look at you," said David shrewdly. "I like the way you look, you know, but you're kind of dark. But you don't have a nose like mine," he added, "nobody in the family does."

"It's a good nose."

"It kind of curves up in the middle," said David.

"Aquiline," explained Susan, "It's the most distinguished kind of nose."

"The kids said it was a Jewish nose. Mom, does anybody of our relatives have a nose like that?"

Not knowing whether to laugh or cry, Susan dried her hands and came and sat beside the boy at the table. "Your grandfather had an aquiline nose," she said.

"Then what'll I tell the kids if they say I'm a kike?"

"Tell them that your grandfather was a Jew, and he was proud of it, and I'm proud of it."

"Gee," said David disconsolately, "I didn't know my grandfather was a Jew. Why didn't you ever tell me?"

"Perhaps we were wrong," answered his mother, "but we wanted to be just Americans. My father and his parents came to this country—"

"Why?" asked her son, interrupting.

"To save their lives," answered Susan briefly.

"Who was going to kill them?"

After a brief pause, Susan answered, "They came from Russia."

"Oh," said David, who was not completely ignorant of European history. "They were kind of playing it safe, huh?"

"Yes," said Susan, "they were playing it safe. They had the idea that in America, people were people, and it didn't matter where they came from. Your grandfather liked that idea. He was a remarkable man. And I wish you could have seen his father, your great-grandfather, when he got old. I remember how he worked in his tiny shop, stitching away

40

in his shirt sleeves, his vest open. He made clothes for gentlemen, and worked from dawn until dark, never complaining, always happy, always interested in what he was doing. David, you'd have loved him."

"Mom, I didn't know your family was like that."

"Of course," Susan went on proudly. "Your great grandfather was smart and shrewd, and his business grew. Now, as maybe you know, my father, your grandfather, is a wealthy man, and owns a big stylish clothing store in New York. You see, your ancestors inherited their flair for business all the way," she finished, ruminating, "all the way from Abraham."

"Who was Abraham?"

Susan looked up. "Don't they teach Bible stories in Sunday school?" she asked.

"Heck, no," replied David, "that's old stuff."

"What do they teach you?"

"Oh, what kind of guys we ought to be, And how to look inside ourselves and see why we don't like Uncle Bill, or somebody. And it's not bad," he added. "It makes you feel better, somehow. You kind of know what you're doing."

"Yes," agreed Susan, "maybe it is good, up to a point, but—well," she murmured guiltily, "I guess your ignorance of the Bible is our fault, your father's and mine. We ought to study it together, but somehow there's just never time."

"Gee, Mom, that would be awful! What if the kids came in and saw us all sitting around reading the Bible! They'd call me a jerk, all right!"

Susan tightened her lips. "Life doesn't have to be governed by what the kids say," she pronounced with dignity. "However, you really ought to know about Abraham. He was a tycoon, a big cattle and sheep man, and all because he was the friend of God, and God helped him in everything he did. It seems to be that way with my father's people, the Jews. I don't know whether it's because they're friends of God, or whether God still remembers Abraham, or what, but when they start a small tailor shop, for instance, it often gets to be a big clothing store."

"Well, gee, Mom, then why doesn't anybody like 'em? And why do the kids call me a kike, and make fun of my nose? Why is that?"

Susan meditated a moment, glancing up at the mountains. "I—I don't know," she said finally, adding in a stifled voice, "Some say it's because they rejected Jesus and had Him killed."

"That sounds like baloney to me," objected David vigorously. "Your father and grandfather didn't kill Jesus. Maybe it's because people are jealous," he added wisely.

"Ha!" Susan laughed briefly and ruefully. "It could be."

David bounced up and ran to the front door as a car drew near and then went on up the street. "When's Dad coming home?" he asked. "Gosh, shouldn't he be home by now?"

Susan's heart jumped into her mouth. But she said comfortingly to her son, "He'll be here, don't worry." She knew that she herself was worrying, fear resting on her ever more heavily as the moments passed.

Evening drew near, and Gideon had not come. The afternoon sunlight was turned faintly gold upon the mountains. He had said—what had he said? She remembered asking him, with an uneasiness not usual to her, "Gideon, you'll be back before rush hour, won't you?"

Gideon had hesitated, looked at her a moment, smiling vaguely, and said, "Oh yes." And then more slowly, looking far away, "I won't—get in the rush traffic, I promise you." What did he mean?

Susan knew something was wrong. Her brain might say it was foolish to worry when someone was late getting home. Her brain could say that perhaps he was making a hospital call, that the bishop had been delayed, that the conference was longer than expected. It did not matter what Susan's brain told her. Her stomach knew with sick and shaking apprehension that something was wrong.

No one but David was at home with her. Josie was spending the weekend with her aunt in San Luis Obispo and, her mother fervently hoped, keeping out of trouble. She would call Mr. Crabtree; he might have a clue. He might say, for instance, that he had asked Gideon to stop downtown to pick up the new church folders. For a fleeting moment, Susan remembered the folders that had been used on Easter. Very "mod" they were, with a scrawled picture on the front that looked at first glance like a purple chimpanzee. Only after examining it in horror and dismay, one saw that it was supposed to be the face of Christ. Susan's mind continued to wander briefly, and she saw in her mind the pictures of Jesus that she had received at Sunday school as a child—beautiful pictures, the Good Shepherd carrying a little white lamb in His arms. What had happened, that now He was pictured like a purple chimpanzee? These thoughts flitted willy-nilly through her mind . . .

Before she could call Mr. Crabtree or the church, however, there were footsteps on the porch. She leaped up and ran to the door, even though she knew it could not be Gideon. These were not his heavy, measured steps. These steps were light, almost prancing, and they brought two people, not one. Nevertheless, she flung open the front door eagerly. Perhaps they brought tidings, good or bad—

There stood Leslie and Lisa Ainsworth. Susan's face fell. "Oh—come in," she said lamely.

They entered, Leslie commenting, "Expecting someone else, huh?"

"Well, yes," said Susan, "I'm expecting Gideon. He's a bit late getting home from Los Angeles."

"Oh, that's nothing," said Leslie with a large gesture, plunking himself into an easy chair and crossing his legs. "Traffic, you know."

Lisa established herself more primly on the sofa, and murmured gently, "I always worry—I mean, when Leslie doesn't come when I expect him."

"Women are like that," said Leslie. "Guess it's a good idea. Us guys, we need somebody to care about us. But look, I just came to cheer you up. You know, I kind of feel you've been concerned about Gideon. He's been a bit down, I know. But that group we went to, it did him a lot of good."

"Did it?" snapped Susan. "Seems to me that ever since that group, Gideon's been more depressed than ever. Don't tell me he hasn't, because I know!" Susan could be cross when irritated, and could be irritated when in the grip of wild alarm.

"You just don't understand," soothed Leslie. "Sure, a guy goes through a bad time for a while, but after a while, he sees, sure, he is kind of a lousy character, and so what? Then he cheers up and doesn't worry about himself anymore, because, you know, we're all like that underneath. We're just better off when we know it."

"I'm sorry, but I don't agree with you," Susan said. "Everyone has a right to certain reserves."

"Oh, that's old stuff," declared Leslie.

Lisa, on the sofa, giggled ineffectually and remarked, "That's what he always says."

"Yeah, it's for the birds," Leslie went on, though what the

44

birds would do with this information, Susan could not imagine.

She felt herself becoming more and more grim inside, and unable to help it. Something else was wrong with the method about which Leslie was so enthusiastic. She could not quite put her finger on it, but there was something. She remembered strange words in the prayer book about being very members incorporate in the mystical body of the Son of God—something like that. Susan's spirit was reaching for a knowledge beyond her grasp.

"Well, we've all got to learn," Leslie was saying as, after what seemed to Susan an interminable call, they prepared to go. "Just thought I'd drop by to tell you not to worry about Gideon. He's all right. He's going through a self-discovery process, that's all. He'll come out the other end just great; you wait and see!"

With these bright words he ambled out the door, waved, and marched toward the car, Lisa obediently trailing after him.

Suppertime came, and still Gideon had not returned. Susan could stand it no longer. She called the bishop's office, and when no one answered, she shakily dialed his home. "I beg your pardon, Bishop Updyke," she said, "but can you tell me what time Gideon left your office? He's not home yet, and I just wondered—"

"Why, Mrs. Bruce," replied the bishop, "I'm afraid there's some mix-up here. Father Bruce didn't see me today."

Susan sat down weakly on the chair beside the phone. "You mean—he didn't come—at all?"

"No—no, he had no appointment today, no."

There followed a long silence. "There, there," said the bishop, not without concern. "Don't you worry. He'll show up. Something's happened to upset his plans, that's all. He'll show up!"

"But—what does one do?" asked Susan. "I mean, I know something's wrong, because Gideon isn't like this. He always does what he says he's going to do. Bishop, if it gets really late and time for bed, and he doesn't come—what should I do?"

"The usual thing, I would think, would be to call the Highway Patrol, and ask them to—"

The police! The Highway Patrol! "Thank you," said Susan faintly, quickly hanging up. But before she had quieted her whirling mind, before she could force her shaking fingers to open the directory and look up the number, the telephone rang, its voice splitting the silence like a buzz saw.

Gideon! It must be Gideon, telling her that the car had broken down, that he was delayed in traffic, that he would be home soon—

"Susan?" It was the voice of her sister Frances in San Luis Obispo. "Has Josie come home?"

Susan's mind stopped working for a moment, then clicked into action, gathering itself to cope with the new emergency.

"Isn't she with you?" asked Susan. "She was coming home tomorrow, wasn't she? I was going to meet the bus—"

"Yes, but—now don't get upset, Susan; she's disappeared."

"Disappeared!"

"This morning, right after breakfast, some friends of hers showed up and wanted to take her for a ride—to Three Rivers, they said. And—she hasn't come home."

"Who was driving?" Susan asked, cold fear stealing through her.

"Oh, a boy—red hair."

"Beard?"

46

"Beard," answered her sister, glumly. "Moustache, long hair, all the rest of it. Too old for Josie, I'd say."

"Anyone else in the car?"

"Well, he said so. At least he spoke of 'we', not 'I'. And Josie said you knew about it, and it was okay. Susan," Frances went on, as there was only silence on the other end of the phone, "didn't you know? Didn't you give permission?"

"No," answered Susan, and then in a sudden agony of new fear, "Frances, go and look in her room!"

Susan waited, but she knew already. Josie had gone away with Leroy. She had deliberately planned it, and where they had gone only God knew—to the hills and caves of the Big Sur, across the desert to the hippie communities of New Mexico? Only God knew.

Frances returned, her breathing quick and heavy, as though she had been running. "I don't see her suitcase!" she gasped. "Oh, Susan, what shall we do, what shall we do?"

Susan hardly knew what she said. There was no answer to give. When Bob had disappeared, no Highway Patrol or police had been able to find him. Now Josie—! Oh Gideon, *please* come home!

For a moment Susan swayed on the verge of collapse. Then the blood of her fathers must have moved in her veins, and out of her frozen fears emerged what could only be courage—an iron invincibility that lifted its head and would not bow down.

Gideon was in trouble, but he was alive! Of a sudden she knew it, almost as if she heard him calling her name, "Susan!" in tones of urgency, but of life, not death. In a flash she knew also that their son was alive, and when he got

47

ready, and when he had learned whatever he had gone to find out, he would return home. And Josie was alive, and there was every hope that she, too, would come home.

Even as Susan's grandfather had gone forth into a new country still trusting the God of his fathers, and even as his forefather Abraham had gone into the mountains willing to sacrifice his only son Isaac in obedience to God, so in Susan the bitter cold of fear became the steel of determination.

She would not give up, not weep and wail and shed tears. Rather, she would go forward, as Moses went forward into the waters of the Red Sea that parted before him. The stern and terrible history of the Jews was not her inheritance for nothing. She would go forward, Susan determined, and in some way the waters of life would open before her!

Chapter Five

Two young people—Jess, dark and bearded, and Ellie, with hair the color of dry mountain grass and eyes as blue as the sea—found Gideon's body crumpled and apparently lifeless, at the foot of a steep mountain gulley.

The rest of their group trailed far behind, their light voices wind-blown across the crags as they sang, "Alleluia, alleluia," over and over. They were not climbing the San Gabriels merely for fun, but with the serious, childlike purpose of passing the peace of the Lord to the mountains and to the San Andreas Fault beneath that unsteady part of California. They had learned about this kind of prayer from their motherly Christian friend, Beth, and were joyfully trying it out on their long mountain hike.

Jess saw the car first, crushed among the sharp desert rocks and bushes in a deep gorge. Then, as they climbed down toward it, Jess saw the man—or corpse. Which was it? He froze in his swift, scrambling stride and put out one arm, as if to warn Ellie away, but with a choked cry, she looked and stood still beside him.

"We ought to—report it to the police, or somebody—" Jess began.

Ellie stopped him, her hand on his arm. "He may be alive," she breathed, gesturing at the still, distorted figure lying at some distance from them among the rocks.

"Hardly."

"But we'd better find out. I mean, we can't just leave without checking, can we?"

"Okay, come on," said Jess. He led the way, and Ellie followed, until the two stood panting and white-faced by the man's figure lying on its back amid the rubble, arms outflung.

"He's dead!" whispered Ellie in horror.

But Jess, kneeling beside the man, his hands upon the chest and pulse, replied after a moment, "I don't think so. Come here; we'll pray for him."

Drifting in and out of consciousness, Gideon heard—or thought he heard—faraway singing: "Amazing grace, how sweet the sound—" Impossible! He was dreaming—or perhaps dying, as he had hoped and planned. But there it was, drifting toward him across shimmering distance: "I once was lost, but now I'm found—" Then Gideon seemed to feel a warm flow of life entering his body, even as life seeped out through his many wounds.

He opened his eyes, groaning with pain and with the jolt of returning consciousness. He had failed again! He had failed in life, and now in attempted death. Once more he closed his eyes, desiring only to drift out of consciousness. Then words came to him, seeming to lift him out of the aching void into which he was sinking. "Jesus, You came to seek and save the lost. Now save this man, and heal him!"

Who were these people, and what were they saying?

Another voice, light and soft, wove itself through the deep tones of the man who had been praying. "Thank You, Jesus! Thank You, Lord! You are real, You are true, and You are right here now, bringing this man back to life!"

Again Gideon opened his eyes, and the world of desert mountains, sharp and bright in the sun, swam around him. The sunlight was shining through something bright—a girl's hair, hanging like a thin golden curtain about her face. Gideon could not see her clearly—only her eyes, blue as the sky and lit with a sort of inner light. Someone whom he could not quite see was behind her. A deep male voice said, "Thank You, Lord, he's coming to life. Thank You, Lord!" The intonation was unusual, and the face, as Gideon steadied his vision and looked, was faintly foreign, dark, and hung with much beard. The world swam before Gideon, pain engulfed his whole body in a black flood, and once more consciousness drifted away.

When he next opened his eyes, the two young people seemed to have increased to many. They stood about him, or knelt with their hands upon him. Some of their lips seemed to move, and others knelt with heads bowed, long hair straggling over their faces. What and who, in God's name? Were they praying? Gideon clearly heard a loud, "Thank You, Lord!"

Gideon realized that they seemed to know he was alive and conscious, but did not know what to do next, which was not strange. Surely he would die if they tried to move him from that wild, crumbling slope. To his great surprise, Gideon found that now he did not want to die. Something deep within him seemed to be coming to life.

He looked above the tousled heads to the steep mountain crags and saw that they were beautiful. Gideon had forgotten. For a long time, he had not been seeing the world around him, only his own darkness . . .

He forced himself to look at the young people, and tried to speak, but no sound came. Then one of them, the girl with the sunlit hair, asked the strangest question he had ever heard. "Do you know Jesus?" she asked.

Gideon moved his split and bleeding lips and managed to answer, "No." He sensed that what he knew *about* Jesus was not what she meant. No, he did not know Jesus.

"He knows you," said the girl, "and loves you!"

"Do you know you're a sinner?" inquired the dark young man, and no, it was not an absurd question. It was quite proper.

Gideon answered, "Yes," realizing that he had never admitted it before, not in words.

"And Jesus, the Son of God, came into the world to save you," said the young man, while Gideon heard small sounds around him, like happy birds singing words he did not understand.

"Will you let Jesus save you and make you well?" asked the youth solemnly, while the girl continued to bend over Gideon, her hands on his laboring heart, her long hair falling upon him like bright rain.

"Please," she said. "Please!" Gideon did not know whether she was entreating him, or the Jesus who seemed so real to her.

Was he willing for Jesus to save him? Gideon dimly wondered. This very morning he had desired nothing but death. Now, with death near, with a broken body and his lifeblood oozing out even while young hands tried to stanch it—now, for no understandable reason, he desired life! Perhaps it was the life he saw in their eager faces. There was a glow about them, light in their eyes . . .

"Say, 'I accept Jesus Christ as my Lord and Savior.' "
The young dark man looked upon him soberly.

Had he not been on the verge of death, Gideon might have
explained that he was an ordained minister, so he did not
need to say such words, but he had no strength to explain.
So he simply murmured, barely audibly, "I accept Jesus
Christ as my Lord and Savior." He said it with long pauses,
and so faintly that the girl bent lower to hear him.

"He said it!" she cried triumphantly, as though this were
some great victory. A sigh, or ripple, seemed to go through
the group in waves. One of these waves reached Gideon,
exploding within him in tiny sparkles of unreasonable joy.
It was ridiculous joy, even mingled with a bit of mirth, here
on the edge of the abyss of death from which he had been
snatched. If they only realized that he was a minister, knowing the mysteries of God before they were born—!

But had he known them? Never before had he said that he
accepted Jesus as his Lord and Savior, and never before had
he known this feeling of new, joyous life entering him, while
here he lay among the scattered wreckage of his car. He remembered, though dimly, how he had speeded up the steep,
savage curve, to make sure the car would hurtle over the bit
of piled earth that was the only road guard, and how his consciousness had mercifully blanked out before he crashed in
the terrifying cliffs of the canyon.

Now that these young people had found him and, it
seemed, saved his life, how could they possibly get him out?
Gideon wondered. He was sure that he had broken bones.
Blood was still seeping from his head and limbs into the
bandages which the young people had made out of their
own clothing and wrapped tightly about him. Also, he
sensed that he was bleeding inwardly from unseen wounds.

Why not? No one could fall as he had fallen and still live.

Gideon heard them talking as he closed his eyes again, in and out of consciousness, but still sensing tiny ripples of new joy.

"How long will it be, Jess?" someone asked.

The dark young man glanced at a watch that gleamed incongruously on the hairy arm below the weirdly dyed sweatshirt. "Not long," he paused, "if they made connections."

"They must have! Didn't we pray for the ranger to be there?" This was the girl speaking, as she lifted her hands from Gideon's chest and shook them a bit, as though they were tired.

"A helicopter is coming," explained Ellie, leaning close to Gideon again and speaking to him distinctly. "A couple of guys took off to the ranger station, and they'll call the rescue unit to lift you out in a helicopter."

"Can you move your arms?" Jess asked.

Wild pain jabbed Gideon as he tried, but the arms did move.

"How about your legs?"

"No," whispered Gideon, not daring to make that inconceivable effort.

"They'll have to hover, and let down the basket," said Jess.

Ellie added, "Don't be frightened. You don't know Jesus very well yet, but just ask Him and He'll take care of you."

"I—can't—" Gideon managed in a hoarse whisper.

"We'll ask Him for you," said Jess, his voice strangely gentle within his black beard.

Gideon had grown up in the church as choirboy and acolyte. He had always heard the Bible, and sung the hymns, and said the prayers of the church. For three long years, he had attended seminary. And here these children told him that he did not know the Son of God very well! Furthermore, they told the truth.

"Come on, you guys," called Jess, looking at the motley group whose eyes shone with other-worldly joy. "While we wait, let's give him the works—good works!" he added, white teeth shining for a moment as he smiled at Gideon.

So they all crowded around again, kneeling on the rough slope and laying their hands on Gideon. Those who could not quite reach knelt beyond, laying their hands on the shoulders of those in front.

Jess, who seemed to be the natural leader, looked up at the sky lit with the gold clouds of sunset, and at the rocky mountaintops splitting the air. He spoke to Someone up there, as though he had no question of His being, as though he could see Him. "Thank You, Jesus," he began, and his words were echoed in the whispers and joyful sounds from the kneeling group. "You love us, and You can heal us, just as You did when You were on earth in a body. And You are here now too, only we can't see You. So now, come, Lord, and do a miracle! This man has accepted You as his Savior. He's been lost for a long time, Lord, and now he's found. Come into him, and mend whatever's broken, and—"

"And kind of wrap him up in Your love while we get him off this mountain," added Ellie.

"And speed up the helicopter, Lord, speed it up, so we can get him out of here before dark," added another.

Gideon's pain increased as they spoke, but, in spite of the agony, somehow there was a heightening of consciousness, a feeling of being upheld like a baby in its mother's arms. He even had a momentary picture of himself walking

55

straight and strong, with new light in him, like the light shining in these kneeling ones around him.

Someone began to sing in a small voice, as light as a whisper. "Amazing grace, how sweet the sound—" Others joined, and they all seemed to surge in the swing and flow of the melody. "I once was lost, but now I'm found, was blind but now I see."

There came a beating in the sky, like the wings of a very large bird. It drew nearer, its beating changing to a great clattering roar, as above them hovered the flying monster that was to lift Gideon out of this wilderness into which he had thrown himself.

"I crashed—on purpose," Gideon whispered, feeling strangely impelled to tell them. Perhaps they would not be so sure that Jesus would save him.

"Oh, sure," said Jess unconcernedly. "We dig that."

"But you see," said Ellie, bending over him, "Jesus wants you here a while longer, and He wants to save you and make you well so you'll really know Him."

Gideon could not answer above the earth-shattering roar of the hovering helicopter, but he managed a smile, for he was already better. Not his body—he seemed hardly aware of his body—but he himself was better. Even if he passed out again when they lifted him, he was better. He had been lost, and now was found.

Chapter Six

The mountains were growing dark, Gideon had not returned, and Susan knew with a cold inner knowledge that disaster had befallen him. Vividly she remembered his departure that morning, not quite usual, not quite comfortable or comforting. She remembered the faraway look in his eyes when she asked what time he would be home and his vague reply, as though in a dream, something about not getting caught in the rush traffic.

Josie, also, had gone away. Surely she would soon be home again! She was just off on a lark, merely a lark . . . Or could she have run away and now be alone in the world or, worse, in the too-close company of some boy, in a cold cave or on some far beach?

"When's Dad coming back?" asked David, wandering in with his slingshot.

"Put that thing away!" snapped Susan, her nerves taut.

"Well, heck—"

Just then the bell rang. Susan darted to the door, her

heart thudding. It was only Leslie, standing there uncertainly, as though he did not know why he had come.

"He's still not home?" he asked nervously.

"Not yet," said Susan. "Come in."

Leslie was already in, walking back and forth with fidgety gait. "I guess he's all right," said he, "but—"

"He's not all right, and you know it!"

"Maybe Dad's totaled the car," said David cheerfully.

"Someone would have found him," Susan said shortly. "The police would have called us." With swift steps she went to the window, as if to see Gideon driving down the street.

"Have you called the police?" asked Leslie suddenly.

Susan nodded. "Nothing," she said, straining forward as a car passed, and then sitting down with a deep sigh.

"Highway Patrol?"

Again Susan nodded. "Gosh!" David sighed forlornly, his tousled hair falling in his eyes. "It's lonesome without Dad or Josie."

"Josie?" asked Leslie quickly.

Susan swallowed hard. "Spending the weekend with her aunt," she said. She simply could not face the fact that Josie might not return.

At that moment the telephone rang. It was Susan's sister. "Has Josie showed up yet?"

"No," Susan said, and dropped back into a chair, her hand limp on the receiver.

"This is the assistant rector speaking," said Leslie, gently taking the phone from her. "May I help you?"

"It's about Josie," replied the voice on the other end. "Has she called or—come home? I'm Susan's sister. Josie was visiting here, and she's gone off with a boy—and her things are gone, too."

58

"I am sure there'll be news from her soon," said Leslie in his professional voice. He held the telephone away from his mouth and looked inquiringly at Susan.

She shook her head. "Tell her I'll call—as soon as I have any news," she faltered.

"Well," said Leslie after complying and hanging up the phone, "Josie shouldn't be too hard to find. Have you—done anything about her?"

Susan, lifting hopeless eyes, replied, "I'm—waiting for Gideon. He—he would know what to do."

Leslie noticed the conditional tense. Gideon would know, if he were here, if he were alive . . .

Again the phone rang. Leslie picked it up. "The Highway Patrol," he said, his lips tight.

Susan was up like a flash, snatching the phone from his hand, and David flung himself from his chair, and bolted into the bedroom to listen on the extension.

"Is your car registration SKJ002?" asked the grave, official voice.

"Yes, yes—have you found my husband? Is he alive?"

"We have found him."

"What—where—?"

"Up in the mountains, way off the road. He apparently drove onto a fire break, not a road at all, and ran off the side. However," the patrolman added, rallying into sympathy, "some kids found him, the rescue unit got him out by helicopter, and he was still alive. They took him to St. Luke's Hospital."

"Is he — still alive?"

"You'd better call the hospital," the patrolman said, anticipating her question.

Susan was already at the door crying, "Hurry, Leslie! You'll take me, won't you?"

"I'll take you," said Leslie, as he hastily hung up the telephone, but then he said, "Wait, the police say we should call the hospital."

"Why call?"

"Maybe they don't know who he is, or—"

"Or what?"

"Never mind, the police said to call."

In case he's already dead, thought Susan, as Leslie fumbled for the number and made the call.

"I am calling about Reverend Gideon Bruce," she heard him say, followed by a pause. "Yes, he is there. He was just brought in by helicopter." He put his hand over the mouthpiece and said, "They're calling emergency."

The seconds stretched on into what seemed years before Susan heard Leslie say, "Yes—yes. We want him to have every care—private room—yes, oh I see. Intensive care, yes."

"Mom!" shrilled David. "He's not—he's not *dying*, is he?"

"Is that what they said?" asked Susan, suddenly frozen rigid.

"They're doing all they can," answered Leslie, swallowing hard and remembering the ominous note in the nurse's voice. We're to go to emergency, or intensive care. What about David?"

"I'm coming too!" shouted David. "Don't leave me here!"

Once more the telephone rang. It was Reginald Crabtree, inquiring after the rector. "The police just called," said Leslie. "There's been an accident and—he's in St. Luke's Hospital. I'm taking Susan there now. Call my wife, will you?"

"Is he bad?" asked Reginald.

"Yes."

"What about the boy?"

"I want to go too!" shouted David.

The senior warden, however, was making a clear decision otherwise. "I'll come right over and get David," said he. "Put him on the phone."

"I'm on the phone," shrilled David from the bedroom, "but I don't want—"

"We've got a good supper ready," said Mr. Crabtree, "and there's a game on TV. Your mother will call from the hospital as soon as she finds out how things are. I'm coming for you now." Whereupon Mr. Crabtree hung up, and David reluctantly did so too.

"I don't want—" he began again.

His mother cut him short. "You're going with Mr. Crabtree," she commanded.

Leslie was already in the car and Susan on her way out, when the phone rang for the fourth time. "Any news of your husband?" It was Bishop Updyke, warmly cheerful.

"There's been an accident. He's in the hospital. The police just called, and we're on our way there."

"What happened?"

"He was driving up in the mountains—why, I can't imagine. He took a wood road—not even a road really, a fire break—and the car skidded or something, and went off into a canyon."

"Just a minute," said the bishop firmly, forcing Susan to pay attention to what he was saying. "Remember, your husband had an appointment with me that was—postponed until five o'clock."

"But—"

"His appointment was postponed," said the bishop slowly. "So your husband, to pass the time, must have gone for

61

one of his favorite mountain drives. The car skidded on a curve—"

"Thank you!" gasped Susan gratefully. And she added, rather surprisingly, "Pray for him, won't you?" as she hung up and ran to the car. To David, standing dismally on the front porch, she called back, "Mr. Crabtree will be right along!"

Leslie sped through the night, veering around cars in front of them, narrowly missing oncoming traffic, till Susan finally ordered him to slow down, and they arrived at the hospital under the illuminated white cross which split the sky above it.

They found Gideon in the emergency room—if it was Gideon. His eyes were rolled back, his head was twisted sideways, his face was slate-gray, and he gasped for every breath. Blood seeped through bandages about his head, and a sheet was drawn up to his chin. A doctor came and went, and a nurse stood beside him, monitoring instruments and a transfusion bottle suspended at the end of the wheeled stretcher, while on the other side stood two incongruous figures—a tall, dark, untidy youth, and a girl with yellow hair. When they were in the way, they stepped back, but at other times, they kept their hands inconspicuously on Gideon's chest and wrists.

Susan stood stock still, not daring to touch him. "Is he—dying?" she whispered to the nurse.

"We have sent for the priest."

The last rites, thought Susan, remembering that this was a Catholic hospital.

At that moment the priest entered—an old man, fully vested for this encounter between a dying man and his God.

"His wife," said the nurse, indicating Susan.

The priest bowed slightly toward her.

"And these?" he asked, glancing at the two young people beside Gideon, saying, "Excuse me, please," as he took their place.

"They came with him," said the nurse. "They—found him."

Apparently the priest accepted them as the good Samaritans of this modern rescue, for he proceeded, bowing and crossing himself, with the gentle sweep and flow of the sacrament. At last he touched the lips of the dying man with a spoon containing the body and blood of Christ, said the final prayers, pronounced the benediction, and departed with slow and stately gait, as though walking in procession. Maybe he was doing just that, thought Susan's stunned mind, for she imagined a company of angels walking beside him, their white wings faintly gleaming in the harsh hospital light.

A tired young doctor hurried back to Gideon's side. "Still hanging in there?" he inquired, laying his hand on the patient's wrist.

"Yes," the nurse replied. "In fact, his pulse seems a little stronger."

"Hm," said the doctor. He bent over Gideon and with a tiny focused light looked into his eyes. As he did so, the lids fluttered slightly and began to close. "Hm," he said again, unrevealingly. "Well, a multiple stabbing is on its way in; we've got to get him out of here," gesturing at Gideon.

"Could he have a private room?" faltered Susan.

"Intensive care," said the doctor briefly to the nurse. "Get orderlies," and to Susan and the others he added, "You'd better leave."

"I'm his wife," said Susan, who had no intention of leaving.

The doctor only replied, "Wait outside then," and went his busy way.

Eventually, by asking one or two harried employees in the corridors, Susan, Leslie, and the young people found their way to the door of the intensive care unit. Soon Gideon came, trundled by orderlies, the nurse from the emergency room leading the procession. There was much bustling and adjustment of equipment. Obviously, while the patient was being established in new quarters, no visitors would be tolerated.

As Susan perched on the edge of one of the molded plastic chairs in the waiting area, the dark young man met her eyes with his and said in tones of quiet authority, "He's not going to die."

Susan's heart gave a great leap of joy, and then returned to its unsteady beating. "How do you know?" she asked.

"Because we're praying for him," answered the young man. "I'm Jess, and this is Ellie." He indicated the young woman beside him. "Do you people believe in prayer?"

"Why, yes—yes, of course," managed Susan, suddenly wondering whether she did or not.

"Do you know how much he's hurt?" she asked of the strangely authoritative young man, wondering as she did so why she did not ask the nurse.

"Pretty well smashed up," said Jess. "Legs broken, one anyway, head hurt, probably bleeding inside—but the Lord can take care of all that!"

"Do you believe in Jesus?" asked Ellie softly, looking directly at Susan.

"Why, I—yes!"

"Then you know He can make him well, don't you? He even raised the dead, remember?"

Leslie cleared his throat.

"We know Jesus is going to raise him up," declared Jess, "because up there on the mountain, he accepted Jesus as his Lord and Savior."

There was a strange sound from Leslie, and Susan looked warningly at him. Whatever these young people thought they were doing, no one should laugh. For who could tell—?

The nurse came to the door, motioning for her, just her, to come in quietly. Gideon's bed was in one corner of the room. Another nurse was beside him. Susan could see no change in Gideon.

"Will he live?" she half-whispered to the nurse as though the nurse were God, able to tell the times of life and death.

"We don't know yet," came the soft reply. "But why don't you sit down?" she added, nodding toward a chair. "And you," looking at the young people who had come in unbidden, "isn't it time you went home?"

"Home?" asked Ellie with an odd little smile.

Jess gravely explained: "We can't. We have no car. They let us come with him in the helicopter to—help hold him, kind of. The rest of the gang had to walk back to where we left the car. They'll pick us up eventually."

"They know what hospital?" asked the nurse, a bit sharply.

"Yes."

"I'll leave word at the desk," said the nurse. "You may wait in the sitting room at the end of the hall."

"Will you be staying with him?" asked Susan.

The capable nurse replied, as though it explained everything, "Yes. This is intensive care."

Jess and Ellie did not stay in the room at the end of the hall. In a few minutes they crept softly back into intensive care and stood beside Gideon, their hands again laid lightly upon him. Gideon sighed, his closed eyelids moving a bit. The nurse smiled but, to Susan's amazement, made no protest, and Susan found herself looking at the young people with new, awed, interest, as they stood there so silently. Why did the nurse, as if she did not see them, let them stay?

Susan turned to Leslie, lingering rather uncertainly at the door. "Why don't you telephone the Crabtrees," she murmured.

"What shall I tell them?"

"Tell them he's going to live!" said Susan, not knowing why she said it.

The nurse looked up with an enigmatic smile. "His breathing is better," she announced.

Jess's white grin split his black beard, and Ellie sighed softly, "Praise the Lord!"

"Put your hands on him, too," Jess commanded Susan. Wondering, Susan laid trembling hands upon her husband's body. Answering her unspoken question, the extraordinary young man explained, "Jesus lives in us, so He uses our hands. Put your hands right on mine," he added.

Susan did so, and she could feel life entering Gideon through those hands, a warm feeling of indescribable energy. "It's like—electricity," she whispered.

"It's light," said Jess, as casually as though they were watching the flow of a mountain stream. "Same thing—life."

Leslie tiptoed back in and stood silently in the shadows.

"You can go home," said Jess, glancing at him. "We can take care of him—and her."

"But I'm the assistant rector," said Leslie with dignity. "So I—"

"Assistant what?" asked Jess.

"Rector."

"That means kind of a preacher like," explained Ellie.

"Mean to say he's a—"

"Yes, my husband's a minister," said Susan.

"That's funny," mused Ellie in her soft voice. "He didn't know Jesus."

"Here comes the doctor," said Leslie, glancing out the open door. Jess, Ellie, and Susan all stepped back while the doctor strode through the midst of them as though they were not there, and laid his stethoscope upon Gideon's chest.

"He's better, isn't he?" breathed Susan.

"You're his wife?" asked the doctor, withdrawing slightly from the bedside. As Susan nodded, he went on, "Then it would be unkind to deceive you. He does seem stronger, but X rays show the left hip broken in five places and jammed four centimeters into the body. The right leg is injured, but apparently not broken. He is cut internally, across the rectum, and there is considerable internal bleeding from this and probably other sources. There are also a couple of fractured ribs, some concussion, and cuts on the head and face. What else there may be, we do not know, but—"

"How long—before you—know?" uttered Susan, her newfound hope shattering.

"Another two or three hours," replied the doctor, laying his hand for a moment on Susan's arm. "You have courage," he said, adding slowly, "I'm afraid you're going to need it."

He glanced past Jess and Ellie, as though not seeing them, and motioned Leslie to step outside with him.

"The doctor believes," breathed Jess, as the two men

67

walked down the corridor, their footsteps echoing hollowly past sleeping doors. "He must believe, or he wouldn't let us stay. Come on, Ellie!"

The two young people again laid their hands on Gideon, the nurse saying nothing, apparently not noticing. Jess looked up at Susan, and matter-of-factly said again, "He *is* going to live!"

"How do you know?" she gasped.

Jess replied, with a little twisted smile, "I just know."

"Praise the Lord!" murmured Ellie, as though this were the only explanation needed, and to her surprise, Susan found herself echoing, "Praise the Lord!" She spoke from an uncertain heart, but there was now within her the feeling of life.

Leslie returned, weariness writ heavily upon him.

"You'd better go home," said Susan. "Get some food and sleep. After all, you've got to look after the parish. Early service tomorrow—"

"We're staying," said Jess, before anyone could challenge him. "We found him, so we've got to look after him, and—we don't have any early service in the morning."

"Call me—if anything happens," said Leslie.

"I'll call. You've been very helpful. I don't know who these young people are—but they'll look after me."

"Yup," said Jess.

"All night, until—" Susan quavered.

"All night," Jess said firmly. "We won't let them run us out, even when the gang comes for us."

"You'll need sleep."

"We can take turns—on the floor, in the hall or somewhere. We're used to that."

"Whew!" sighed Jess to Ellie as Leslie departed. "We'll

get along better without him. She believes," he added, nodding toward Susan, "but he doesn't. I bet he hoped the doctor would kick us out."

"How about that doctor, not kicking us out?" marveled Ellie.

"Like I said, it could be, he believes, only he can't say so," Jess conjectured. "Doctors aren't usually as tough as ministers."

"You can say that again," replied Ellie. "Good thing we didn't know he was a minister." She gestured with her chin toward Gideon, her hands still upon him.

"He accepted Jesus just the same," said Jess, "and let me tell you, Jesus accepted him."

"How do you know?"

"God's been telling me," said Jess, "And He's told me this man's going to get well."

"How can God tell you things like that?" asked Susan, the hushed conversation apparently not disturbing the patient or the nurse. "God doesn't *talk* to you does He?"

"No, but I *see* this man well; that's the way God tells me," Jess explained lucidly.

Susan looked inquiringly at the nurse, who said primly, "This is a Christian hospital. We have no rules against prayer. But—" her somewhat homely face was lit by a smile, "we'd better be as discreet as possible. You are tired," she added to the young people, "and I think you should rest in the waiting room. I hope your friends will come soon."

Ellie straightened up and rubbed her hands. "I am tired," she sighed, and turned gladly to the door. "Coming, Jess?"

"Call me if—if he—" Jess said.

"I will," said the nurse, her hands upon Gideon's wrist, and the young people went out. "Now you rest too," she said to Susan, indicating the one chair in the room.

Susan sank gratefully into the chair, resting her head against the wall, and closed her eyes. "Do you really think he'll—live?" she whispered, when the nurse came close to her.

Expert with long training, the nurse replied, "I make no decisions; I only do my duty. But come to think of it," she added after a moment, "I think it would be better for you to rest outside, with the others. This is intensive care, you know," she added with significance, as though it were the holy of holies.

So Susan went humbly to the small room at the end of the hall furnished with a few easy chairs, two straight ones, a bare table, and a rack of magazines. The very atmosphere was tight with the tension of many who had waited there in fear.

"Bad vibes here," said Jess, as though reading Susan's thoughts.

"Jesus can get through any vibes," said Ellie softly.

Susan cringed. It seemed unsuitable to speak thus familiarly of the one whom she had learned to call, with downcast eyes, "Our Lord."

"How is it that you know Him so well?" she asked Ellie.

"I was down and out, see?" said Ellie. "You know, booze, and drugs, and boys and—even girls. I didn't care. Anything to get hold of money for drugs. I mean, you know, they cost a lot."

Susan did not know, and she looked with horror at this innocent-appearing young woman, old beyond her years, who had apparently sold herself, body and soul.

"Well, some of the kids from the coffeehouse, Jess and some others, they found me on the Strip. I was wandering along, not going anywhere because, you know, I was pretty

70

well stoned. They came up and asked me if I knew I was a sinner. I did, all right; I sure did know that! Then they asked did I know God loved me? And I said, 'Hell, no! Nobody ever loved me.' You see, my mother, well—she had a lot of men, and didn't really know who my father was. I was just a drag to her, see? That's why I ran away, me and my girl friend. We hung around back of bars, and swigged whatever was left in the empties—beer or anything. I don't know what happened to her. Somebody picked her up, I guess, and took her off.

"Anyway, these kids told me that God loved me, and He sent Jesus to die for my sins, so I could be forgiven and start all over again. It was real heavy, and I didn't believe it exactly, but then they began to pray for me—"

"Right there on the street?" gasped Susan, horrified.

"Sure! There wasn't any other place."

"Wasn't there a church?"

Jess snorted or laughed, Susan couldn't tell which.

"We wouldn't go into one of those," said Ellie.

"They'd run us out," explained Jess.

"So then I began to cry," went on Ellie. "They asked me if I was sorry I was a sinner, and I sure was! I always had been, because it really isn't any fun, only I didn't know how to be anything else. Then—they asked me if I accepted Jesus as my Lord and Savior. And I did!"

"Just like the man did—your husband," said Jess.

"What happened then?" asked Susan, for in the midst of her dreadful fear for Gideon, something within her cried out to know about these young people.

"Then I felt so happy—oh, man, it was cool! I seemed to see Jesus, like He was right there. And I was healed! I mean, I didn't want drugs or booze, or anything! I mean, I was healed right then. That's why we know your husband will be healed," Ellie concluded. "He accepted Jesus too!"

"Is he really a minister?" asked Jess in his deep voice. Susan nodded, having no words.

"What kind? I mean, there are different kinds of ministers, aren't there?"

"Episcopalian."

"Man, that's heavy!" said Jess cryptically. "And what was that other guy doing downstairs—all dressed up fancy, with the lighted candles and the spoon, and all that?"

It took Susan a moment to realize that Jess was speaking of the priest who administered to Gideon the last rites of the Church. Candles? She fumbled in her mind. Yes, there were candles, on some kind of stand. "He was a Roman Catholic priest," she explained.

"Oh, wow!" remarked Ellie. "What was he doing?" she persisted.

"In the Roman Catholic Church," Susan explained, "they bring a person communion if he—seems to be dying."

"Why?" asked Jess and Ellie together.

"Communion is for the forgiveness of sins," she began.

"You mean that's what he gave him in the spoon?"

Susan nodded. "When you two were praying for Gideon—" she said, "that's my husband's name—"

"I dig that name," nodded Ellie approvingly.

"There was sort of—life, coming through your hands," Susan went on.

"That's the life of Jesus," said Ellie evenly. "I felt it when they prayed for me on the street."

Jess nodded, then asked, "How come, if Gideon's a minister, he didn't already know Jesus?"

Ellie explained, "We asked him if he knew Jesus, but he said he didn't."

Susan had no answer.

Chapter Seven

Gideon drifted in and out of his world of light, darkness, and unthinkable pain. From time to time, snatches of song rang through his mind. In the midst of thick darkness, the jingling tune of an old nursery rhyme beat within his unawakened brain: "Go tell Aunt Nancy, go tell Aunt Nancy, go tell Aunt Nancy, the old gray goose is dead."

"Who is the old gray goose?" a faint voice wondered.

From somewhere in the black pit of his nether awareness, another voice answered, "God." And he laughed—or something seemed to laugh.

This must have been while he still lay on the mountainside, for he dimly remembered awakening there to pain and then drifting off again—and then, some centuries later, or so it seemed, he remembered faraway, sweet singing. There was a girl with long golden hair, and a bearded youth towering over her—

No, she was here, and if he dared to open his eyes, he would see her. But Gideon dared not, for fear that, after all, she would not be there.

"Gideon!" she seemed to be calling, but that was absurd; how could she know his name? The girl on the mountain did not know him. But he was no longer on the mountain. Sharp rocks did not pierce him when he tried to move. His whole body was full of pain—but it lay on a bed, not on jagged rocks.

Then, without decision, Gideon opened his eyes. The world swam about him—not the wild world of the mountains, but ceiling, walls, and tubes hanging from somewhere and apparently attached to him. And there was the young woman, her face gradually coming into focus through the hair that hung about her in a shining cloud.

"Hi," she said. "Do you know me? I'm Ellie."

His lips formed the name. "Ellie." Yes, Gideon knew her. In fact, he seemed to remember life flowing from her hands— He also remembered, or perhaps dreamed, being far away in a shining world, and hearing someone call him. Was it the girl Ellie—or Susan? Then he would come back unwillingly into this world of pain, and another woman, the one in white, rustled around, and there would be a prick somewhere, and the pain would drift away while he sank into fathomless depths. It wasn't really sleep; it was just not being quite aware of anything.

"Gideon!" This was not Ellie's voice but another. He opened his eyes and carefully slid them around toward the voice. Susan stood there, taut and still, the lines of strain upon her eager face frozen into quietness.

"Susan!" he murmured, and her dark eyes flashed with joy. He lifted one hand, finding a tube attached to his wrist, and tried to reach for hers. "I'm sorry," he whispered, and tears came to his eyes, whereupon Susan wept. Throughout their married life, Gideon had hardly seen her weep, but these were tears of joy, her smile shining through them like sunlight through quick rain. "It's all right," she said. "Now that you've come back, it's all right."

"But—" There was something else. Gideon groped in the veiled recesses of his mind and found words from far away. "I'll never walk again," he murmured.

"But you will!" This was the golden-haired girl, her voice surprisingly strong and clear.

"How do you know?" Gideon formed the words painfully.

"Jesus told me." Ellie made this statement with such quiet simplicity that it could not embarrass anyone. Normally Gideon would have cringed to hear the name of his Lord spoken as though He were a real person standing close by. Now, perhaps after all, Jesus was exactly that—a real person, standing close by—

Being full of drugs, Gideon then slipped away into a never-never land somehow dimly true, a land in which Jesus was a real person who smiled upon him.

Surely, thought Gideon, through his half-dreams, he had always known Jesus. As a little child, he loved to look at the Sunday school cards with that gentle figure, draped in blue and white, carrying a placid lamb in His arms. Sentimental the pictures might be, but the child never forgot them. Surely he had always known Jesus, and as a minister he had taught Jesus to his congregation! So mused Gideon semiconsciously, while a voice within seemed to say, "Have you?"

Next the nurse was standing over him. "Come now," she crooned, "try to drink a little of this. It will do you good." Obediently, Gideon tried to drink through the crooked tube that she held. He looked and saw that the golden-haired girl was gone, but Susan was standing by the bed.

He had no way of knowing whether she had been there all the time. With her was a little boy, looking at him with big, wondering eyes. "Hi, David!" said Gideon, letting the tube go from his lips.

The child's face broke into a wide grin. "Hi, Dad!" he replied, "Thought you'd never wake up, but I'm sure glad you did!"

"Me, too," replied Gideon. Then he looked beyond David, feeling vaguely that someone else should be there. He looked at Susan and said, "Josie?" inquiringly. He saw Susan's face tighten, and something like a veil dim the clear shining of her eyes.

"She'll be home soon," said Susan.

"Where—is she?" asked Gideon.

"You remember," Susan replied. "She went to visit Frances, and she—she's staying a little longer than I thought, but she'll be back soon."

Gideon, nodded and closed his eyes to think about this, for something in Susan's tone troubled him.

It must have been night and day and then night again, though it was hard to tell in Gideon's half-world. Then came another day, on which he awakened completely conscious. Everything that had been drifting and formless, in and out of darkness, in and out of light, suddenly became solid and real.

The doctor was beside him, studying his chart, and muttering uncertainly, "Hm," and again, "Hm! Any pain here?" asked the doctor, lightly pressing Gideon's left hip.

"No," responded Gideon.

"And here?"

"No."

"And here?"

Gideon shook his head.

"Well—can't believe it!" the doctor muttered. "Five breaks in the hip—never set them. We never did anything to them; it was impossible. Well—we need further X rays." And he walked off, much perplexed, the nurse at his heels.

The sixth day after the accident, Gideon Bruce was sitting by the window in a wheelchair, bathed, shaved, and thin in the somewhat inadequate hospital gown. He looked down on a bright California courtyard where grew red hibiscus and roses of several colors. Mockingbirds were singing on the patio, and the sun shone through a dim veil of only slightly smoggy mist.

Strangely, there was a heaviness within Gideon. He almost wished that he were back in bed, living in that half-world of dim consciousness where there was no need for thought and where he had no responsibility—not even to sleep, for if he needed sleep, it was provided. But Gideon could not stay in bed forever. He had been declared a miracle and told that if his healing continued as it was, he would soon be going home.

The dreadful thing was that Gideon did not want to go home. The thought of facing the parish again—Mr. Crabtree, Angela and Doris, Leslie and Lisa, and all who sat patiently in the pews Sunday after Sunday—made his heart fail. True, Susan had told him of Bishop Updyke's kind though mendacious statement that because of the postponed appointment Gideon had gone on a drive to pass the time. The bishop meant well, thought Gideon, but no one would believe it. He might as well tell the truth. But what was the truth? "Don't think about it now," he told himself, but something deep beneath consciousness would not let it rest. What was the truth?

77

The truth was, as far as he could tell, that he had not wanted to live; he simply could not face life . . .

These thoughts were interrupted by a small sound at the door, and Gideon turned to see Susan pausing there, her eyes wide with joy, her face alight. A rush of tenderness arose in him as he looked at this stalwart woman who loved him without question or doubt. He held out his hand to her with a little smile. "See!" he said. "The doctors are calling me the miracle man!"

Susan bent over him, gathered him into her arms for one swift moment and then, as usual, controlled herself and drew up a chair to sit beside him, only holding his hand in hers.

Something's on her mind, thought Gideon—something besides me. "Josie?" he asked, looking at her. "Is she home yet?"

Susan paused, her eyes flickering away, and back again. She smiled and replied steadily, "No, not yet. She picked up a touch of flu, and Frances thought she should stay until she's better."

"When will that be?" persisted Gideon.

"I don't quite know," said Susan. "I'll call tonight, and find out."

"Maybe you should go up there and drive her home," said Gideon, picturing his daughter ill and feverish.

"Maybe so," replied Susan evenly. "But we'll wait a day or two until we see how things are."

Was she telling him the truth? Gideon did not quite know. However, his mind veered away from the subject. Let it wait a day or two. Let him not face any more truth yet—not just yet.

Gideon could not speak to Susan of his strange unwillingness to come home, but it lay upon him like a burden and he longed to share it. Ellie, he thought briefly, would understand. At first he had thought her a child, but now that he had seen her more, he realized that she was older than she looked. Whatever age she was, she had learned more than many people ever learn—that much, Gideon was sure of.

He must have dozed off, for when he next opened his eyes, Susan had gone, and Ellie herself stood in the doorway.

"Hi," she murmured with a little smile.

"Hi!" said Gideon, himself smiling.

"And look at you, up in a chair!" said Ellie, coming to sit in the place lately vacated by Susan.

"Yes," said Gideon, his voice heavier than it ought to be. "I'm up."

"I almost didn't make it today," said Ellie abruptly. "The thing is, Jess didn't want me to come. He's—I don't know what's the matter with Jess." She paused and looked at Gideon from under her golden eyelashes. "Maybe he thinks I sort of care too much about you. You know, you can get that way when you pray hard for a person. Sometimes it seems as if you just care too much. It's weird."

"Can you care too much?" asked Gideon gently. "It's only the love of Jesus, isn't it?" he added, surprising himself by speaking thus. "I don't see why Jess should object to that."

"He's been acting strange lately," said Ellie with a sigh. "He doesn't come to the coffeehouse any more, because he says he doesn't want Beth telling him what to do. Beth is our leader. She's a beautiful Christian, sort of a mother to all of us, and she runs the coffeehouse," Ellie explained, glowing as she spoke of someone who obviously meant much to her.

"Does Beth tell Jess what to do?"

"No, not really," answered Ellie, "But, after all, she's a lot older, and she kind of teaches us. I mean, she doesn't sit with a book and teach us that way, but she does tell us things. She's the one who found us, and we don't have anyone but her to help us."

"What about—ministers?" asked Gideon hesitantly.

"Oh, ministers don't know much," answered Ellie, unconscious of the insult.

"Don't you think they know something?" asked Gideon.

"Oh, they probably know about the church. I mean, they've made up some rules and things, and they kind of have meetings. But they don't really know that Jesus heals, do they?"

"Ha!" Gideon laughed weakly, and agreed, "Maybe not." Meanwhile, a thought stirred at the back of his mind, the shadow of a memory. Beth, who was Beth? "What's Beth's other name?" he asked Ellie.

"Fisher," said the girl. "We kid her about being maybe a fisher of men, like Jesus said."

"And when you and Jess put your hands on me and prayed, it was Beth who taught you to do that?"

"Yes, only there isn't anything you do, really. You just know that Jesus is alive and real, though we can't see Him, and when we believe, He sends His life into the one who is sick and makes him well, just like He always did," finished Ellie, ungrammatically but sincerely.

"But why can't people simply pray for themselves, and get well?"

"Oh, I guess they can, but sometimes it's too heavy, you know, and they need someone else to be a sort of channel. You know, like the paralyzed men in the Bible, and the lepers and blind men—and you on the mountain."

Beth. Beth Fisher. Gideon had heard that name before. He wanted to remember, but did not want to, and though he closed the door of his mind, still he remembered. Some years before, a little boy in his parish was suddenly taken ill with spinal meningitis. The desperate parents had mentioned to Gideon a woman named Beth Fisher, said to have healing powers, and had asked whether they might get her to come and lay hands on their child. Gideon had forbidden it, revolted by the thought of some strange woman practicing weird rites of healing on a member of his congregation. It savored of medicine men and witch doctors, he thought, and it was definitely not endorsed by the bishop. Could not he, the rector, do all the praying that was necessary? He did mention the child at the Communion service, and also went more than once to the hospital, expressing his hopes and praying that God's will be done. But the child had died.

"What's the matter?" asked Ellie, looking at his knitted brows.

"Has anyone ever been healed of spinal meningitis through Beth's prayers?" he asked intently.

Ellie nodded. "Oh yes, germ things always seem pretty easy," she said, "especially with a child. Of course, Beth doesn't do a lot of this kind of thing. She's too busy with the coffeehouse. But one of the kids got meningitis a few months ago, and Beth laid hands on him and prayed, and he got well."

"He might have recovered anyway," muttered Gideon, who felt as though he were fighting for his life.

Ellie only said, "Sure," bade him goodbye, and went away.

That night Gideon could not sleep. If he had permitted those parents to call in this strange woman, would their child be alive today? Was this one of the many ways in which he had failed his parish? Was this failure and others like it, the prod below the surface of consciousness that had caused him to break forth into senseless irritation before the altar at Easter, and that led later to his near fatal mountain drive—?

What could he do? It was too late to go back through time and save that little boy . . . I won't ask Ellie! he thought resentfully. But he did, on her next visit to him in the hospital.

"There's only one thing to do," said Ellie, matter-of-factly, sitting across from him in the straight hospital chair while he told her the story. "Tell Jesus you're sorry, and ask Him to forgive you."

Gideon almost laughed. "And ask Him to forgive me for all the other things too?" he inquired. "I mean, driving off the road on purpose, and—"

"All the other things too," said Ellie gravely.

"But—" Gideon did not know how to explain the absurdity of this oversimplification. Surely forgiveness was the entire teaching of the church; it was the whole purpose of the Communion service; it was the basic theological fact that he himself pronounced at every service!

"But you haven't believed it," said Ellie, quite as though she could read his thoughts.

"Of course I've believed it!" retorted Gideon, searching wildly through his mind for theological phrases to support him.

"With your mind, maybe, but not down inside," explained Ellie, ignorant of the correct psychological terms.

"And how do you know?"

"Because you're not happy," she said simply, looking directly at him with a little smile.

Gideon pondered this baffling simplicity. "Well, okay," he said finally, "so how do I get the idea across—inside?"

"It's easier if someone else gets it across," said Ellie.

"How?"

"Well, if you'll let me, I'll—I'll just do it. I'd rather do it than try to explain."

"Go ahead," murmured Gideon, feeling foolish but resigning himself to this feeling which apparently was becoming habitual.

Ellie arose, went out and looked up and down the hall, and then returned, closing the door almost shut behind her. "No good shutting it entirely," she said with a little grin. "Then they'll be bound to come poking in to see what we're doing." At this, she stood beside Gideon's chair, placing herself between him and the door, laid both hands on his head, and spoke to Jesus just as if He were there with them. "Jesus, help Gideon to tell You all that is on his mind making him unhappy, so that You can take it away," she said. Then, as Gideon remained silent, not knowing that this would be required of him, she said gently, "Go ahead; just tell Him!"

"I'm sorry, Jesus," said Gideon, thinking only that the faster he did this absurd thing, the quicker it would be over. "I'm sorry I wouldn't let Mrs. Fisher see the little boy, and that he died. And I'm sorry that I tried to kill myself. And, I'm sorry most of all that I didn't stop on the freeway—to help that little girl—" and then to his own horrible embarrassment, Gideon wept.

"That's enough," said Ellie, as though understanding. Again she spoke to Jesus, still standing beside Gideon but no longer touching him. "Now Jesus," she said, "You've heard what Gideon said." Neither of them thought it strange that she used his first name. "I know that You want to forgive him, because that is why You gave your life on the Cross—so that You can keep on giving Your life to us every time we call for help. So I just thank You now that You are doing it.

"I can sort of see Your joy and peace flooding Gideon, healing all the bad memories of worry about the child in the hospital and the one on the freeway, and wanting to kill himself, and everything that has been hurting him on the inside. I mean, the way it's going to be, Jesus, is that he'll be able to remember these things, but they won't give him the same feelings. Instead of worrying, he will feel happy about them, because they are past, and they can't hurt him anymore. Thank You, Jesus! We know it's being done, and these old things—all the things that he should have done and didn't, and all the things he did that he ought not to have done, like driving off the mountain—they can't bother him any more. Thank You, Jesus!"

Only much later did it occur to Gideon that Ellie, who had never attended an Episcopal service or glanced at the prayer book, had pronounced a perfect absolution!

Chapter Eight

Gideon awoke the next morning with a strange feeling which he later identified as happiness. It was a free, spontaneous flow of joy, not ecstatic but deep and quiet. Moreover, he awoke to the tune of an old song, and as he listened to it, the words came, old words, long forgotten.

"What can wash away my sin? Nothing but the blood of Jesus. What can make me pure within? Nothing but the blood of Jesus. Oh, precious is the flow, that from His side doth go—" No, that wasn't quite right. He could not remember the rest, but he had remembered enough. Gideon knew that the melody had floated into his mind because this exact thing had happened to him. He knew that the guilt and remorse for all his past failures had somehow, mysteriously, been washed away and transformed into gentle peace. This was incredible, but it was so. He even tried to resurrect the old, bad feelings, and could not. The burdens were gone, having simply disappeared into thin air! Why? Gideon knew very well why. It was because of the prayer of a young woman who in utter simplicity believed that Jesus Christ, the Son of God, forgives sins.

Oh, he thought, groaning audibly, if only the church knew this! If only he had known it all his life! If only all ministers dared say, "Thank You, Jesus, that You forgive sins." At this, Gideon snapped out of his half-waking condition, his eyes wide open and a slow flush creeping into his cheeks. It was possible, not only possible, but true! For centuries, penitents had confessed their sins, priests accepting their forgiveness with complete belief and finally dismissing them with those most comforting of all words: "Go in peace. God has forgiven all your sins." Wasn't this exactly the substance of what Ellie had said to him?

Even he himself, Gideon now realized, had made such statements. Though confession was now considered by many a bit amusing, an ancient relic not to be taken seriously, nevertheless, someone did occasionally come asking to make a confession. Gideon honored such a person with dignity, by putting on his vestments, going into the chancel, and hearing the confession seriously. Even, according to the old custom, he sometimes gave a penance, the reading of certain psalms, for instance, and finally he said the traditional words, "Go in peace. God has forgiven all your sins."

"What can wash away my sin? Nothing but the blood of Jesus." Again the words sang themselves through Gideon's mind, and the slow flush upon his face deepened as he remembered his own fresh experience of forgiveness. Now he realized that, "Go in peace. God has forgiven all your sins," are the most powerful words anywhere between earth and heaven, and that the blood of Jesus Christ can mysteriously, actually wipe away even the thought patterns and emotional grooves caused by old sins. So by prayer, a person can be set utterly free from any effect of sin or sadness, in time or eternity. In a flash, Gideon realized that this most powerful tool was always his, as a Christian and especially as a minister, and he had not even known that he had it!

Strangely, he did not grieve as this realization crashed over him, castigating himself for his blindness. Rather, he could do nothing but rejoice. No longer need he be afraid to go back to his church. Not only were the old wounds healed so that he could step forth totally free, chains fallen from him, but now he knew that this tool of prayer belonged to him, and that in the name of Jesus Christ, he would use it! Praise God, thought Gideon, that this understanding came to him before he left the hospital, so that he no longer dreaded going home.

"You'll be glad to get home, won't you?" So had crooned Angela and other women of the parish who dropped in, bearing flowers and cookies.

One more potted plant and I'll have to move out! Gideon had thought grimly.

"Home in a few days—great!" Mr. Crabtree had boomed. "You'll feel like a bird out of a cage, huh?"

No, he would not feel like a bird out of a cage, Gideon had thought inside himself. In spite of all the annoyances—rattling food carts, nurses awakening him at dawn with a washcloth, needles being poked into him—Gideon had found the hospital not a cage but a refuge, a hiding place from reality.

Reality! Bob, Josie, Stan—*Stan!* Of all these, Stan lay the most heavily upon Gideon's heart. Could Ellie, he wondered, possibly help Stan as she had helped him? "Lord, let her come just once more," he prayed.

By the time he had, with some help from the nurse, bathed,

dressed, and was sitting by the window, Ellie did come, to say goodbye.

"Do you suppose," asked Gideon slowly, "that you or Beth or somebody could possibly help Stan?"

"Who's Stan?"

"Stan is the father of that little girl killed beside the freeway, remember? I told you about her."

Ellie nodded, remembering very well Gideon's faltering account of this incident that had precipitated him toward sudden death.

"Do you suppose you could tell Stan about Jesus?" asked Gideon eagerly. "Stan is not smashed up outwardly, but on the inside. You know what I mean. Suppose you could help him?"

"I'll try," answered Ellie soberly. "I'd like to try."

"Of course," Gideon went on meditatively, "we know that what Jesus did for me through you was not only the miraculous healing of the body but the healing of my soul as well, mostly by the forgiveness of old sins. So far as I know, Stan isn't brooding on old sins, as I was. He is simply grieving over two tragedies: the death of his wife three years ago, followed now by the loss of his only child."

"The same power works for both," said Ellie with assurance. "I mean, you know—" and she sang softly, " 'There is a balm in Gilead, that makes the wounded whole; there is a balm in Gilead, that heals the sin-sick soul. . . .' You see," she added earnestly, "it's like magic, but it's real power, like light that shines back into darkness and reaches those places in our minds that we try to forget, and heals them. It's just like magic," she repeated.

"I know," said Gideon gratefully. "Look, after I've been home a few days, come and see me, at the church. We'll go to the garage together, and I'll introduce you to Stan, and tell him how you and I got acquainted while I'm buying some gas, and—well, you can take over from there."

Ellie's face brightened. "The Lord will take over from there," she said.

"Gideon!" Susan was standing in the doorway, her eyes alight. "You look like a new person!"

"I am a new person," said Gideon, a wide smile upon his thin face.

Susan waited during the tedious delay until the doctor came to sign his release, and at last, in solemn procession, Gideon in a wheelchair escorted by a nurse, they trundled out into the blinding sunshine. The hills were hazy, and farther mountains invisible, but all near objects shone with unbelievable brilliance. Gideon looked about with a strange feeling that he had never seen the world before. They drove along Orange Grove Boulevard, where blue jacarandas lit the gray blue sky, and finally turned toward the mountains into their own street. Gideon hardly spoke, looking with amazement upon a world that was new and shining and beautiful!

Finally, a catch in his voice, he asked, "What about Josie? When is she coming home? Look," he added as Susan hesitated, "I know you've been keeping something from me, and I guess I really didn't want to know while I was in the hospital, but I'm strong enough now. Tell me about Josie. I know she hasn't been with Frances all this time."

"She's there now, though," answered Susan quickly, "but you're right. She was missing for a while, with that Leroy and a bunch of other kids, I guess. She told Frances some story about where they were going—I forget where—and

89

that they would be back by evening, but they didn't come back. Frances called me, of course, but that was the very time you—" Susan's voice trailed off, as she remembered those ghastly days.

"Tough for you," said Gideon gently.

"Yes," Susan agreed, swallowing hard, "it was. At first Frances thought that she had gone for good, and taken her suitcase, but later she found it in the back of the closet. And—and Josie did come back."

"Where was she?" asked Gideon slowly.

"At some sort of Be-In, whatever that is. You ask her when she comes home."

"When will that be?"

"She has had flu; that much is true," said Susan, "but she's all right now, and I think not later than tomorrow Frances will bring her home."

Somehow, none of this surprised Gideon. He sat in silence, just wondering about Josie. Would she follow the vague, obstructed, dead-ending pattern of so many of her contemporaries, or could she possibly swing back into being her old self, the daughter whom he loved so dearly? She, too, would have to become a new creature, thought Gideon, or else— He did not complete the thought.

Susan parked on their narrow drive, opened the door for Gideon, and started to help him out. "No," he said, "I want to do it myself."

"Crutches," said Susan, getting them from the back seat and holding them for him.

Gideon replied, "I don't even need crutches. Look!" Slowly, wavering a bit, but nevertheless walking, he crossed the bit of lawn, climbed three steps, and entered the front door. Inside, he sank into the nearest chair, sweat

90

on his forehead. It was not a sweat of pain, only exhaustion. He had walked alone! When the doctors had finally decided that he would live, they had told him he would not walk again. Then, as he began making his amazing recovery, they had added, "Maybe with crutches," and still later, when X rays showed the leg perfect, they told him to use crutches for at least a month. But he had walked into the house without them.

"You'd better use them anyway," said Susan, fluttering over him like an anxious hen.

"Don't worry," replied Gideon, "I will when I really need them."

"The doctor said—" Before Susan had time to quote the wise physician, the doorbell tinkled and in came Mr. Crabtree, grinning broadly. Gideon rose to meet him.

"Can't believe it," rumbled Mr. Crabtree, looking down at Gideon's quite useful legs. "Can't believe it!"

"Well, want a demonstration?" Gideon walked three steps to the fireplace and back again.

"Sit down!" said Mr. Crabtree hastily. "Didn't know if we'd ever get you back or not. It's wonderful!"

"It is a miracle," replied Gideon clearly. "The doctor said so."

"Well—uh, that's great, just great! Your accident really worried us."

"Accident?" questioned Gideon.

"Yes, accident, yes," said Mr. Crabtree. "The bishop told us, you know. He had to postpone your appointment, so you went for a ride in the mountains and—had an accident."

"Oh, yes," responded Gideon absently, remembering that Susan had told him of the bishop's charitable words. "But you know," he went on, "that's not really true. It's kind of the bishop, but—"

91

"Look here, my boy," Mr. Crabtree interrupted. "What Bishop Updyke says is true. It's got to be; he's the bishop. And after all," he added, "the thing that's kindest to the parish and your family, that's truth!"

"I see what you mean," Gideon replied.

Mr. Crabtree, his heavy face lightening with relief, sank down in a chair and murmured gladly, "That's it! Well, they'll all be coming to see you—all the ladies, and everybody—so I won't stay long. Take it easy, hear? Don't try to do anything—not for a week anyway. We've got the services all fixed up. Leslie's doing all right, and he'll be in presently to talk with you. You just stay here and rest."

"I take it those are orders," grinned Gideon.

"They are," said Mr. Crabtree, "orders!" and he clumped away and swung heavily into his car.

"I wonder what he really meant," said Gideon to Susan. "They're not too keen on having me stay. They let me know that much before—"

"Yes, but now you're a new man," Susan reassured him. "You just wait and see."

Come, behold the works of the Lord! thought Gideon, and he laid his head back in the soft chair and sighed. He was a new man, and what the Lord would work in the new life opening before him was more than he could tell!

The first crisis Gideon would meet was his own daughter, and the first enemy to be overcome was his fear for her. He did not sleep well, waking twice that night with wild dreams of Josie screaming beside the freeway. No, it was not Josie, but in the dream, the fleeing girl became Josie, and in the dream, Gideon himself ran after her, and lifted her in his arms, and brought her home.

The next afternoon, before the traffic thickened, and before Gideon's heart wore itself out with beating, Josie came home. He heard her footsteps on the porch, and rose out of the easy chair. The door was flung open, and Josie ran ahead of her aunt and rushed into his arms. Gideon gratefully lowered himself back into the chair, his arms around her, holding her tight. "Oh, Daddy," Josie sobbed, "are you all right?"

"Sure, Baby," Gideon answered, using a pet name that he had not used for years, patting her dark, curly hair, "sure I'm all right. Every now and then one or several doctors would pop into my room, telling each other to come and see the miracle man. That was me!"

"Oh, great!" cried Josie, snuggling close to him. "I was afraid maybe you were worrying about me, and that was why—the accident happened."

"No, child," Gideon reassured her, "As a matter of fact this—uh, happened before I knew you had gone with Leroy."

"I'm sorry, Daddy," Josie whispered in a choked voice. "I'm really sorry. I wouldn't have done it if I'd known."

Gideon put his hand under her chin, lifting her face so that he could look directly into her eyes. "Josie," he said, "I'm sorry too. I wouldn't have done what I did, either, if I'd known."

"You mean, you did it on purpose?" breathed Josie, looking straight at him, her eyes wide.

Gideon nodded. "You forgive me, and I'll forgive you, okay?"

"Okay," said Josie with deep relief, and then she asked, "Why did you?"

"It's kind of hard to explain," said Gideon, listening a moment and realizing that Frances and Susan were chatting comfortably in the kitchen. "I think it was mostly because of

93

old memories inside me that hurt a whole lot, you know, and nobody could take away the hurt. It was worse, being a minister, because I was supposed to be able to take away other people's hurts. At least Jesus was, but I was His agent, you might say. I knew there ought to be some kind of power, something I could do, but for all my looking, I couldn't find it."

"Wow! That's weird!" said Josie, scrambling out of his arms and perching on a footstool beside him. "You know, Dad, that's about the way I felt! And that's really why I went off. It wasn't so much that I was crazy about Leroy. Oh, he's sort of my best pal, and every girl's got to have some guy, you know. But it wasn't so much that; it was the things he said."

"What did he say?" asked Gideon.

"Well, he said—we're the New Age people, you know. We kids can't be satisfied with the old establishment, and the way they live—go to the office at nine, come back at five, have a few cocktails, eat dinner, watch TV, go to bed. Leroy said there's got to be more to life than that. There's got to be something else! I told him that's what preachers say in church, but Leroy just laughed. He said, yeah, that's what he figured they say in church, but the churches don't feel different from anyplace else. And preachers just say words. They're no different from anybody else either, no happier. The thing is, people in churches think they've got it. But we New Age kids, we know that's not all there is."

"So—you went with him," meditated Gideon slowly, "to find what else there is."

"Yeah, that's right. It was a Be-In—a thing for kids to come to and just be."

"Did you find it?"

"No!" Josie bounced up from the footstool, and down again with a plop, as though to emphasize her words. "No, Dad, it was pretty—pretty rough."

"What was it like?"

"Oh, we went to a—a park, sort of, and more and more kids came, and everybody brought guitars, and things like that. Some even brought babies. The babies cried," added Josie piteously. "One baby there, it cried and cried, and I guess it was real sick. After a while—it stopped crying. Dad, you know, I think it died."

"Died!" cried Gideon in real horror.

"I—I think so. They wouldn't tell us, see? They wouldn't tell us anything, but it didn't cry any more—and they sort of took it where we couldn't see."

"Weren't there any police?" demanded Gideon furiously.

"Oh, they were around, but what could they do? They didn't know about the baby; I mean, what could they do?"

"Why didn't they just tell you all to get out of there and go home?" asked Gideon.

"We weren't doing anything bad," said Josie, "not really bad—only it was kind of miserable, see? First everybody sang and laughed and played their guitars, and it was sort of fun. But, Dad, you know you can't keep that up all night—singing and laughing and carrying on. After a while, I got so sleepy I could hardly stand it, but there wasn't any place to sleep, and I couldn't leave, because there was no place to go. Anyway, we were too crowded, and the car was jammed in, and we could never have gotten out of there—not in the middle of the night, we couldn't. So—Leroy had some grass—you know, marijuana—and—"

"What!" cried Gideon hoarsely.

"Well, yeah. He told me to smoke it and I'd feel better, and I did—"

95

"Feel better?" asked Gideon grimly.

"Yeah, sure, you know, for a while I felt fine. I laughed and sang and felt just fine, but after a while, I got terribly sleepy again. So then Leroy said, 'Here, I know how to fix that.' And he gave me a little red pill."

"Oh, my God!" said Gideon shuddering.

"Well, gee, Dad, it wasn't that bad. I just kind of went to sleep, see? The stuff helped me go to sleep, and that was better than staying awake and being miserable all night."

"What next?" asked Gideon heavily.

"Next day the cops came, and they kind of broke it up. They told us to break it up, get moving, go home. So we began moving—and was I glad! Some of them fussed and fought a little, but I was glad to get out of there! I looked around to see if I could find that baby and its mother. It never seemed to have any father, just a mother not much older than me. But I couldn't find them. Then we left, and I began to feel just terrible, you know, all hot and cold, just terrible. By the time we got back to Aunt Frances' I was sick! But I'm okay now," she added. "Don't worry about me, Dad, I'm all right."

Gideon leaned forward, put his arms around his daughter, and drew her head against him. "Remember when you were a little girl," he said, "and you used to sit in my lap while I told you stories?"

Josie nodded, her arms tight about him. "About Mowgli," she said, "and the Wizard of Oz!"

"Yes" said Gideon gently. "Maybe someday I'll tell you a better story."

"What about?"

"About Jesus."

"Oh," Josie sounded disappointed as she untangled herself from his arms and sat up. "I've always known about Jesus—Sunday school and church, and all that."

"But He's real!" said Gideon. "Do you know He's real? Do you know He's alive and can do miracles today?"

"Is that what happened to you?" asked Josie, new understanding coming into her eyes.

"Yes," said Gideon, his face shining, "that's what happened to me. Remember the man that couldn't walk, and Jesus told him to get up, pick up his bed, and go home? Look at me, Josie, look at me!" Whereupon Gideon rose from his chair, and with the merest tremble walked across the room and back again. "The doctors said that leg was broken in five places, with the hip bone jammed up into the body, and there were cuts inside and out, too—but look at me!"

"Wow! How did it happen?" said Josie.

"There was a girl," responded Gideon. "She doesn't seem much older than you, but I guess she really is. There was a whole bunch of young people, but she is the one I remember best. They came singing on the mountain, and—"

"Why in the world were they singing on the mountain?" asked Josie.

"It was kind of funny," Gideon agreed. "I asked Ellie about it when she came to the hospital. She used to come and see me, so as to keep on praying for the leg. She said they were singing to sort of comfort the San Andreas Fault and tell the mountains that Jesus loves them. It is their way of praying that there won't be bad earthquakes. Isn't that—weird?"

"Yeah," exclaimed Josie. "But you know, those kids were probably looking for something, the same as Leroy and I were."

"I suppose so," said Gideon thoughtfully, and reached forward to take Josie's hand in his. "When you were little, you were the funniest kid, always looking for something!" Gideon's voice grew deep and tender with memories of the small, rosy-cheeked child who would scramble into his lap and cuddle in his arms. "We'd turn around and you'd be gone! Where was Josie? We'd go and search for you up and down the street. The place where you went most often," he added, chuckling, "was the barbershop."

"I don't remember that," said Josie, "but I think I remember one time when I went to the police station. Something about my tricycle?"

"It certainly was!" laughed Gideon. "You weren't more than four. We couldn't find you anywhere. And then you came, pedaling along the sidewalk on your tricycle, perfectly happy. You said you'd left it out and couldn't find it, so you went to the police station and asked them, and they had it, so you came home!"

They sat there, father and daughter, laughing together. "You see, both of us ran away," said Gideon, "looking for something. You found your tricycle, and I've found—something else."

The second Sunday after his return, Gideon Bruce conducted the service. He was thin and drawn, yet a radiance shone from him as he stood to read the lesson that he had chosen—the story of Elijah fleeing from Jezebel, the furious queen who threatened his life. Gideon read from the nineteenth chapter of the first book of Kings:

"He arose, and went for his life, and came to Beersheba, which belongeth to Judah, and left his servant there. But he himself went a day's journey into the wilderness, and came and sat down under a juniper tree: and he requested for himself that he might die; and said, It is enough; now, O Lord, take away my life; for I am not better than my fathers. And as he lay and slept under a juniper tree, behold, then an angel touched him, and said unto him, Arise and eat. And he looked, and, behold, there was a cake baken on the coals, and a cruse of water at his head. And he did eat and drink, and laid him down again. And the angel of the Lord came again the second time, and touched him, and said, Arise and eat; because the journey is too great for thee. And he arose, and did eat and drink, and went in the strength of that meat forty days and forty nights unto Horeb, the mount of God."

Gideon continued the story of marvelous things happening to Elijah. The Lord Himself asked him, "What doest thou here, Elijah?" And Elijah complained of the children of Israel, their evil deeds and rebellion against God.

Finally Elijah said, "I, even I only, am left; and they seek my life, to take it away."

Gideon finished the chapter, said, "Here endeth the lesson," and sat down.

When the time came for the sermon, he looked at the congregation, reminded them of the Bible reading they had just heard, and said, "I, too, have sat under that juniper tree, and I have longed for death, and sought it. You know that. But God will not let us hide forever under a juniper tree. He bids us come forth and climb the high mountain of faith, to stand before Him. As we take our stand firmly in Him, the forces of this earth will do their best to dislodge us. There may come a mighty wind blowing from the dark clouds of this troubled, troubling earth. There may come an earthquake, shaking us to the very foundations of our being. There may come the fire of the anger of those still hiding under the juniper tree who are fearful of our new stand in faith.

"But the Lord is not in these destructive forces. If we stand fast and resist them, the time will come when we will hear His still small voice within us, and will know that He is not only King of kings, and Lord of lords, but also the breath of our own being—the Father who, having begotten our spirits of His own glory, abides forever within us, our Comforter and Guide."

And thus began a sermon which many of Gideon's congregation never forgot.

Chapter Nine

Some days later, Gideon entered the bishop's office and sat in a deep leather chair facing the desk. Bishop Updyke, who had summoned him, put his fingertips together, and looked at him from under lowered brows. Other bishops, handsomely photographed and framed, looked down from the walls between bookshelves full of holy tomes, and plaques of the saints, and of gnarled hands uplifted in prayer.

"What's happened to you?" demanded the bishop, omitting all preliminaries. "Since your—accident, you look like a new person!"

"I am," said Gideon, remembering a verse, which he fully understood for the first time: "If any man be in Christ, he is a new creature; old things are passed away; behold, all things are become new."

"Tell me what has brought this about," the bishop asked, looking at him with warm intentness.

Remembering Ellie's words, Gideon replied simply, "I've found Jesus."

"That's a strange answer," said the bishop after a considerable pause. "You're supposed to have known Him since you were a child brought up in the church, and you are, after all, a priest."

"I know, Bishop," Gideon agreed ruefully, "but the truth is, I never really did know Jesus until now."

"Well, tell me all about it," the bishop encouraged him. "I really want to understand."

"Jesus Himself must have been looking for me," said Gideon quietly. "You know, Bishop, though you were kind enough to cover it up, I was running away from the Lord and from life. Did you hear that I was found, and my life was saved, by a group of young people?"

"Hippies, I gather," said the bishop unenthusiastically.

"You might call them that," admitted Gideon, "or maybe Jesus People. I don't know whether they, in their simplicity, call themselves anything. They know Jesus, that's all."

"Being what they are—or what we think they are—how can they?" demanded the bishop.

"Through desperation, I suppose," returned Gideon with a gentle smile. "When they were at the bottom, someone told them that Jesus loved them, that He was alive and real and could make them new people, healing drug addiction and forgiving sin. They were just simple enough to believe it!"

"Hm," said the bishop reflectively, and then went on after a moment, "Hasn't the Church always taught this?"

"Yes," agreed Gideon, "and it is very perplexing that though the Church has taught it, very few people, church members or not, believe it. Or perhaps," he added, "they believe it with their minds but not their hearts. The only way people can really *get* it, I guess," Gideon went on pensively, "is the same way I did—through healing, through a miracle. That's what it was, you know," he declared, "a miracle. Look at me!"

The bishop hesitated. "You do look fine," he said with a smile, "but I suppose one might say that the doctors' original diagnosis was wrong."

"That's not what they say," objected Gideon.

"Are you sure you are in a position to know what the doctors say?" the bishop persisted, but not unkindly. "After all, your mind was unstable, and probably had been for quite a while, as I happen to know. In fact," he went on, "I sent for you today because your vestry, and especially the senior warden, are somewhat—concerned about you."

"Concerned?" asked Gideon. "They had plenty to be concerned about before, but now I'm well!"

"Mm—well, yes," said the bishop, "but it is easy for a person in deep—depression, to swing into a somewhat—what shall I say?—exalted state—a sort of temporary euphoria. To tell the truth, your vestry are worried that this may be the case with you."

Gideon's heart sank into his stomach. "So what do they want?" he inquired.

"They think a lot of you," the bishop hastened on. "They are truly fond of you—but right now, you puzzle them."

"Because I know Jesus!" mused Gideon. "Yes, I can see that such a thing might puzzle a vestry."

"They're wondering whether, for a while, it might be wise for you to be—uh, under a bit of supervision."

"What do you mean by that?" demanded Gideon, his throat tightening.

"Well, that you avail yourself of the advice and care of a psychiatrist," said the bishop. "After all, that's what psychiatrists are for. We sometimes need doctors of the mind, as well as of the body."

"My mind does not need a doctor," stated Gideon.

The bishop answered, "That's what you think, at the moment, but one's own opinion, at a time of transition like this, is hardly to be trusted. However," he added hastily, "I don't insist, not now. I only suggest it for your own good, and for the reassurance of the parish."

"Bishop Updyke," said Gideon, in a voice that trembled only a little, "have you ever had any such experience—I mean a—a sort of confrontation with our Lord?"

"I am confident that in my more conventional way I have met Christ," the bishop replied, speaking the last words with precision, as if they were in quotation marks.

"Then," said Gideon with quiet emphasis, "since you know Jesus, you do know that He is still here and still does miracles, don't you?"

"I have been hearing a lot about miracles," said the bishop, looking directly at Gideon, "and frankly, I don't either accept or believe all of it. There may be considerable exaggeration."

Gideon shook his head. "I wish, Bishop Updyke, that you would talk with my doctor. X rays can't be exaggerated. Get from him a complete statement of my condition when he first saw me, and of the progress of my healing. That's fair enough, isn't it?"

The bishop pondered, his chin resting upon his cupped hand. "That does seem—reasonable," he said. "Yes, it seems quite reasonable. And if he thinks that you should also see a psychiatrist?"

"Then I will."

On this note, Gideon returned home, and at the first opportunity challenged his senior warden. "So, you got the bishop wondering about me, did you?"

"Only for your own good, my lad," replied Mr. Crabtree. "We just want to make sure you don't rush ahead too fast, that you get plenty of rest, and time to—sort of come back to yourself."

Seated in Gideon's office, they could hear the choir practicing in the church, and Boy Scouts racketing out of the parish house. "I'm not sure I want to come back, completely, to my old self," he murmured. "I'm a whole lot happier now."

"Something's happened to you, no question about that," replied the senior warden, a bit doubtfully. "I guess it will turn out all right in the long run. But right now, I don't know; the change is so sudden. You—you kind of frighten people by being so—sort of exuberant."

"What do you suggest?" asked Gideon.

"Well," replied Mr. Crabtree deliberately, "if you just wouldn't—talk about the Lord so much, and in such familiar terms."

"Oh?" said Gideon wryly. "Is there something improper in talking about Jesus? I—um, thought that was part of my job."

"Yes, yes," said Reginald hastily. "And if you would just refer to Him, you know, with dignity, as 'Our Lord,' that would be fine. But there is something—disrespectful about just saying 'Jesus,' as if He were somebody you'd just said hello to around the corner."

"But He is!" cried Gideon, "He is! However," he added courteously, "I do see what you mean. The bishop said something like it—that people might be frightened by such a sudden change in me. I really will try to moderate my transports for a while."

"When you say, 'Jesus,' the way you do," inquired Mr.

Crabtree, curious in spite of himself, "what do you sort of see in your mind? You look far away, and you smile—"

"Well, it's hard to say," murmured Gideon, for actually what he was seeing at that moment was a young woman's guileless face, her blue eyes filled with unearthly joy. He could not tell Mr. Crabtree this, but it was through this girl, Ellie, that the love of Jesus had shone for him, and it was through her that the light of the Holy Spirit had come into him. She would not always stand between him and Jesus, Gideon knew, but for the present, she was like a glass, through whom he saw his Lord as never before.

At the end of this interview, Gideon drove home, parked the car, and limped into the house, his chin protruding belligerently. "What's the matter?" asked Susan, coming from the kitchen, dish towel in hand.

"Oh, they think I'm crazy," said Gideon.

"Well—?" Susan sat down, looking at him with twinkling eyes.

"What do you think?" asked Gideon. "But listen to this: Both the bishop and the senior warden think I should see a psychiatrist."

"So why not?" asked Susan calmly.

Gideon sat up straight, his blue eyes flashing. "You think I'm crazy, too?"

"No, I don't," said Susan. "I think you're just your usual, somewhat unusual, lovable self! However, if a psychiatrist says you're all right, then they won't worry any more."

"Yes, but—"

"You're just afraid of psychiatrists, that's what," said Susan gently.

"I guess I am," Gideon laughed briefly.

"Lots of people are afraid of doctors," Susan went on.

"If they have suspicious symptoms, they won't see a doctor for fear of what he will say. That's stupid. If they do have something bad, they *should* see him, the sooner the better, and if they don't, he'll say so. Then their minds will be at rest, and their friends can fuss about something else."

"Well!" Gideon laughed, rubbing the back of his head. "Okay," he conceded, "but let's wait until after the bishop has talked with my doctor."

"And if he then says to see a psychiatrist, you'll go?" questioned Susan.

"Well, I guess I'll have to, won't I?" Gideon said, smiling.

Susan went back to the kitchen and set about making a casserole. She knew very well that Gideon was not mentally disturbed. However, she thought tight-lipped, there was no question that he was emotionally upset. How much of it was Jesus, and how much Ellie, Susan did not know. Beneath the barriers of reserve in which both of them grew up, Gideon's love for Susan and hers for him ran deep and true. Nevertheless, she resented his present preoccupation with Ellie. Standing at the sink, she turned on the hot water furiously, and then turned it off, wondering what she had intended to do with it.

Gideon was no woman's man. He bore with the women of the parish, but did not understand them. Their solicitude he found annoying and their notions frustrating. He did not delight in their company. He consulted the men of the vestry upon every subject, but dealt with the women as little as possible, even seeming to neglect them. He tenderly loved the little girls of the parish, just as he loved the little boys, but as they grew older, he retreated behind his barricade of dignified reserve.

Now here was this girl, who looked hardly more mature

than Josie. Gideon could not speak of her without tenderness in his voice. She and her friends had saved his life, Susan knew that. She and the tall Jess, whom Susan had met at the hospital, had, in Gideon's own words, led him to Jesus. But that, she thought was ridiculous! Surely, Gideon had always known Jesus!

What then was this change in him? It was definitely good, a change for the better, Susan reflected honestly. So whatever it was, her practical nature asserted, she had better rejoice and be glad in it.

At this point, Josie came in, flung down her school books, and sat casually on the table.

"Had a good day?" asked Susan automatically.

"Oh sure," said Josie, "more or less." Crunching a potato chip, she added suddenly, "Leroy's kind of mad at me."

"Good!" snapped Susan, "Glad he is!"

"Yeah, I know," said Josie. "You never liked him. Well, now he doesn't like me much."

"Why?"

"I guess because I don't want to run around with the gang and smoke grass, you know."

Susan drew in her breath. "Marijuana?" she asked in a whisper, as one might speak of death.

"Yeah, but I—I just don't want it any more, Mom. You know, it makes you feel good for a while, but then you get dull and sleepy, and—oh, I just don't want to bother with it."

"Thank God!" said Susan, and launched into what she had heard of the evils of drugs, which might lead to insanity, which might lead to death.

"Lay off, Mom," said Josie. "They give us all that in school, and it only makes some kids more anxious to try it. They want to show off, see, and prove that they won't fall into all these traps."

108

"Anyway," sighed her mother, "I'm really glad that you don't want it." Then she asked abruptly, "Have you met this Ellie that your father talks about?"

"Sure," said Josie, "at the hospital."

"What do you think of her?" Susan could not resist the question.

"I don't know," said Josie. "She asked me if I knew Jesus. If that's not the darndest question! I've seen those Jesus kids before, you know. They roam the streets and ask anybody they see if they know they're sinners, and if they know Jesus. That turns me off!"

"I can see how it would," said Susan with a short laugh. "It does me, too, but I guess sometimes it helps people."

Josie nodded. "You know, Mom," she said, sitting in a chair, her elbows on the table, "I'm kind of worried about Florrie."

Susan often worried about Florrie herself. "Here, cut these up for me, will you?" and she handed her daughter a bowl of mushrooms. "What is it with Florrie now?"

"Well, you know, she's always been crazy about boys; even when we were little, she wanted to play getting married, and things like that."

"I remember," laughed Susan. "Once she and that tiny, dark-haired boy were playing getting married. They called to you to come and play with them. Do you know what you said?"

Josie shook her head, popping a bit of mushroom into her mouth.

"You were only four, and you said, 'I can't get married; I've just been born!'"

Mother and daughter laughed together. "Well," Josie continued, "Florrie's still got boys on her mind. And I tell you, Mom, this Marcus she goes with—I don't like him a bit. You remember him?"

"I'm afraid so," responded her mother. "Didn't he and Florrie and you and Leroy go to that—Live-In, or whatever it was?"

Josie nodded solemnly. "Yeah, and you know, Marcus is always telling how he takes drugs and they don't bother him a bit."

"He does!" With a horrified jerk Susan turned around from the sink.

"Oh, only pot as far as I know," said Josie. "I don't think he uses hard stuff."

"What about Florrie?" asked Susan.

"Gee, Mom, I don't really know. She acts queer sometimes, you know, sort of half asleep."

"She always did act half asleep," commented Susan, interrupted by a shout from the front door.

"Josie, come on out!" called a boy. Josie sprang up and started out of the kitchen.

"Come right back here!" commanded her mother. "He can come, too, if he wants to. Tell him you've got to help me. I want to see for myself what they're like."

"Okay," said Josie, surprised at her mother's interest. "Come in here, gang," she called out.

"You come out!"

"No, got to help Mom. Come on in! Mom says so."

Florrie then appeared at the kitchen door, a small pale girl with lank brown hair. "Hey, that's a neat outfit," said Josie, eyeing her somewhat peculiar garb. "Have a seat. I'll be done soon; just got to help Mom."

With a shy smile, Florrie dropped into a chair. "Wait for you outside," said the tall boy, Marcus, lurking in the doorway.

"No," said Josie, "here's another chair. Sit down! Have a coke." She went to the refrigerator and got refreshments, while the tall youth grudgingly sat down, tossing his head to get the hair out of his eyes. There was a look of truculence about him, dark unfriendliness, that made Susan cringe.

"What's going on?" asked Josie, wiping dishes and putting them on the shelves.

"Got a neat idea!" cried the boy. "How about you and Leroy coming with us tomorrow?"

"Where to?"

"Haven't quite doped that out," answered Marcus, carefully casual. "Some of the guys say it's neat out in the desert this time of year. I mean, it's really cool. We thought it'd be cool, you know, just to start and see where we end up. What do you say?"

"Tomorrow," said Susan primly, "is a school day."

"School—ha!" Marcus snorted slightly and tossed his hair, peering from under it with dark eyes that never seemed to look directly at a person.

"School!" repeated Marcus, "Boy, I've had enough of that jazz. What's the use of school?"

"Some people think," said Susan coldly, "that it's a good idea to learn things like reading, writing, and spelling."

"Oh, I can read and write," responded Marcus, "and nobody cares how you spell. I'm not going to keep on with this school jazz much longer."

"And what do you plan to do in life?" asked Susan.

Josie looked at her mother quellingly, and pursued the subject more lightheartedly. "Yeah, that's an idea, Marcus," she said. "What're you going to do?"

"I don't care whether I do anything," growled Marcus.

111

"I might just take off. Do whatever comes into my head."

"Oh, come on!" said Josie.

Florrie smiled admiringly, and murmured, "That's the kind of guy he is, Josie! Really!"

"Yeah, but that doesn't make sense," said Josie. "You've got to have something to do."

"Yeah? Who says? That's what the establishment says," proclaimed Marcus, answering his own question and rising to lean against the doorjamb, arms folded, with an air of extreme wisdom. "What good have they done? The whole country's a mess. I'm not going to join them, so I might as well quit right now."

Florrie looked at him. "Just have adventures, huh? Like those people that came out west and started everything—"

"By hard work," interrupted Susan forcefully, "building houses and roads, finding water, clearing land—hard work!"

"Aw, that's all gone out of style," proclaimed Marcus. "Us New Age kids, we don't do that!"

"So who's going to feed you?"

"Oh, we get along. You know, we don't eat much. That's another trouble with the establishment—you eat too much. We're learning we don't have to."

"What would you live on?"

"You know, greens, fruit—things that are easy to get. We don't eat meat and that stuff. Eating meat isn't right."

"Where do you get that?" demanded Susan. "Not out of the Bible. Jesus didn't tell people not to eat meat." As soon as she spoke, Susan realized that quoting the Bible was a mistake, but she was so accustomed to the Bible as the final authority that the words came unbidden.

Marcus doubled over in merriment. "Never mind Jesus," he said. "He isn't a New Age kid! Gosh, He lived way back! Why pay any attention to Him?"

Josie flung down her dish towel, and faced Marcus. Her cheeks were flushed. "Okay—so where do you get your ideas?" she demanded.

"I dunno," drawled Marcus. "A lot of us kids think like that, and I know some guys on the Strip—you know, the ones with long yellow robes and their hair in pigtails, sort of. They know the wisdom of the far east. Those guys are really weird, but they're cool. They tell it like it is. And they don't eat meat."

"Buddhists!" exclaimed Susan shortly, again turning her back upon this uncouth youth.

"Whatever they're called," growled Marcus, "they've got new ideas, like ours. That's why we call ourselves the New Age kids."

"New!" Susan exploded again, whirling about. She had intended to say no more, but this she could not stand. "It's thousands of years old, much older than Christianity."

"That makes no never-mind," replied Marcus. "Maybe it's old, but it's new nowadays, and that's the way us kids want to live."

"So who's going to pay for what you do eat? Who do you think pays the taxes for your food stamps while you goof off and don't work?" Josie pursued the argument. "It's the people who work that take care of you. It's the establishment!"

"Okay," said Marcus, "they've got it coming to them. Come on, Florrie, we don't want to stick around here. Josie, you coming with us or not?"

"I'm not," said Josie as they drifted out.

"Good riddance!" breathed Susan, her face a white flame of anger. "Josie, I don't want you to have anything more to do with those two."

"I don't want anything more to do with Marcus, that's for sure," said Josie. "But Florrie—we've been friends since we were kids. And you know, Mom, I'm scared about her!"

"I am too," said Susan soberly.

"I wish I could keep her away from Marcus—sort of take care of her."

Susan poured a cup of coffee and sat at the table beside her daughter. "I wonder if Florrie would listen to—oh, you know, Ellie, the girl that helped your father."

"I wonder." Josie meditated, chin in hand. "Florrie, she believes anything anybody tells her, and Ellie's as far out as Marcus is—only in a different way. Why don't we ask Dad?" She looked hopefully at her mother. "Maybe he'll know what to do."

Chapter Ten

Gideon drove to the garage on Foothill Boulevard followed by Ellie in the rattletrap car used for the work of the Christian coffeehouse. When they had talked in his office before starting, Ellie had said quite casually that no doubt what Stan needed was the Baptism in the Holy Spirit, to which Gideon had reacted with shocked amazement. "Good heavens!" he exploded. "You don't mean that you'd pray for the Holy Spirit to comfort a hard-bitten mechanic bereaved of his wife and now also of his child? Why, for all I know, he doesn't believe anything about God!"

"Is there any harm in praying for him to have the joy of the Lord?" Ellie said softly.

"No, of course not—but how could he?" asked Gideon incredulously.

"I mean a magic kind of joy, not dependent on anything in this world," Ellie explained, looking far away, as at something invisible. "After all, it's what Jesus promised. It's His Holy Spirit."

She spoke as innocently as if she were offering a plate of good food. Indeed, the first day she had come to see Gideon in his study she had laid her hands on his head, as though she were the priest and he the candidate for ordination, and prayed for the Holy Spirit to come upon him, giving him all gifts of the Spirit that were best for him. Theologically, Gideon believed that he had already received the Holy Spirit in his ordination, and for that matter in his confirmation and baptism, and he told Ellie this quite definitely. "But you don't have Him," she had returned, equally definitely, "not all of Him."

This there was no denying, and Gideon had found from the beginning that to argue with Ellie was fruitless, so leaving theology aside, he permitted her to pray. The joy of the Lord did indeed enter him, a sort of icy barrier somewhere in his diaphragm melting away and a warm, soothing current of life coming in. He felt it! Its tenderness moved him to tears, and then the tears burst into joy, and he laughed aloud in delight. No wonder Gideon's face shone when Angela and Doris saw him emerge from his study, and he didn't care! Ellie had gone ahead, padding light-footed down the hall and disappearing through the heavy swinging doors.

Now she was following, and Gideon, glancing in the mirror, wondered whether the disreputable car would make it to the garage. It did, and Ellie parked by the sidewalk while Gideon made the first approach to the glum mechanic whose head was under the hood of a car.

"What if he won't talk?" Gideon asked Ellie nervously. "What if he has a customer, and can't?"

"We'll just ask the Lord to open the way," said Ellie, "and if this isn't the time, we'll try again."

"Find something wrong with your car for him to check," suggested Gideon.

Ellie replied laughing, "That wouldn't be hard."

So when Gideon indicated his friend's car was having problems, Stan said briefly, "Okay, put it over there," jerking his thumb to a corner of the lot. Then he inserted his glum face, strangely handsome above a blue shirt which matched his eyes, into the car's inner regions, and emerged shortly with grim disapproval. "Mean to say this heap still goes?" he demanded.

"Well, sometimes," faltered Ellie, pleading in her voice.

Stan's eyes narrowed, looking at her more keenly. He turned to Gideon and asked bluntly, "Who is she?"

"She and her friends found me on the mountain," replied Gideon, gratitude pulsing in his voice. "Their prayers saved my life."

"She doesn't want to see what's wrong with the car; she damn well knows that," Stan grumbled. "She wants to see what's wrong with me." He turned on his heel, as though to leave, but then he whirled back and looked at Ellie, his eyes softening and misting over with a gentleness that Gideon had never seen in this tormented, taciturn man. At that moment, Gideon decided later, Stan fell in love with Ellie.

"Take over," said Stan with a jerk of his head to the boy minding the pumps, and he led the way to the little shop behind the garage, motioning Ellie to a seat on a high stool. "Pile of tires there, Rev," said Stan to Gideon, his eyes remaining on Ellie. Gideon perched upon the tires, and Stan, leaning against a partially dismantled car, said to Ellie with frightening directness: "Shoot!"

Never was the way opened more abruptly for the entrance of Jesus Christ, and never was the setting less suitable—never save once, in a stable long ago.

Ellie drew a long breath, and began with sledgehammer directness: "Do you know Jesus, Stan?"

"Nope," said Stan. "My mother used to take me to church, and they talked about Him, but He never did anything."

"He does, if people believe Him," said Ellie leaning forward, her bright hair incongruous against the backdrop of tools and grimy rags. "Look what He did for Gideon."

"And look what He didn't do for my kid!" Stan's voice was harsh, and he added, "Or my wife. She looked a little like you," he said abruptly, "just a little."

What could Ellie possibly say, wondered Gideon, to the ancient, unanswerable problem of evil suddenly flung in her face?

"If Jesus had been there, those things wouldn't have happened," she said steadily.

"Thought He was supposed to be everywhere."

"Only if there's somebody He can work through." Ellie explained in her own way the elements of faith. "We've got to be His workers—like the boy there at the pump. If he's not on the job, the customers won't get gas."

"If Ellie and her friends hadn't been on that mountainside, I'd have died," said Gideon.

"But why?" asked Stan, throwing away his cigarette as though to give his whole attention to this matter—or to Ellie. "Jesus is supposed to be God, isn't He, or the Son of God, or something? Then why can't He do whatever He likes, whether anybody's there to help Him or not?"

"Maybe He does sometimes," said Ellie, her face tense with thought, "if it's a place with good vibes, or something. But, you see, most places don't give Him a chance. The vibes are so bad."

What could she mean, thought Gideon, and what would

Stan make of it? To his amazement, Stan seemed to understand perfectly. "Yeah, I know," he said slowly, "like some of those movie places—or topless joints. Just go in them and you want to do something bad. But a mountain—nothing bad about a mountain. Hey, what were you kids doing up there? Nobody goes there except coyotes, and nuts like him." Stan grinned briefly at Gideon, who felt gratified that he was worthy to be called a nut.

"We were singing to the mountains," said Ellie simply.

"Now I've heard everything! Why sing to the blasted mountains?"

"It's a way of praying for them," explained Ellie softly, "giving them God's love, sort of, so they won't get all upset and have earthquakes."

"Is she nuts?" demanded Stan of Gideon, jerking his thumb toward Ellie.

"I'd think so, except that I'm alive," grinned Gideon.

"It's like this," explained Ellie, "some people think they hear God warning them there's going to be an earthquake, and they should run away. But maybe they don't quite get it right, see? Maybe God's really telling them that the earth is all upset, and there might be an earthquake, so they'd better pray for it to quiet down. That's what we do."

"So that scares the earthquakes away, huh?"

"Who knows?" said Ellie quite simply. "It certainly doesn't do any harm. We might as well try it."

With narrowed eyes and quizzical expression, Stan looked at Gideon and asked, "What's *with* this gal anyway?"

"God, maybe," said Gideon, surprising himself.

"Do you think up these notions all by yourself?" inquired Gideon of Ellie.

"Oh no," she replied. "Beth teaches us."

To this Stan asked, "Who's she? Another nut?"

"Could be," laughed Ellie.

Gideon explained to Stan, "Beth is a woman who runs a sort of coffeehouse where kids that need help can—"

"We just sort of drift in," elucidated Ellie. "You know, it kind of happens."

"What happens?" At least Stan was interested—or was he interested only in Ellie, asking questions just to keep her there?

"Well, see, we were all hooked on pot and stuff, really stoned most of the time. So, we'd kind of feel better when we went there and got a coke or something. After a while, maybe we'd ask Beth what it is that feels kind of good in there, and she'd tell us it's the love of Jesus, and ask whether we'd like Him to come into us and really fix us up, you know. By that time, we like Beth so much, you know, we say, 'Sure. We're washed up this way, so He might as well.' So—"

"So what?" asked Stan, throwing down a freshly lit cigarette and grinding it on the garage floor with his heel.

"So—Beth puts her hands on us—"

"Why?"

"She just does, and asks Jesus to come in and fix us up."

"Damnedest thing I ever heard," growled Stan, his gaze on the floor.

"Wouldn't you like Him to come into you?" asked Ellie simply, while Gideon sat with his heart in his mouth.

"No!" shouted Stan. He leaped to his feet and stood swaying a little in the doorway.

Ellie shrank back, her blue eyes hurt and surprised. "Why?" she asked in a low voice.

"Not your fault," answered Stan gruffly. "See, when I was

a kid, my mom used to take me to revivals. She made me go to the altar and—accept Jesus. That's the way they talked, see? Well, I had to," he went on, "with the minister breathing down my neck, and everybody groaning and shouting and carrying on. But nothing happened—not then, or afterward, or—ever."

"What do you mean nothing happened?" asked Ellie while Gideon looked away in embarrassment.

"Well, in the Bible—my mother used to read me the Bible, see?—when Jesus got into the picture, things happened. Lame people walked, and things like that."

Ellie asked another question. "Did you ever ask Him to make a lame person walk?"

"Heck no! Who would *I* be to ask Him? But all those people yammering about Jesus, they didn't either. When people got sick, and even died, they just said it was God's will—so what the heck! I caught on that the whole thing was a con game. The preacher beat it off with the collection, and everybody was left just where they were before."

"We asked Jesus to come in and fix us up," said Ellie, lifting her head and turning her blue gaze to Gideon. "When I was a kid, my mom never took me to church. She was usually drunk anyway. So we didn't learn wrong things about God."

Stan turned to Gideon, jerking his head toward Ellie. "She *must* be nuts."

"She's not," smiled Gideon, his eyes alight, "and I'm here to prove it."

"That's the only reason I'm staying cooped up here listening to you guys. Look, you're a preacher, huh?"

"We call them clergymen," said Gideon, stalling for time.

"Okay, clergyman, Jesus salesman, huh? Well, I'm a car

121

fixer and salesman, and when I sell a car, or send it out after I've worked on it, it's darned well got to run, see? But in your church—when you ask Jesus to do miracles, does He do them?"

"Well, some miracles of the soul, I guess," floundered Gideon.

"What do you mean, miracles of the soul? I'm talking about honest-to-God miracles, like you walking after being all smashed up. Do things like that happen in your church?"

Gideon bowed his head, and all he could say was "no."

"I guess you're like my mother's preacher guy—don't really believe what you're talking about."

"But the people in your church—" Ellie chimed in anxiously. "Don't they accept Jesus as their Lord and Savior? I mean, when they belong, when they—"

Gideon grimly supplied words. "We—prepare them for confirmation. That's when they join our church," he explained. "We teach them—" Gideon paused. What did he teach them? The creed, the Lord's prayer, the ten commandments, and where to find them in the prayer book—the meaning of the vestments—the history of the church (with certain glaring omissions), how to receive communion—"No," said Gideon flatly, answering Ellie's question.

"Don't they ever accept Jesus?" asked Ellie incredulously.

"In baptism, when they're infants," said Gideon faintly.

"You've got to be kidding!" said Ellie. "No baby can accept Jesus."

"Through their sponsors—"

"Who are they?"

"Godmothers and godfathers—"

"What a lousy deal," Ellie exclaimed. "You mean, other

122

people, not even the kid's own father and mother, stand up and say that he accepts Jesus?"

"They do," asserted Gideon, trying to pull his thoughts together. "Then the priest puts water on the child's head, and—" He paused, wanting to frame in words his vague belief that this rite does have significance, that something really happens to a baby's soul.

Ellie shook her head. "No wonder miracles don't happen in your church," she said sadly, inexorably.

Stan lit a new cigarette, said with a dry grin, "See what I mean?" and started to stroll out.

"I'm sorry," said Gideon to Ellie.

But even as he spoke, Stan turned back to her. "Come again," he said throwing the words over his shoulder as he left. "Like to talk some more someday."

"Praise the Lord!" sighed Ellie. "He won't forget—"

"You've certainly given Stan something to think about," Gideon said through Ellie's car window, as she got ready to leave. "He can't deny that my healing's a miracle."

"Why don't you do one?" demanded Ellie, easing the car into gear.

"One what?"

"Miracle!" she shouted, as the car clattered into the boulevard.

Good heavens, thought Gideon, he do a miracle! Yet he could almost hear Ellie saying, "Why not?" Certainly he visited the sick, and the fatherless and widows in their affliction, as the Bible said, and he spoke comfortingly of God's grace and mercy, expressing hopes for their recovery. Occasionally he read the Office of the Visitation of the Sick, which solemn service was enough, he thought grimly, to put anyone in the grave. But to demand and expect healing!

Sweat broke out on his forehead at the thought. But he knew with bleak presentiment that some day he would have to do it.

The time came sooner than he expected. Gideon was hardly home before David burst in, his face white as a sheet under dirty smudges. "Dad! Dad!" he cried, hurling himself upon his father and holding on for dear life.

Susan hurried in, dropped on her knees, and endeavored to gather the trembling boy into her arms, but David clung convulsively to his father, trying to speak. With one hand Gideon motioned Susan to silence, and with the other stroked the dark, tousled head and murmured, "Okay, David, take it easy. Quiet down now, and tell me what's wrong."

David lifted his head, drew a dirty hand across his tear-stained face, and gasped, "Sammy and I were on our mini-bikes, and—"

"Hold it a minute, and sit down," said Gideon, dropping to the sofa and drawing the boy down beside him, while Susan dabbed at his face with a dish towel.

"See," gasped David, "we were up the canyon, you know, where there's lots of room." Gideon nodded, picturing the area of rocks and sand, hurled into wild confusion by rain-storms, covered with precipitous motorbike tracks. "Sammy was on his bike," sobbed David. "I yelled at him to get out of my way, but he just laughed and wouldn't, and—"

"You ran into him," said Susan gently, and Gideon smiled at her, grateful that she did not add the, "I told you so," which must be in her mind.

"I couldn't help it," wailed David. "Honest! He could have got out of my way, but he didn't—and he kind of swerved and went over the edge into the stream, only there wasn't any water in it, just a lot of rocks—"

At this moment, Josie rushed into the room. "I told you—" she began excitedly. Plainly she knew about the accident. "Yeah, I was there," she answered her mother's questioning look. "I yelled at David to stop—"

"I tried to!" the boy gasped. "But it just wouldn't stop. It sort of skidded and went faster. I didn't mean to hit him, honest!"

"You must have hit the gas instead of the brake," said Josie disgustedly. "Jerk!"

"How badly was Sammy hurt?" asked Susan.

David was unable to answer, but Josie, who had collapsed into a chair, replied, "Gee, I don't know, Mom. People ran back and forth, and after a while, the ambulance came and took him away."

"What hospital?" asked Gideon quietly, for he saw what was coming. Josie did not know.

"Wouldn't the police know?" asked Susan.

"Yeah, Dad!" cried David, lifting his face from the protection of his father's arm. "You go and do a miracle, huh?"

Gideon thought, and almost said, that this was the end, the very end!

"Didn't you come into our Sunday school class two days ago and tell us to stop making those dumb pots and listen to a true story about Jesus making people well?" demanded David.

It would seem, thought Gideon, that he had done his usual church school visiting perhaps with more enthusiasm than wisdom.

"You're the minister, and that's sort of like Peter and Paul and those guys, isn't it? Okay," the boy concluded, "go and make Sammy well!"

"Better go, Dad," said Josie wisely. "You know David when he gets an idea."

"Who is Sammy?" asked Gideon, still stalling.

"I don't know. His name's Bernstein, or something. His father runs that cleaning shop where you go, Mom."

"I know him," said Susan, stroking David's head. "He's a nice little man." Her eyes met Gideon's, and he knew he would get no help from her in evading his children's campaign.

"But they're Jewish," Gideon objected. "They might not appreciate my butting in."

"I guess people didn't appreciate Jesus butting in either," said Susan, "until He did miracles."

Jesus did miracles, thought Gideon, and look where it led Him . . . Nevertheless, He did them, knowing it would make trouble with the top brass—just as it might for him if he were to rush into the hospital and demand to pray for a Jewish boy who, for all he knew, might be at the point of death.

"Dad, you're not going to chicken out, are you?" asked Josie, her enigmatic dark eyes fixed upon him.

Gideon rose and called the police, and after some moments of inquiries, announced to the family, "He's at St. Luke's, the same hospital I was in."

"It's the nearest," said Susan.

"How badly is he hurt?" asked Susan.

"All I could find out is that they're taking X rays."

Josie, frowning at her brother's tears, said, "He's not going to die, you dope! Isn't Dad going to pray for a miracle?"

"I'll go with you," said Susan gently. "We're David's parents, that's all. You won't even have to say you're a minister."

When they reached the hospital, they found their way to

Sammy's room, not unlike the one Gideon knew so well. In the doorway, a dark-haired woman sobbed inconsolably, while her husband stood by the bed, looking down at the unconscious lad. The sorrow on his face struck Susan's heart. It was the face of one who expected the worst, because the world had always dealt him the worst.

As Gideon and Susan hesitated in the doorway, a nurse gently drew Mrs. Bernstein out into the corridor. "We can't let you stay unless you quiet down," she said.

"He knows nothing!" wept the anguished mother. "Oh, my God, he knows nothing!"

"Of course not," soothed the nurse in a voice familiar to Gideon. "Until we get the X rays, we know nothing either," she went on, forestalling the next question, "but we can—hope."

Gideon spoke the nurse's name, remembering.

"Oh!" she cried, with amazement. "You! You're well, you're walking—!"

"Of course!" said Gideon, smiling widely, and he added, "Let us go in and see him. You remember my wife, Susan."

"It's against the rules. You aren't family, or—"

"We *are* family," said Gideon firmly. "They are of God's human family, so we are kin."

"If the doctor comes—" the nurse wavered.

"If the doctor comes," said Susan, divinely inspired, "we are Sammy's Uncle Gideon and Aunt Susanna. You had no choice but to let us in."

Abruptly, Gideon forgot himself entirely and spoke words that came apparently from without. "Mrs. Bernstein," he said gently, yet with such quiet authority that the stricken woman quieted and looked up at him, "our son caused your son's accident." Mrs. Bernstein started to wail again. "Now look at me," commanded Gideon. "I want you to see me walk."

The very absurdity of this request caught the woman's attention, and she looked while he took a few steps and came back to her. "So you walk," she said bitterly. "My son does not walk."

"He will," stated Gideon. "I know, because six weeks ago— Was it six weeks?" he asked the nurse. She nodded and Gideon went on. "Six weeks ago, I lay on a bed right here in this hospital, and the doctors said I would never walk. Now look at me!" He strode swiftly down the corridor and back again. "In fact, the doctors didn't think I'd live, did they?" Again he looked at the nurse and she shook her head. "Your injuries were far worse than this boy's," she said, "so far as we can tell. The X rays aren't back yet."

"Then how do you walk?" asked Mrs. Bernstein, puzzled.

"There is another doctor," said Gideon, pointing upward. "He healed me."

"Ah, God!" cried Mrs. Bernstein, to whom God was a whimsical being who must be obeyed no matter what He chose to do. "The Lord gives, and the Lord takes away—"

The sad-faced father had by now become aware of the colloquy at the door, and stepped toward them.

"What is this?" he asked.

Gideon repeated the facts of his own healing, again calling on the nurse for corroboration. "I—I can do this," he ended. "I am nothing, but because I believe, I can be a channel for God's power. If you will let me go in there—and stand by your son—and—"

"And what?"

"Pray." There was no avoiding the issue.

Mr. Bernstein started slightly, and then seemed to freeze

128

inwardly, gathering into himself as he stepped into the corridor and closed the door behind him. "We are Jewish," he said.

"So am I," said Susan softly beside him. "Part of me is Jewish, and it's a big enough part so that I know how you feel."

"Who are you, anyway?" Mr. Bernstein asked, not taking his eyes from Gideon's.

"I'm a minister," said Gideon, blood rushing into his face. He remembered the long empty years, and his own retreat from life. "I haven't been a good minister," he went on. "I tried to kill myself—but someone who knew God's power came and prayed for me, here in this hospital. Like the boy in there, I knew nothing—but I lived. So now I know God's power, not because I'm anyone great, but because I am someone so very small."

"He is like a doctor who might offer to make your son well," interposed Susan. "Wouldn't you let him try, without asking whether he was goy or Jewish?"

Making a slight gesture of relinquishment, Mr. Bernstein stepped back and opened the room door. Gideon did not see whether or not the parents followed, for he looked neither to right nor to left but went straight to the bed. He laid both hands upon the boy's laboring chest, and prayed.

"Heavenly Father, creator of heaven and earth, You created this child, and You can re-create him. You are his Father, and You love him as his other father loves him."

He paused. He always prayed, "in the name of Jesus Christ." Should he say it now? His inner wisdom knew that he should not. When Jesus prayed for healing, what was it he said? "Arise and walk!" Yes, but Gideon did not feel able to say those power-packed words here. As a channel of God's power, he was not great enough. He would only say what he could.

"God, I ask You to heal this boy," he prayed on and felt the sweat rolling from him in the effort of concentration. He felt the light-power course through his arms and hands. "Thank You for Your healing life now coming into him," he continued, "mending any bones that may be broken, healing any internal bleeding, and making him whole. Thank You for helping the doctors, too," he added, "guiding and blessing all their care of him."

Silence all about. Susan stood on the other side of the bed, her hands upon the boy inconspicuously, half hidden by the sheet, touching him lightly. The mother had crept in, startled but unresistant, and stood beside her husband at the foot of the bed. The nurse was at the door, as though to ward off intruders. All waited in tense silence. Gideon felt the need for yet more words, while remaining in prayer beside the child, and as words came, he spoke them, hardly realizing that they were not English—

"God help me!" he exclaimed inwardly. "I'm speaking in tongues!" Nevertheless, he made no effort to break off the sounds that rolled quietly but in sonorous beauty from his lips.

They ceased at last, and when he ended with, "Amen," he was shaking from head to foot.

The child on the bed opened his eyes. "Hi, Dad," he said in a tired little voice.

At this, his mother fell upon him with outcries of delight, only slightly modulated by the nurse's cautions.

"He lives!" said the father. "My son, he lives!"

"I'll call the doctor—" murmured the nurse.

She ushered the rest of them outside, leaving only Mrs. Bernstein sitting by the bed holding Sammy's hand.

"How did you know there was internal bleeding?" the nurse asked Gideon in the hall, drawing him slightly to one side, while Susan and Mr. Bernstein beamed at each other like old friends.

"I didn't," replied Gideon.

"But you prayed—"

So he had, Gideon realized. "I only said what came to me," he replied, adding, "The bleeding will stop now."

"Yes, I know," agreed the nurse.

By this time, other relatives had arrived—aunts, uncles, cousins, and friends—all held at bay by the protecting nurse.

"What do I tell them?" asked Mr. Bernstein, following Gideon and Susan down the hall as they tried to leave.

"Don't tell them anything!" said Gideon hastily. His heart gave a lurch of fear as he wondered—what if this were only temporary, and the boy became unconscious again, and— "If he ever seems to need me," he said to the father, "I'll come back."

Mr. Bernstein took him by both hands. "He will not need," he said, "but come—come!"

Looking upon his dark, gentle face, Gideon loved him as a brother. He remembered how Jesus said He had not seen such faith, no not in Israel. He, Gideon, had not seen such faith in his church nor, until this time, in himself.

"It is the Lord God who works," said Mr. Bernstein in wonder, "the God of Abraham and Isaac and Jacob—"

"It is," echoed Susan, her face shining.

"You spoke Hebrew!" cried Mr. Bernstein, suddenly recalling Gideon's last prayers. "You spoke the Hebrew of Moses and David and God Himself, through His people. Blessed be His name!"

Hebrew? Was that the language God had given him? What then had he been saying when those sonorous sounds flowed unbidden from his lips?

131

Mr. Bernstein, seeing them to the elevator, repeated in English what Gideon had been saying in Hebrew, all unknowing, beside Sammy's bed: "The Lord is my light and my salvation; whom shall I fear? The Lord is the strength of my life; of whom shall I be afraid?"

Chapter Eleven

Gideon and Susan drove home in strained silence. Hot summer had settled upon the land, and the skies were murky. Even the fragrance of eucalyptus and orange blossoms that floated in waves out of flowering backyards could not dispel the acrid, irritating smog.

Gideon turned on the air conditioning, as they swept from Orange Grove into Rosemead, and turned left into Foothill on the green arrow. Finally Susan spoke. "What's all this," she said in an ominously stilted tone, "about you speaking Hebrew?"

Gideon swallowed, hard. "I don't know," he said. "I just sort of prayed as the words came to me—"

"And where did they come from?"

"Well," Gideon endeavored to explain, "when I'm preaching in church, see, on those rare occasions when I'm really on God's wavelength, I sort of unconsciously listen to the words in the air. I hear them just before I say them. So, as I was praying for Sammy, other sounds came to me. I didn't know what it was, but what I heard, I said, that's all. And—it turned out to be Hebrew! After all," Gideon went on lamely in the face of Susan's unsympathetic silence, "you know I had a bit of Hebrew in seminary."

"Yes, but you couldn't possibly remember it," his wife spoke truly. "The fact is, you didn't know *what* you were saying back there in the hospital."

"No, that's the strange part of it, I didn't. But look, Susan. Do you believe in God—or don't you?"

A slight sniff was her only answer. Gideon went on. "Okay, if you believe in God, then why can't you believe that He put Hebrew words into my mind for the comfort of those Jews? It made quite a difference to Mr. Bernstein, you know." In spite of being nervous about Susan's attitude, Gideon could not help smiling, his blue eyes shining, as he remembered how the light came to that Jewish father's face, how he raised his head and stood as tall as his small frame could, and how he said in hushed tones, "You spoke Hebrew!"

"That could have been it," said Susan dubiously, "but isn't that what people call speaking in tongues?"

"What if it is?" asked Gideon.

"Did you know you had the gift of tongues?" Susan persisted.

"Well, no—not exactly," her husband replied, fumbling for words.

"What did Ellie pray for that time you and she were in your study?"

With a jerk, Gideon stopped for a red light. How did Susan know? "Angela and Doris told me," she said, answering his unspoken question. "After Ellie left, they saw you come out of your study, and they said you were shining

134

like a light. So now come on and tell me what went on!"

"What went on," said Gideon, "was high, holy, and I might say, completely biblical. Ellie prayed for me to receive the Baptism in the Holy Spirit, the same thing that happened to Cornelius and his family in Acts 10 while Peter was preaching to them. 'The Holy Ghost fell on all them which heard the word . . . for they heard them speak with tongues and magnify God,' " quoted Gideon. "No wonder I shone like a light," he added, "because I felt a light come on inside me. That's just what happened."

Again there was a long silence while the car trundled east—to the right, freeways and cities, to the left, high mountains, at this moment veiled in haze. At last, they reached Monrovia, and Gideon went more slowly, as they neared home. Susan spoke. "I don't like it," she said in a small, stifled voice. "Gideon, I don't like it at all. I know it happened in Bible times, but these things aren't supposed to happen today."

"They do though," Gideon said, and the surging joy would not stay out of his voice. "They happen in little groups all over the place. They happen among the Jesus People, the Christian kids."

Susan pronounced her dictum: "They do not happen in Episcopal churches," said she. "Furthermore, you know very well that the bishop has said they're not to happen in this diocese, and that no priest in this diocese is to speak in tongues."

"I know," said Gideon uneasily, "and you may be sure I won't speak in tongues publicly. But when the Holy Spirit overwhelms one, and words come forth, apparently by God's will and for His purposes, what can one do?"

"You have a point there," admitted Susan. "Yes, you have a point."

Silence again until they reached their own house, where Susan walked ahead and opened the door while Gideon closed the car and followed. As he entered the living room, his wife whirled upon him and spoke again. "I don't approve of it," she said. "I think it's tricky, and dangerous. I'm not even absolutely sure it *is* the work of the Spirit. It could be a counterfeit, you know. But Gideon, if you have this, why—" the words burst from her—"I want it too!"

"Praise the Lord!" said Gideon. He flung his arms around her and held her close.

"Don't go praising the Lord to me," said Susan, somewhat huffily untangling herself from his strong, encircling arms. "I don't want you sounding like a Pentecostal. You're not one, and you're never going to be. You're an Episcopal priest, and don't forget it!"

"Yes, but I'm also a man, and your husband," laughed Gideon, "and I'm glad, Susan, I'm glad! I'm wading out into deep water, and you don't like it, you don't approve of it, but you're coming with me—isn't that great?"

Susan relaxed and laughed too. "Yes, it's great," she said. "I'm coming in with you! So can you—pray for me to have this gift?"

"Oh, good Lord!" cried Gideon aghast. "Gosh, no! I'm like a baby just learning to talk. No, I wouldn't know how to pass it on."

"There isn't any 'how' is there?" asked Susan. "Don't you just ask for it?"

"I don't even know that," said Gideon. "I don't know anything. Tell you what: why don't we get Ellie and Beth, or somebody from that coffeehouse, to come and pray for you just as Ellie did for me?"

Susan shook her head vehemently. "Fine thing," said she, "Ellie and her friends traipsing in here, talking all kinds of gibberish, and doing who knows what kind of funny things! In might come Josie, and David, or Leslie, or Mr. Crabtree—The thing would blow up with a bang you could hear all the way to Washington! The bishop would hear about it, and you'd be out, Gideon! No, whatever we do must be in private." Having issued that ultimatum, Susan charged into the kitchen.

"Well," pursued Gideon, "the only other thing I can think of is for us to go to the coffeehouse that Ellie has talked about so much."

"Ellie!" grumbled Susan from the stove. "Always Ellie!"

"I know," said Gideon contritely, "it must irritate you. But look, Susan, you know me better than to think that I'm falling in love or something. This girl has sort of waked up in me the love of God, and I connect her with it. So I guess I do love her in a way, but the Bible word is 'agape,' Christian love."

"Okay," said she, "okay. I guess I might as well jump in head first, and let them give me the works."

"You're a good sport," said Gideon, grinning. "You always have been." Then he closed his mouth quickly, lest he should again exclaim, "Praise the Lord!"

The next day, therefore, having cleared some time and called the coffeehouse, Gideon and Susan set forth. They wound through unknown back streets of Pasadena, and finally located the small house marked inconspicuously, "Koinonia." Gideon mused aloud, "I vaguely recall that means fellowship, or brotherhood, or love—something like that."

"Well," Susan replied brusquely, for she was distinctly uneasy, "let's go in and find out."

They knocked timidly and entered the little house through

137

the partly open door. It had a wide living room opening into the kitchen, whence issued the refreshing odor of coffee. The living room was sparsely furnished with a few rickety chairs, and many cushions casually tossed upon the floor. Young people with lank locks or heads of unruly hair, beards and moustaches, were lounging about. Upon the wall hung, absurdly, an enormous elk's head. "Old Rick," offered one of the young men, noting Gideon's inquiring gaze. "This used to be a club, or something, and he's always been there, Old Rick has." The youth grinned cheerfully and returned to his guitar.

Susan was looking about with distaste. The young people's clothing was casual in the extreme, and rather ridiculous, she thought—girls in blue jeans with boys' shirts drooping over them, or some absurd top not unlike a baby's dress, their faces innocent of any makeup, their hair brushed straight down. Only a few years back, thought Susan, these same girls might have affected bright red lips, eyes painted lugubriously blue and green, and hair piled on top of their heads like beehives. From one extreme to another, she thought. But she had to admit they looked clean. Even the boys, if you could see under their hair and beards, looked clean!

As Susan and Gideon stood there somewhat uneasily, a middle-aged woman bustled out of the kitchen, brushing damp hair back from her forehead, and shook hands with them. With her came Ellie, light shining in her eyes as she greeted them timidly. "I'm so glad," she whispered, "oh, I'm so glad you came!"

"Something worrying you, Ellie?" asked Gideon in a low voice. Ellie nodded, and tears came for a moment to her eyes.

"Never mind though," she said, turning to Susan. "Tell me first: is it really true that you'd like us to pray for you?"

Susan gulped, and answered valiantly, "Yes—yes it's true. I don't know what it's all about, but I figure the best way to find out is to try it and see."

"O taste and see that the Lord is good!" murmured Ellie, and somehow the words did not sound foolish to Susan. Spoken with such sincerity and simplicity, they rang true. "Beth," Ellie called to the older woman, "are you ready?"

"Sure!" Beth answered with a wide smile. "Ruth, you keep an eye on things, okay? See if the boys want more coffee." She looked around the living room. "No place in here, I guess," she said rather ruefully, for one of the young men was twanging a guitar, and others were talking. "Well, let's go to my bedroom."

Susan stiffened, but there was no help for it. Into Beth's bedroom they went. She motioned Susan and Gideon to rather stiff chairs, while she perched on the edge of the bed and Ellie sat cross-legged on the floor.

"Do you know anything about the Holy Spirit?" Beth asked, turning to Susan.

"I thought I did," she said, "but apparently there are things I don't know." She nodded toward her husband. "He's got something I don't have. Nine chances out of ten, it will get him into trouble. But— I'm his wife, and if he's going that way, I want to go with him. Maybe that's not a very good motive," Susan concluded lamely.

Beth smiled broadly. "Believe it or not," she said, "I'm an Episcopalian, too, and I know just what you and all of them are up against. You see, in one way we *have* received the Holy Spirit. Gideon, you're a minister, so when you were ordained, the whole Church, represented by a bunch of

139

bishops, prayed for the gifts of the Spirit to be quickened in you, didn't they?"

"They did," nodded Gideon.

"Did anything happen?" asked Beth.

"Must have," answered Gideon, stoutly defending the Church, "though I didn't feel anything particularly—miraculous. I felt good, and—happy, sort of. But certainly there was no rushing mighty wind, no tongues of fire—or any other kind," he added.

"Just the same," responded Beth, "because I believe in God and His word, and because I also believe in the Church, I know you did receive the Holy Spirit then, and that wasn't the first time. When you were confirmed, didn't the bishop pray for the increase of the Holy Spirit?"

"More or less," grinned Gideon. "You know how it is. It's been kind of—watered down. The word mostly used is 'grace.' 'Defend, O Lord, this thy child with thy heavenly grace—' "

"That's a good, safe word," agreed Beth, "because nobody knows what it means. However, at least they do mention the Holy Spirit, so confirmation was another time when you received the Holy Spirit, wasn't it?"

"Surely," agreed Gideon, "and yet—"

"I know all the 'and yets,' " added Beth with a sigh. "But look, confirmation wasn't the first time either. What about your baptism? Isn't there a prayer that the Holy Spirit be poured out upon this child—something like that?"

Gideon nodded as Susan interposed, "But no little baby can—can speak with tongues, and all that."

There was a giggle from Ellie sitting on the floor. "Maybe babies speak in tongues better than grown people," she said. "Who knows what they're saying when they talk?"

Susan cocked her head and looked at her doubtfully, wondering whether she could be serious. Beth was continuing, "Surely anybody who has been baptized did receive the Holy Spirit then."

"Something really does happen at baptism," nodded Gideon. "I'm glad you know that. To somebody like Ellie, who wasn't brought up in the church, it may sound silly, but I guess any minister could tell you it's true. Several times in my ministry, I have been called to baptize a baby who was said to be dying, and every single time, as soon as the baby was baptized, the fever went down, the disease abated, and it got well."

"So, what is lacking?" asked Ellie from the floor. "When we found Gideon up on the mountain, he had just tried to kill himself. He didn't know any more about the Holy Spirit—why, he didn't know anything!"

"The trouble was," said Beth, "his heart knew—or whatever you want to call it. Something inside him knew that he was a child of God. Paul said in Romans 8, 'The Spirit itself beareth witness with our spirit, that we are the children of God.' But his conscious mind didn't know it, so he was always—"

"I was always looking for something, and didn't know what," said Gideon, interrupting. "Then, of course, I was terribly unhappy about old sins, and didn't know the power of Jesus through the Holy Spirit to forgive sin and set me free."

"Exactly," said Beth. "In one sense, you had received the Holy Spirit, but in another sense you hadn't. It is like receiving a present, and then forgetting that you have it. A friend might meet you on the street and ask, 'Did you like my present?' And you think frantically, 'Oh yes, there was something, all wrapped up in paper and ribbon. Where did I put that thing?' You see," Beth went on, turning to Susan, "in a sense you already have the Holy Spirit, but you don't know that you do, and you're not using it. You might say it is still wrapped up in paper and ribbon. Does that make sense?" she asked.

Susan breathed a sigh of relief. "You know, actually it does," she said. "I'm really relieved! I—I didn't expect it to be like this."

Beth laughed her great, hearty laugh. "I know," she said, "you expected us to gather around you, and gang up, and shout and clamor and whoop and urge you, and push you, and prod you, and jiggle your face—"

"Something like that," Susan smiled. "Oh, I am relieved!"

"When we get to praying for the Holy Spirit, I won't guarantee that we won't do a bit of holy shouting, because, you know, we get so happy, it's pretty hard to prevent it! Of course we wouldn't do it in a church. You're not supposed to be really, really happy in church! Here in our own place, though, we might have a little holy fun, but certainly there won't be any of what you might call 'carrying on.' We'll just simply pray, that's all. So come on, Ellie—want to get anyone to help us?"

"How about Jess? Is he around?" said Gideon.

A cloud came over Beth's face as Ellie bowed her head and said, "No—not Jess."

"Is something the matter?" asked Gideon. "I haven't seen Jess for a long time, but when he came to the hospital, I thought he was pretty great."

"He was—pretty great," said Beth. "Too great to please old Satan, I guess, but now he's—he's lost."

"What do you mean, lost?" asked Gideon.

"I mean literally that," answered Beth. "He has taken a

wrong path, and gone out for every kind of funny business you can think of. It started when he announced that God had told him that Ellie was to be his wife. Well, that didn't witness to any of us, least of all Ellie, and we told him so. He got furious and slammed out of here, and the next thing we knew, he got mixed up with some sort of Buddhist group. He went to one of their meetings, and they gave him a piece of paper and told him to make a little shrine for it. Then he was to squat down before it, you know all twisted around like those statues of Buddha, and rock back and forth and chant 'om' or 'um,' or something. Well, Jess tried it for a while, and worked himself into sort of enjoying it, but that wasn't sensational enough, and he heard of other things—"

"Terrible things," whispered Ellie, her head still bowed. "Terrible!"

"Such as—what?" asked Gideon.

"Never mind," answered Beth hastily. "Let's forget about that now, and not distract our attention. That's just what the devil would like us to do, distract our attention. We simply won't! No—let's get Ruth and, Ellie, if you see one or two others that you think would help, bring them too."

Ellie scrambled to her feet and went out into the living room. "Why do you have to have two or three or four?" asked Gideon with curiosity.

"Same reason you do in the Episcopal church," said Beth crisply. "When you were ordained, didn't you have three or four?"

Gideon grinned broadly. "Eight or ten would be more like it," he said.

"Okay, same idea," answered Beth. "It just makes a wider channel for the power to come through. You see," she added to Susan, "it really is a tremendous power."

143

Gideon repeated softly after her, "It really is!"

Ellie returned with her friend Ruth, and two boys, lanky and hairy, but with a light that could not be denied shining in their eyes. They stood around Susan, and Beth said to Gideon, "Come on, you too."

They laid their hands upon her, and Beth led them in a prayer, very simple and direct, that the Holy Spirit, already in this woman through the offices of her church, might be quickened and increased within her.

"Now, Lord," said Beth, "You promised this, and we hold You to it. You said that if we who are evil know how to give good gifts to our children, how much more will our heavenly Father give the Holy Spirit to them that ask Him. So now, quicken into life the Holy Spirit that is already in this woman. Fan it like a smoldering fire, until little flames shoot up. Bring it to life, and pour out upon her first of all, Lord Jesus, those gifts that You Yourself promised—holy joy, the peace that passes understanding, and the knowledge of truth. Thank You, Lord," Beth went on. "Oh, thank You, Lord! Oh Lord, we rejoice in You!"

A chorus of voices joined in, saying "Amen," and "Oh, thank You, Jesus!" From that, they went into other sounds that Susan could not understand, until it was a bit like a chorus of birds twittering around her.

At first, Susan unconsciously resisted, hiding behind her barrier of reserve, but somehow she could not continue to resist. Something in her heart seemed to melt and soften, and great joy welled up within her. Tears even came into her eyes. "Oh," she breathed. "Oh! This is what I hoped it would be! This really is what I hoped it would be!" To her own complete amazement, she opened her lips and said with the others, "Thank You, Lord!"

144

"But I didn't speak in tongues," said Susan, when the murmurings about her ceased, and the little group melted away, dropping their hands from her and standing in silence but with joy that could almost be seen as a light around them. "Or did I?" she asked. "Were those funny little sounds that I made speaking with tongues?"

"Maybe," said Beth. "It doesn't matter. I know that some people insist that a person speak in the heavenly language right away, but we don't. We're looking for something much greater than that."

"Oh yes, I know!" exclaimed Susan, who could feel joy surging through her. "But will I speak in tongues some-day?" she asked rather wistfully, because all of a sudden, for no reason that she understood, she found herself longing for this mysterious gift, whatever it was.

"You will," Ellie reassured her softly. "You will!" And she looked upon Susan with the same shining love that she poured out upon Gideon. Susan saw it, recognized it, and smiled. This was no ordinary love, but that "charity" that comes from Christ. She knew it now, and would no longer be afraid.

"You know you've both got to start testifying," said Ellie, uttering these alarming words most matter-of factly.

"We've got to *what?*" asked Susan.

"You know," Ellie explained. "If you're going to keep it, you've got to give it to others. That's the way it is!"

"Oh no!" Susan moaned. "How could we?"

Gideon muttered grimly, "You don't know the Episcopal church!"

"She does." Susan indicated Beth. That indefatigable lady was on her way to the kitchen, but she turned around in the doorway and smiled.

"By the way, what church do you attend?" asked Gideon.

"I used to go to St. Stephen's," said Beth, "but—"

"You don't go any more?"

"Not very often." Beth shook her head ruefully. "I find I'm not—particularly welcome. You see, I—keep the wrong kind of company." She motioned to the young people with her, who blithely commented, "Praise the Lord!"

"What do you think will happen to me, if I testify about the Holy Spirit?" Gideon demanded of Beth.

She fixed him with an enigmatic look. "Do you want to testify?" she asked.

"Frankly, no."

"Then," said Beth gently, "we will pray for the time to come when you will want to, because Ellie is right. If you don't find some way of giving it away, you're not likely to keep it. But wait," she called, halting their progress toward the front door, "wait until the Lord shows you the way!"

"And you," said Gideon to her, as they again started to leave, "in order to do this work, you've given up your church life. Is it worth it?"

"Yes, it is," said Beth firmly. "Those boys who were just praying with us both used to be mainliners."

"Mainliners?" asked Susan faintly, thinking briefly of certain suburbs of Philadelphia.

Beth nodded. "Injecting heroin into the veins," she explained. "One of them, Pat, is only about sixteen now, and he was a mainliner from the time he was twelve."

"Do they live here?" asked Susan.

"Oh no, they just pop in. Pat goes to school, and the other kids work in garages, grocery stores, or somewhere."

"Why do they come?" asked Gideon.

Beth looked at Ellie, who was standing quietly by. "Why, Ellie?" she said.

"We don't try to figure out why," said the girl gently. "It's just that everything here is kind of peaceful and happy, see? The kids sing, but they never sing bad songs. They just don't want to, here. If they have a guitar, they may play it, and there's coffee, and—well, it just kind of feels good to be here. We start coming, and then we bring other kids, and after a while, Beth talks to us and tells us about Jesus, and—then we're changed. Everything's changed."

"Do you mean to tell me those boys are really healed of drugs?"

"Sure," said Beth, almost nonchalantly. "As soon as they get the Holy Spirit, they're healed of taking drugs right away."

"Amazing!" Gideon meditated aloud. "The government spends millions. The church doesn't know what to do. And this works right away! No withdrawal, no de-tox, just Jesus."

"Yes," Beth nodded casually, "though sometimes it takes a while for all the symptoms to clear up. Pat was in really bad shape. His whole body was sort of going to pieces. His gums bled, and the doctor and dentist couldn't do anything about it. His knees were so weak he could hardly stand. Everything was wrong, so we had to throw in a lot of healing prayers, too. It took a while, but he's fine now."

"I can see that," said Gideon, looking over his shoulder at the tall lad lounging on the floor and strumming a guitar. "But it doesn't always work," he said. "Jess—"

Ellie shook her head with a look of great sadness. "Jess— well, he just got lost, you know. He went the wrong way. There was no personal power or glory in our thing. It all belonged to Jesus, and everything went to Him. Jess wanted it for himself. So, what he's doing now—" her voice sunk to a whisper— "he calls it devil worship," she breathed.

147

"Good heavens!" cried Susan, while Gideon shut his eyes for a moment.

"The worst of it is," said Beth, "Jess has the idea that Ellie belongs to him. That's why we keep her here, and we all keep an eye on her, but as a matter of fact, I don't know how safe she is even here. You two—" and here Beth looked squarely at Susan and Gideon— "can join us in praying that Jess will not be able to harm anyone, neither Ellie or anybody else. Will you do that?"

"We will," they both agreed solemnly, and made their way out.

Chapter Twelve

In pursuance of his duties, Gideon next day went to see an elderly parishioner, Mr. Green, ill with terminal cancer in a veterans' hospital. He drew up a chair beside the bed, in due time took the old man's withered hand and laid his other hand on his forehead, making the sign of the cross as he did so. He prayed for God's presence to be with him, and for the peace, light, and joy of the Spirit to enter him and take care of him in all ways that were best. He then turned, leaving the old man smiling contentedly, and started out of the four-bed ward.

In the bed next to the door lay a young man, obviously very ill, beside whom sat two somber women, apparently his wife and mother. All three were silent. The young man's eyes were closed, and he labored for every breath. Gideon, as he passed the bed, could actually feel the heat of his fever. Now *that* man, he thought, could get well! The thought flitted into his mind, and out again, hardly catching his attention. He was not the young man's pastor, nor had he been asked to pray for him. The very idea terrified him, and he hurried out of the room.

The next moment, however, he found himself back again, standing beside the bed. How he got there, he could not have told; he was simply there. Moreover, he laid his hands upon the young man, and spoke to him. "You can get well," he said.

The eyelids fluttered, and for a moment the eyes opened. "Huh uh," said the man, and closed his eyes again.

"I'm sure you can," Gideon persisted, not knowing whence the words came. "There is a power that can heal, you know—God's power—and if you'd let me pray for you—" The young man moaned slightly, saying nothing. Gideon continued, amazed at himself. "Do you mind?"

The older woman nudged the sick man. "Let him pray," she said. "Come on, let him pray for you!"

"Oh, all right," moaned the man, his eyes closed.

Thereupon, Gideon, laying both hands upon him, called for the power of Jesus Christ to enter, search his body and find the cause of the infection, destroying it at this moment, and making him well. How he knew what to say, he had no idea, but the words came as simply and naturally as if he were offering someone a drink of cold water to relieve his thirst. Though afterward he was horrified, remembering what he had said, at the time, he felt nothing except quiet assurance. He ended his prayer with, "Thank You, Lord! I believe that You are making him well." Then he turned abruptly and left the room.

When he reached his car, Gideon was shaking. "Why in the world did I do that?" he said aloud. "I went there to pray for old Mr. Green. I ended up praying for a perfect stranger in desperate condition, and I really believe he will get well!"

A week later, in making his hospital rounds, Gideon again entered that room. There was the young man sitting up in bed and whistling softly, his eyes shining. "Oh," breathed Gideon, "you're better!"

"Yup, sure am!" said the man. "Doctors don't know what happened, but I'm okay. Going home tomorrow."

"I'm glad," replied Gideon simply.

"So am I." the soldier replied. "But you know, it wasn't dying—I didn't mind dying so much. Even in the war, I wasn't scared to die. Because there was something else in me that was already dead, if you know what I mean, and now it's come to life again! Do you know what that could be?" he asked the minister.

"Yes," said Gideon, "that was your spirit," and the young man sighed a deep, happy sigh.

There were no words to express the joy and thanksgiving of Gideon's heart as he turned toward the bed of his own parishioner. "How goes it?" he asked Mr. Green.

"Better," replied he, "better! It doesn't hurt anywhere near as bad, and I kind of feel happy inside."

"That's good," smiled Gideon, adding, "thank You, Lord!" Again he prayed for the peace and joy and glory of God to fill Mr. Green, but even this time it did not come to him to pray that he should live. He was old, and alone in the world, and had no place to go if he did live. It might be the Lord's time to take him quietly to his heavenly home, where He could take care of him in the best way. So after his prayer, Gideon departed, wondering greatly.

Gideon did not know that later that day Mr. Green's nephew came to see him, nor did he dream that the old man would tell his nephew how the rector prayed for the young fellow next door, and how he recovered and was about to go home. Later the story got back to Gideon, but it did not dim the light in his eyes and the joy in his heart, because every day, more and more, he was walking in glory.

A well of joy seemed to have broken free within Gideon, and when he thought about it, he realized it began when Ellie had prayed for the forgiveness of his sins, the healing of his memories. Tiny bubbles of joy began seeping into his consciousness, and in spite of all difficulties, wonderings, and worries when he went home from the hospital and resumed life in the parish, the joy within him only increased. It arose at unexpected moments. When he looked at the mountains, his heart would lift up, and he would be filled and flooded with the sense of being part of God's creation. It was a mysterious feeling, as though God's life flowed through him and also through the mountains and trees, through wild coyotes yelling upon the hillsides, through little birds singing in the trees—one life, one Creator, one joy.

In spite of the pressure of people, and their varying and often unhappy needs, when Gideon entered his study, he seemed to be greeted with a quiet kind of joy, as though a part of himself were waiting for him to return.

In quite a different way, this glory seized upon him when he went into the church, and especially when he mounted the pulpit to preach. He carefully refrained from telling the congregation everything, and yet light shone around him, and rang forth in his words. "The Lord Jesus is alive today!" he would say. "He lives, and He can move and work just as He always did. The only difference is that two thousand years ago He appeared in a physical body, and the power of God moved through that body of flesh in which He lived and walked. Nowadays, He also appears in bodies of flesh, many of them—or it should be many—wherever He can find those who believe in Him. Then Jesus Christ, the Son of God, can enter and do mighty works, even as He did of old."

The people would look wonderingly at Gideon, but as they looked, he somehow touched their spirits with his. He was doing more than saying words. He was pouring out power. He was praying for his people, even as he preached. Some faces were closed against this power, some lips were downdrawn, disapproving, some eyes were filled with doubt. But others beamed upon him as he spoke, and he could feel the power going from him to them, from them back to him, echoing, re-echoing, and the church filling with spiritual light and spiritual presence.

Once, looking upon the congregation, Gideon saw far back near the door two people who had never come before —Stan and Ellie. After the service, he looked for them; they were gone, probably having slipped out during the last hymn, but their presence gave him joy.

His own wife, Susan, was there at every service, sitting behind him in the choir. Gideon did not quite know what Susan felt. He believed that she received at least the beginnings of the entrance of the Holy Spirit in Beth's coffeehouse when the group prayed for her, but the power had not yet crashed through all the barriers in her mind.

Gideon told Susan about the healing of the young man in the hospital. "Where does he live?" she asked.

"I didn't ask."

"You'd better look him up, hadn't you?" said she.

Gideon replied slowly, "I—suppose I had. I don't know whether he belongs to any church, or has a pastor."

"Much good if he does," observed Susan in her quick way.

"You started this job, Gideon, and you'd better finish it."

Gideon learned the young man's address from the hospital, and called on him. "How are you doing?" asked Gideon, as the two sat on the front steps of the bungalow where he lived, chatting in the sun which now had a touch of autumnal coolness.

"Well—not so good," said the soldier. "I'm mad!"

"Who're you mad at?"

"Oh, I'm mad at the Army. See, now look, they owe me a whole lot of back pay, and I think they're trying to gyp me, and I'm not going to take that! I told them so, and it makes me feel all kind of sick inside, being mad like that."

"Look," said Gideon, "do you want to stay well, or not?"

"Of course I do," replied the man.

"Okay then, you've got to forgive the Army." Gideon did not know how he knew this; perhaps it was self-evident. "You said it made you sick inside. So, if you want to be well, then you're just going to have to forgive the Army!"

"That's heavy," grunted the young man.

"Want me to pray about it?" asked Gideon.

"Might as well." And so, sitting on the steps while the traffic rolled by, Gideon prayed for the love of Christ to help the young man forgive the Army.

Not long afterward, Gideon, looking down into his congregation, saw his new young friend sitting there, looking up at him hopefully.

The story got around in other quarters, however, and a streak of trouble entered Gideon's joy. "What's this I hear about you running around to hospitals doing miracles?" inquired Reginald Crabtree, a tinge of sarcasm in his voice.

"I didn't do any miracles," answered Gideon.

"How about what old Mr. Green said, how you went to see him, and prayed for some young chap you didn't even know, and he got well?"

"Oh, that's true," smiled Gideon, "and it seems to me Jesus must have prayed for some people He didn't really know, when the multitudes came to Him."

"Okay, then if you can do that, why didn't you pray for Mr. Green so he'd get well?"

Gideon could not answer, and, in fact, there were many questions that he could not answer. Why did not all the sick in his parish manage to get well? If this power worked for some, why not for everyone? Why did he, Gideon, sometimes feel that it would work and at other times know that it would not? Was this his own weakness, or a variation in the will of God?

"Oh Lord, show me!" prayed Gideon, but the Lord did not show him. However, some days later, the Lord brought him a way of finding out, and strangely enough through his assistant, Leslie.

"Say, I just heard of a new kind of conference," said that enthusiastic young man.

"Not another!" moaned Gideon, half to himself.

"Come on," coaxed Leslie, standing in the church parking lot by the rector's car, one arm on the open window. "Listen, Gideon; this is different. In fact, it sounds like just exactly what you'd really like, the way you're going now. It's called a School of Pastoral Care, and it's for clergy."

"Put on by the bishop, no doubt," said Gideon with a touch of sarcasm.

"No, it's not. That's the funny thing. It's just put on—I don't know, by some little group. They have them all over the place, but this one's going to be in California, and the leaders are going to be a priest from the east coast called Paul Forrester, and John Masterman, a psychologist from the south. The thing is, it's on healing."

"Well!" ruminated Gideon. "I just might go to that."

Later, asking Susan what she thought of the five-day conference, he said, "Do you suppose you could go too? They say wives are allowed, even though it's primarily for the ministers."

"No, you go," Susan replied. "Leslie can look after the church, and it could be just what you need, but I'd better stay here and take care of things."

With a certain relief, Gideon prepared to go. On the whole, it would be easier to be there without his wife wondering what he thought and how he was reacting. Having registered by mail, he arranged to ride with a Methodist minister who was also attending.

They drove out the San Bernardino freeway, taking the Yucaipa turnoff into the mountains. Higher and higher they climbed up the craggy hills to where the spruce trees grew tall, snowcapped peaks showing between them. Gideon disliked meeting strangers, so it was with a certain shyness that he entered the rather crude camp buildings. After registering, he found his bedroom, equipped with double-decker iron bunks, and then went down again to the large room where the meetings were to be held.

The School of Pastoral Care began with no preliminaries to the lectures, no time taken for each person to tell who he was or why he had come. The first lecture was scheduled for four o'clock, and it began at four, with only the briefest introduction from the young Methodist minister who seemed to be the host. Then a man wearing the black garb and white collar of an Episcopal priest arose and began his talk. From that time on, Gideon felt that he had come home.

Paul Forrester was lean and lank, and his black hair tended to droop untidily over his forehead. His nose was rather long and indeterminate, and his features were in no way distinguished, but his brown eyes shone with warm light. There was a twist to his sudden, wide smile, and to look at him somehow lifted one's heart.

"No doubt most of you," he said, "have come here for the same reason that I first attended a School of Pastoral Care. That is, you have begun to suspect that there is something in Christianity that you don't have, some greatly needed power that you don't know how to use. This, at least, was my reason for looking into the matter of Christian healing. I was not depressed, as some ministers are. I felt no temptation, as some ministers do, to quit the ministry. Such men have good and understandable reasons—namely, they're trying to do the works of the Holy Spirit without having His power. No, I was completely contented with myself, completely satisfied with my understanding of the church, completely able to accept the Bible. I drew the lines more and more narrowly around my faith, so that I could live peacefully within those lines. I put God into a box, carefully made for me through the centuries, with theological bounds that could not in any way be stretched, and with even tighter bonds of a church system which could not be changed. Then I nailed down the lid on the box into which I had put God, and told Him to stay there. But He did not stay there!

"It was an emergency that made me aware of my utter nakedness and deep need. There was a young man in my parish in deep depression. I now know how to pray for such as these. As far back as I can remember, not in a single in-

157

stance has such a prayer failed, though sometimes more than one prayer is needed. Anyway, I did not know how to pray when this young man came to me with dim threats of committing suicide, and I comforted myself, most untruthfully, by saying that those who say they're going to commit suicide never do. I gave him sound advice—oh, it was very sound advice! But it didn't work. One day he came to see me, and as usual I failed completely. He went away and killed himself. This awoke me to the fact that, whether or not I liked it, other people look to the church and to God's ministers for healing of soul and mind and body. So it was up to me to learn how to pray the prayer of faith. I simply had to!"

Here Paul Forrester paused, and his wide smile shone forth. "Don't go looking for it in the Prayer Book," he said. "The prayer of faith is not a special prayer written down in words. It is simply the way to pray for a specific result, with the belief that it is going to happen. I feel some of you thinking, 'But how can we believe that, when in fact we *don't* believe it?' That was exactly my problem, and I learned some ways of teaching myself to believe. In other words, I learned how to pray the prayer of faith. So listen now, and I will tell you."

Using a blackboard to jot down his four points, Paul Forrester explained a way of praying what he called "the miracle-working prayer," illustrating each point with stories, and building up in his listeners the dawning of belief that when Jesus said, "Verily, verily, I say unto you, the works that I do shall ye do also," He was telling the simple truth. His disciples were to do these works. It was up to them to awaken to the powers that He had given them, so that they actually could do them!

Paul closed his talk with a prayer, and Gideon noted how very simple a prayer it was. "Enter into us, Lord Jesus, and increase our faith and the power to heal, so that the time will come that when we stretch forth the hand in Your name, the lame *will* walk and the blind *will* see. Thank You, Lord. We believe this will be so! Amen."

Paul then perched on the desk with his legs dangling and asked if there were any questions about what he had said.

Gideon surprised himself by being the first to raise his hand. "How do you know *when* to pray this way?" he asked, thinking of his own puzzling experience of going to the hospital to pray for a parishioner and finding himself praying for a total stranger.

"That's a good question," said Paul. "The way you know is to ask. Let's do it right now. Think of someone for whom you would like to pray the prayer of faith, someone who you believe can be healed during the five days we are together. Let's make it that definite. Then be quiet a minute; I'll be quiet, too. In silence, let's all hold the one for whom we would like to pray up before the Lord, and then listen, and see whether He tells us yes or no."

There were a few murmurs from the group, and then a wistful voice inquired, "But how are we going to hear Him?"

"God hasn't lost His voice," smiled Paul. "If we practice this kind of listening every day, and give Him time, we'll become able to hear Him speaking inside us. Before we leave here, we may have a practice session together in listening to God. However, perhaps right now in the beginning, you won't be able to hear Him in words. Your unconscious is so unused to hearing the words of God that it may have closed the doors, but He will find some way of telling you. The simplest way, perhaps, is by your feelings. If you feel a good, warm, happy feeling inside about praying for this person, very likely God wants you to do it. If, on the other hand, when you think of this person you feel dull and heavy, as though you were up against a blank wall, very likely God is telling you no."

"And why would God say no?" asked another voice." I thought you people had the idea that it is always God's will to heal."

"Primarily, I believe it is," answered Paul. "That is God's original will, but there is also His circumstantial will—the best that can be done under the immediate human circumstances. For instance, the amount of faith available to God in a given situation may not be sufficient to channel His power into it. He knows all these factors better than we do. Therefore, we must always listen to Him, and get His guidance clear."

After a few more questions, and a prayer for guidance, the session closed, and the ministers gathered to chat in the lounge or put on their jackets and went out to breathe the chilly mountain air. The retreat center was a mile high, and the snow glistening on the mountaintops was not too far away. The wind sighed gently through the tall firs, and the air was rich with indescribable mountain fragrances.

After a fifteen-minute break, the ministers came together for the second lecture, given by John Masterman. He stood up, grinned shyly, fingered his shirt collar, and began in a rather faint voice. Not a trained speaker like Paul Forrester, he made a slow start, but once he got going, he moved the group like a strong wind over the treetops.

"It was need that brought me to this also," he began, "but my need was entirely different from Father Forrester's. I was a wounded soldier in an Army hospital. I was, and am, Jewish, but I knew nothing about religion—only that there

160

was supposed to be a God, though I didn't believe it. I had been two years in that hospital, my left thigh shot to bits, full of osteomyelitis and dripping and smelling day and night.

"Then someone came to me, an ordinary little woman pushing one of those carts that the volunteers trundle through the wards. She offered me candy, comic books, a kind and motherly word, but somehow I felt that there was something different in her, flowing through her. You've already guessed who the woman was, haven't you?" John interpolated, with a new warmth in his voice. "She's the one through whom God saved my life, and later she and her husband started these Schools of Pastoral Care.

"One day I asked her, 'What is this that you have?' She was amazed that I had sensed it without her telling me. She was very shy of speaking to us soldiers about the power of God, and only did it under direct guidance. However, when I asked, she answered me in the most simple words. Instinctively, she must have known that I could accept very little, and therefore she gave me no theology. She only talked about God and His power, and then she laid her hands upon me, under cover of comic books and stuff on the bed, and with her eyes wide open and a smile on her lips as though we were merely chatting, she prayed the prayer of faith for the healing of my leg. I felt such tremendous warmth that the sweat broke out all over me.

"I asked her what it was that I was feeling and she said, 'That's the power of God!' Then she told me that I must learn to do this for myself. I *had* to, because she couldn't be there every day. She would see me again the next week, but meanwhile I must practice.

"Thus she taught me the prayer of faith, in almost the

same words that Father Forrester just used—which isn't strange, because I'm sure he learned it from her, too. Therefore, I struggled to concentrate as I called for this power and connected with it, and tried to imagine my leg perfect. The power began to work, and—to make a long story short—in six weeks my leg was perfectly well! In getting well, it shrunk a bit, but it was completely usable.

"That is how I learned, and having learned, I knew that I couldn't keep this to myself. I wanted to help others as I had been helped. I considered going into the Episcopal ministry, because later this lady's husband, a minister, baptized me and prepared me for confirmation. However, I knew that the ministry wouldn't be suitable for me. I didn't have the background. Therefore, I decided to become a psychologist, because then people would come to me without considering my religion, and I could help them in whatever way seemed best, combining the prayer of faith with the knowledge of psychotherapy."

"Can you really do that?" asked a voice from the group.

"Oh, yes," answered John with a wide smile, and at the close of his lecture, he concluded the session with a few instances from his own experience of how prayer and scientific knowledge work together for healing.

Thus the School of Pastoral Care proceeded, with lectures morning and evening, and afternoon appointments with individual leaders, followed by a prayer clinic in which members of the group practiced prayer with the laying on of hands for one another.

One afternoon, Gideon had the opportunity of an appointment with Paul Forrester. Sitting before Paul in the rather bleak upstairs room reserved for small meetings, Gideon, amazed at how easy it was in the atmosphere of the conference to open his heart, said quite simply, "It's just that I don't know whether to stay with my church, and keep on trying to wake them up, or whether to give it up as a bad job."

"What would you do if you did give it up?" asked Paul.

"Well, you know there are lots of little groups these days, all kinds—from free-wheeling kids to house churches, informally led by ministers who have gotten out of the organized church. I wonder whether God wants me to do something like that. I mean, the institutional church can be so deadening and confining I don't know whether I can stand it!"

"Did it ever occur to you," asked Paul mildly, with his one-sided grin, "that the Holy Spirit requested to be institutionalized?"

"What do you mean?"

Paul nodded. "Yes, long ago. You'll find it in Exodus, Leviticus, and Numbers. The Lord told Moses to build Him a tabernacle. Furthermore," said Paul, tossing back his head and almost laughing, "it seems to me that the Lord was very fussy about His tabernacle. Not merely any kind of place would do; it had to be made just so, said the Lord, giving the exact proportions. Moreover, He desired it to be hung with purple and fine-twined linen; the priests' robes were to be decorated with bells and pomegranates of gold."

"But why?" blurted Gideon. "Why?"

"I wonder," mused Paul. "I wonder also why the idea of making the place of worship full of beauty and glory did not die out with Moses, but persisted and grew even until the present day. I wonder why the Gothic cathedrals—amazingly built, with a magnificence that we can hardly believe even when we see it, and built moreover without our modern construction techniques—I wonder why they were built thus? I wonder what drove men to do it."

163

"Maybe," said Gideon thoughtfully, "it helps them to think of heaven."

"Ah, you've got it," said Paul, delighted. "That's it! Not everyone can grasp this, but I'm sure of it. To adorn a place of worship helps the spirit to remember the beauty and glory of heaven, whence we came."

"Do you think we came from heaven and not earth?" asked Gideon.

"Of course! Oh, the body came from the earth, formed in the womb of the mother, but the spirit, or spiritual body as I like to call it, certainly came from heaven. There is no other way of explaining the little glimpses of things we remember, the feelings that don't make sense any other way, the urges inside us, urges that shake us to pieces if we don't recognize them and work them out. Certainly the spirit comes from heaven!"

"So now," Paul went on, "to get back to your question, consider: would you really feel comfortable if you were limited to celebrating communion with little groups in people's houses, maybe on the kitchen table?"

Gideon shuddered. "I'd hate it!"

"Of course you'd hate it," Paul agreed, "and you'd be right. Maybe you've visited some of those little groups, as I have, and heard them testify to Jesus in all kinds of holes and corners. That's wonderful, but could you be contented with it? Wouldn't you miss the beauty and dignity of the church?"

"Well, yes," said Gideon uneasily, "but the church often seems so cold and stiff—"

"That's for you to change," declared Paul. "The framework of the church has been built by architects and contractors, but we, the people, have to create the feeling, the atmosphere, of the church."

"But how?" asked Gideon. "Why, I couldn't even talk to my people about the things we discuss here. If I said anything about the Holy Spirit, they wouldn't know what I meant. By the way," he interrupted himself, "do the people here—I mean, do you have the Baptism in the Spirit?"

Paul smiled. "As far as I understand it," he said, "I received the Baptism in the Spirit at my confirmation, and a greater measure at my ordination. For that matter, I had the beginning at my baptism."

"What I mean is," said Gideon, getting down to brass tacks, "do you speak in tongues?"

"Certainly I do," answered Paul directly, "though I'm not sure that this is an accurate measure of how much of the power of the Holy Spirit one has."

"Nobody has mentioned tongues here," said Gideon.

"It is not the purpose of this School to emphasize tongues," explained Paul. "The gift of healing is just as 'charismatic,' and that is what we teach here. We'll speak of all the gifts of the Spirit before we get through, but we don't encourage the use of tongues in our meetings, though anyone is perfectly welcome to speak in tongues privately if they like."

"Oh, good!" sighed Gideon with relief. "So let's get back to my question: how can I build up the atmosphere of the Holy Spirit in my church?"

"Use His power," said Paul. "Use it! All the gifts of the Spirit are tools to help us build the spiritual house of the Lord. When you build a house, you don't need to display your tools and boast about them! Anyone can see what has been accomplished. Use the power of the Holy Spirit by filling your church with the prayer of faith, and you will find that as the spiritual light begins to fill your church, people will come to it more and more. They'll slip in singly to say their prayers, and they'll gather in little groups of two or three, quite spontaneously. You provide the power in the church, and you won't need to exploit the tools by which it is conducted. In due time, your people will find out for themselves. And if you like," added Paul, "we can have a prayer together right now for your guidance and power in doing this."

So the School went on, the feeling of love and fellowship and the power of the Holy Spirit growing from day to day. There was no outer, purposeful stimulation of this feeling. Most sessions began and often closed with a hymn, accompanied on the piano by one of the group. These were not modern choruses, but from the hymnbook, beautiful and stirring. Nor were the members of the group asked to shake their brothers by the hand, or to put their arms around anyone and tell him that they loved him. It was not necessary to do this, for the love of Christ spontaneously filled the place.

Each evening after dinner, time was allowed for questions and discussion, a session conducted by one of the leaders. Gideon noticed with a bit of amusement that when the questions verged on the controversial or inconsequential, the leader would call for a hymn, and so the subject would be changed.

On the next to last evening, one of the ministers remarked in this discussion period, "I don't understand it; it's perfectly amazing. Here we talk about things that—why, in some groups, if we even spoke of such things, we'd be at each others' throats. But here we can discuss anything in complete freedom!"

"That," said Paul, "is the power of the Holy Spirit."

By Friday morning when the conference came to an end, Paul and John, two apostolic figures, had, between them, expounded and taught particularly three aspects of Christianity: the word of wisdom, wherewith to understand the mysteries of God; the word of knowledge, wherewith to grasp with the spirit a particular bit of truth or direction that the mind alone would not be able to comprehend; and the gift of faith, which comes directly from the Holy Spirit and is learned by practicing the prayer of faith.

They also discussed the varying gifts of healing given to different people. Another subject was other kinds of miracles besides healing, and great longing was expressed in the group to actually see miracles in the outside world such as are so often mentioned in the Bible—the burning bush, the stilling of the storm, the rushing, mighty wind of Pentecost. However, the group decided that at present they did not have authority to pray for such miracles, but could only long wistfully for that authority and power, or for miracles to come unbidden.

They were also taught about the gift of discernment of spirits, including the dismissal of evil spirits so that the full gifts of God might come in. Naturally, they also discussed glossolalia, the gift of tongues and their interpretation—mysterious gifts that seem to be chiefly for the benefit of those using them.

After consideration of all the gifts of the Holy Spirit, the final morning was to conclude with a service of blessing, with the laying on of hands and prayer for the increase in each person of those gifts of the Spirit most needed for his life and work.

It was a bright sunny morning, not too chilly in the unheated chapel, and so the group went to this building, its

167

tall windows letting in the sunlight and framing views of the trees standing all around like silent guardians.

Paul Forrester, wearing his vestments, led the service which began with the singing of "A Mighty Fortress is Our God." Then he prayed for the School of Pastoral Care and for all those present, that the Spirit of God might be poured out upon them anew for their use as ministers of the church, shepherds of the flock. John then read from the second chapter of Acts the story of the first Pentecost.

At this moment, the church was filled with the sound of a rushing, mighty wind. The windows shook and rattled with so great a noise that John's voice could no longer be heard. Indeed, he ceased reading and looked up, as all of them did, many with arms outstretched, as though to grasp the power in their midst. Gideon thought that it might be an earthquake, but it was not, because the floor did not move. (Later someone checked at the seismic center to make sure, but no earthquake was recorded that day.) The rushing, mighty wind continued, no one could tell how long, for it seemed that time had ceased to be. Finally it died away, and the ministers one after another rose to give thanks to God, or to read other instances from the Bible when signs like these proclaimed to man the presence of his Creator.

The power of God was manifest during all the rest of the service, while the leaders laid hands on all who came to kneel at the altar rail, praying for the quickening within them of the gifts of the Spirit. Soft, evanescent light shone upon everyone, and even the atmosphere of the chapel seemed to change, as though a heavenly fragrance were wafting through it.

Thus did the glory of the Lord fill His temple.

Chapter Thirteen

Gideon left the School of Pastoral Care in a blaze of glory. He had invited Paul Forrester to come home with him and rest for a couple of days before the long flight back east, and Paul had gladly accepted. There was room for both of them in the same car which had brought Gideon to the School, and so they were delivered at the doorstep of the little rectory in Monrovia.

As Susan darted out to meet them and saw the light on Gideon's face, her own eyes shone with joy, and her welcome rang out with her customary strong happiness, ready to meet life when life met her.

After a cup of coffee, Gideon went to the church to check his mail and appointments, and Paul retired to his room to rest. There soon came a knock on his door, and there stood a small boy with dark hair and serious brown eyes. "Are you the minister?" he asked.

"Yes, I'm Paul Forrester," Paul smiled, "and who are you? Come on in and tell me about yourself."

The lad entered and perched casually on the bed, as Paul seated himself in a wicker chair. "I'm David," said the boy. "You know, I belong here. Do you like being a minister?"

"At one time I didn't like it at all," replied Paul, speaking with the absolute seriousness with which he always addressed children, "but now I do."

"I don't think my dad likes it very much," said David. "That's what I want to ask you—do you think he's going to like it better?"

Paul thought a moment, quite seriously. "I think—he's going to," he said.

"You don't think they'll kick him out?"

"No, I don't think so," Paul replied.

"Gee, that's good!" David sighed. "Church is getting to be a lot more fun."

"Fun?"

"Well, you know, not exactly fun but, I mean, there's a lot more to it than there used to be. Us kids don't make those pots any more in Sunday school, you know."

"Pots?"

"Yeah, for a while the other guy—minister—he said children couldn't understand about God, so we were making pots."

With a sound between a groan and a laugh, Paul dropped his head in his hands. "Go on," he said weakly.

"That was stupid, see? But now Dad knows more about God, and it's pretty neat. I mean, it's really cool!"

"Very cool," agreed Paul. "And what does your dad tell you now about God?"

"He doesn't teach the class, see, but he kind of comes in. And you know, when the teachers get together and rap, Dad tells them Jesus is real! Can you beat that? That's what

170

he tells them. And he tells them Jesus can do things, like He used to. Boy, that's really something!"

"So—does Jesus do things in your class?"

"Well yeah, I mean, one Saturday it told in the paper about a kid that was lost. So when we came to Sunday school, the teacher said what do we want to pray about? When you pray about something, you're asking Jesus to do it. Do you dig that?"

"I dig it," replied Paul solemnly.

"Yeah, well, so I said let's pray for them to find that kid. Do you know, in just about an hour they did! He'd got stuck in the snow, and kind of slid down a canyon, and boy! They don't usually find people that slide down canyons. But they found him! Seems like Jesus needs us to kind of help Him, you know. I mean, Jesus couldn't go on His legs. It was the rescue squad guys that went, but Jesus must have somehow showed them where to go, do you think?"

"I think," replied Paul, "that's a very good description of how prayer works. You like that, huh?"

"Gee, anybody'd like that! It's a lot of fun. The kids think it's great."

"Don't you think the grown people also like it?" inquired Paul.

"Well, some of them just want to go to church and sing and listen and go home."

"I know," said Paul sadly, "but when they wake up and learn about Jesus, then they'll change. I'm glad you understand these things, because you'll be a real help to your father."

"Mom digs it, too," replied David proudly. "But Josie, my sister, you know—Josie, oh boy, she's a nut!"

"In what way is Josie—a nut?"

"Oh, I don't know. She's always messing around with dumb kids. They don't want to do anything they're supposed to do. If they were taught to go to church, then they don't want to, see? If they were taught to take baths, they don't want to. Well, I don't want to do that, either," David grinned. "If they were taught they mustn't take drugs and that kind of stuff, then that's just what they want to do."

"Uh—does your sister do that?"

"I don't know," replied David thoughtfully. "She's gotten kind of sneaky, but she's a pretty good kid, I guess. When girls get to be her age, I guess they're always kind of sneaky, don't you think?"

"Perhaps sneaky isn't the right word," mused Paul, letting David share his thoughts, "but at a certain age they are apt to be a bit secretive, and we just have to understand it and keep on loving them, until after a while they get over it."

"I guess so," agreed David somewhat reluctantly as they heard Susan call that dinner was ready.

When they sat down to the simple meal, there was one empty place.

"Josie will be along presently," said Susan, adding with a quick glance at the front door, "I hope!"

Gideon's mouth tightened a bit. "Where is she?" he asked.

"Out with the gang," said Susan.

"She'll come back," said Paul gently, and presently there was a slight scuffling at the front door, a gay shout, "Be seeing you!" a bang, and Josie appeared, bright-eyed and pretty, with her curly hair and hazel eyes. Paul, who himself had two daughters, looked steadily upon her. Not yet, he decided, not yet, but his new friend Gideon had better pray earnestly and with continuous faith for his daughter Josie.

Later that evening, Gideon took Paul to see the church, and the two men spent an hour together talking quietly in the study.

"Tell me about your older son," said Paul. "After all, I'm staying in his room, and I've been looking at his things, and I've wondered— Where is he?"

Gideon groaned. "God only knows where Bob is. He left home months ago—months ago. Actually, I took him for my special prayer project at the School of Pastoral Care. Remember you suggested that we each take a "special intention" on which to try out the prayer of faith. Of course nothing has happened yet, but it's only a few days since I started, and I'm going to keep on praying for Bob."

"What exactly are you praying?" asked Paul gently.

"That he'll come home," answered Gideon simply. "Just that he'll come home."

"And are you willing to face the situation when he does come home—whatever were his reasons for leaving—friction in the family, disillusionment about the world or our own country, turmoil within himself—whatever it was that made him go? Surely you know," Paul went on, "that the young man who returns will not be the boy who left."

"Yes, I know that," Gideon sighed. "I'm sure I was too hard on him about doing chores, getting cleaned up for church, and all that—and wouldn't let him buy an old car that he wanted. But now, if he'll *just come home!*" Gideon almost broke down as he said it.

"When you pray the prayer of faith," said Paul, "then you must be willing to face any difficulties that may come with the answer to your prayer."

"How do you mean?"

Paul replied, "Let your imagination dwell on Bob, and let pictures of him come into your mind, possibly in some foreign country, or Canada, or Hawaii—"

"Hawaii!" ejaculated Gideon, he did not know why.

"All right, what would he be doing there? Will he have found work? Where will he be living? Will he have friends? Will he perhaps have picked up some girl?" Paul paused, giving Gideon time for thought between the questions, at the last of which Gideon made an involuntary sound of protest. "No, but you must face that," said Paul firmly. "It may be just exactly what has happened, and if so, what will you do? Keep on with your prayer project, my brother," he concluded soberly, "but prepare yourself to meet all the problems as they come."

On the second evening of Paul's visit, dinner was interrupted by the shrilling of the telephone. Susan answered it, returning to the table with a twist to her mouth and her eyebrows raised disapprovingly. "For you," said she to her husband. "It's Stan."

"Stan?" cried Gideon. "What in the world?"

"Better go see," and Susan nodded in the direction of the bedroom.

Gideon closed the bedroom door, sat on the edge of the bed, and picked up the phone. "What's up, Stan?" he asked.

"Look here, Rev," said a stern voice, "we got trouble here, and you better come and straighten it out."

"What are you talking about?" asked Gideon, "And where is 'here'?"

"Here is this coffeehouse, Beth's place," said Stan grimly, "I'm out here seeing Ellie, and you'd better come quick!"

Gideon's heart gave a leap and settled again. "Okay, but what's up?" he demanded.

"It's that Jess. He's here, raving crazy, and what's more, he's scared to death."

"Oh, look," remonstrated Gideon, "they've coped with him before. He's just on dope. When he comes to, he'll be okay. I don't have to come for that."

"Oh yes, you do, Rev," answered Stan firmly. "This is different. He may be on dope or he may not, but he says the devil's after him. In fact, he says the devil's *in* him, and I never saw anybody so scared in my life. He's shaking from head to foot."

"Isn't there anybody who can—uh, cope with him?" asked Gideon.

"Just Beth and a bunch of scared females," responded Stan. "They're trying, praying all over the joint, you know, but it's no good. Got to have somebody stronger than that. Now look, Rev, all this you've been feeding me about Jesus, and the Holy Spirit, and all that, see, is it true, or isn't it? If it's true, it's got to work now!"

Gideon asked Stan to wait a minute while he called Paul and consulted with him in the bedroom. "Bring him to the church," said Paul after the briefest description of the problem.

"The church!" exclaimed Gideon.

"Yes, the church."

"Couldn't we sort of see him at the coffeehouse," asked Gideon, with visions of Angela and Doris sweeping in to decorate the altar, and finding a raving young man prancing up and down the aisles.

"No," said Paul, "my hunch is that this needs all the power we've got, and if the church hasn't any power, and the altar of the Lord doesn't mean anything, then we'd better shut up shop. No, have him come to the church. I'll go with you," he added reassuringly. "No problem. It'll work, you'll see."

"Okay." Gideon took his hand off the mouthpiece and spoke to Stan again. "Bring Jess to the church," he said, "right now, if you can make him come."

"Oh, he'll come all right," said Stan. "This man's scared to death, you know. If we say come, he'll come!"

"Fine!" said Gideon. "I have a friend here who's handled this kind of thing before. The two of us will meet you at the church. The lights will be on. Come right in the front door."

"Good deal!" answered Stan, and the phone clicked off.

"I'm sorry to break things up," apologized Gideon, as he told Susan of their appointment. To his surprise, Susan laughed. He was beginning to realize that his wife was more than he thought she was. She liked a good holy fight!

"That's all right," she said. "For two cents, I'd come and see the victory."

"You'd better not," Gideon replied.

"No, I wouldn't really, but anyway, it's okay."

"I'm sorry to bring you problems after such a strenuous week. You ought to be resting," said Gideon to Paul as they entered the empty church and turned on the lights.

"I guess so," answered Paul, "but somehow I like a challenge like this!" As they put on vestments, he said to Gideon, "Now, let's make like an altar guild—candles, communion vessels, the works."

"Why?" asked Gideon, gathering the required articles. "I mean, I'm glad to and all that, but why?"

"Why do you suppose we have these things?" inquired Paul. "Candles on the altar, seven-branch candlesticks on either side, all shining and twinkling, the communion vessels in the middle decently veiled with an embroidered cloth—why do you suppose we have them?"

"Well," hesitated Gideon, "there's beauty in them, and dignity—"

"More than that," Paul broke in. "They impress on the subconscious mind that this is the house of God, and that God is here. Your friend Jess may be crazy, but when he comes into the church, his subconscious is going to feel something, and whatever spirit of darkness is in him is likely to get panicky in an effort to escape." With a gesture of unconscious dignity, Paul swept his hand toward the altar, now glimmering with candles.

There was the sound of scuffling and voices at the front door, and down the aisle streamed a bedraggled procession. First marched Beth with her large kitchen apron over slacks and sweater, for she had forgotten to remove it. With her was a trembling group of young folk, Ellie in their midst. Last of all came a shivering, wild-eyed figure, upheld and firmly escorted by Stan on the one hand, and a bearded youth whom Gideon did not know on the other.

"Take over," said Paul to Gideon. "You know what to do. Have them kneel at the altar rail. Later I'll step in, if you like."

"I do like," said Gideon. "God help me!" he added, and he was not speaking lightly.

"Okay, you start, and then I'll add whatever comes to me. But of course," Paul added, "it's not just the words that matter. You are a priest. You are a channel of God's power. You are a man of ordained authority, and this is your house of prayer. Anything that enters must obey you. Remember that!"

Gideon was reassured. "It's going to be all right," he said to Ellie, who was standing near him, weeping and trembling like a terrified child.

177

"All of you come forward," Gideon said in a tone of command. "I want you kneeling here in front of the altar."

At this, Jess broke away from the two men and ran screaming toward the door. "I won't go there!" he shrieked in a high voice, quite unlike his own. "I won't go near that place!"

"Catch him!" thundered Gideon, and the two men seized him just before he gained the door and brought him back. Gideon came down the aisle and faced him. "Don't be scared, Jess," he said. "Just tell me, what is all this?" But Jess was unable to speak. "Ellie, you tell me," said Gideon.

"He and that crowd, you know, up in the canyon, they decided to worship Satan."

At this, Jess himself spoke. "It's real, it's real!" he sobbed, shaking from head to foot.

"You see, they weren't sure the devil is real," Beth soothed in her motherly contralto, "so they were trying some stunts they'd heard of in order to find out. They didn't think there was any real harm in it. So Jess, he did some black magic. He started saying the Lord's Prayer backward, making it a prayer to the devil, and halfway through—"

"The devil came in," gasped Jess in a harsh, shrieking voice. *"He came in!* He's inside me! He's got me!"

At this, the older minister intervened. "He cannot have you," said Paul calmly but firmly. "Didn't you once give yourself to Jesus?"

"Yes, I did," sobbed Jess, "but, you see, I was just trying everything."

"Didn't you once pray for the Holy Spirit to be in you?"

"Sure, I did," said Jess shivering, his eyes seeming to start out of his white face. "Sure, but I wanted every kind of spirit to be in me. I was trying to see what it was like."

178

"That was bad," said Paul. "Nevertheless, at one time you did give yourself to Jesus. Therefore, in His name, I say—" he drew himself up to his full, slender height, and pronounced loud and clear—"I say that the devil cannot have you!"

Jess gave a convulsive shriek and tried to scramble free again. "Hold it," commanded Stan, "cut it out! Listen to the man, hear! Do what he says!"

"I only say what the rector has said," said Paul quietly. "You are to come forward. Bring him, men, bring him."

So they brought Jess, struggling and fighting, but not able to withstand them, to the altar rail and made him kneel at its very center. Gideon stood there, the cross shining upon his vestments. "Hear the word of the Lord," he commanded, and read from the fifth chapter of Mark how Jesus spoke to the evil spirits controlling a man and commanded them to leave, and how he was from that moment healed. "Jesus has not gone away," said Gideon. "Jesus is here, though we cannot see Him now, and we who are His priests are commanded to do what He did. He has given us the power to rebuke the devil so that he will flee from us. So—" and he turned expectantly to Paul.

Paul stood directly before the quivering man at the altar rail, raised his right hand, and spoke not to Jess but to the evil spirit within him. "I speak to you now, you spirit or spirits," said Paul, "and in the name and power of Jesus Christ, I command you to come out of this man. Come forth!"

Jess's body froze, as though he were turned to stone, and a low moan escaped his lips. His eyes were wide and glazed. "You know that you *must* obey this command," Paul continued, speaking not to Jess but to the tormenting spirit.

"I hold up the cross of Christ before you, and you know that you cannot withstand the cross of Christ. So now, come forth! That's right," he added, as though he sensed something departing. "Come all the way, all the way out! Bring out every bit of any tentacle of evil that may be left in him, and come all the way out!"

Jess gave a great sigh and crumpled, his head upon the altar rail while his two friends supported him. Paul then turned and faced the altar, stretching forth both his hands. "Now, Lord Jesus," he said, "I place these departing things in Your hands. It is not for me to pass judgment upon them; Yours is the power and authority. Therefore, Lord, take into Your own hands whatever evil spirits are now departing from Jess. Take them in Your own hands, Lord, and absolutely forbid them ever to return to him, or his friends, or this church, or to any place upon this earth.

"And now, Lord Jesus, come quickly, quickly, and fill up with Your love all the empty places in Jess. Enter, Lord Jesus, and reclaim what is Yours!"

There was a deep, quivering sigh from Jess. He raised his head, and murmured, "It's gone!" looking around wonderingly. "It's gone! O-o-oh!" His face relaxed, and he looked like himself again.

"Thank You, Lord!" murmured Beth.

"Oh, thank You, Jesus!" whispered Ellie.

"Good job!" growled Stan.

"Finally, Lord Jesus," Paul continued praying, "surround Jess with a circle of light. I call for Your guardian angels to be beside him on the right hand and on the left, so that nothing evil shall ever again enter into him, and so that from this time on, he may be wholly Yours. Thank You, Lord."

Paul turned and nodded to Gideon, who raised his right hand and pronounced the benediction.

"The Lord bless you and keep you, the Lord make His face to shine upon you and be gracious unto you, the Lord lift up the light of His countenance upon you and give you peace, now and forevermore. In the name of the Father and of the Son and of the Holy Ghost, Amen."

"It's gone," whispered Jess, standing up, and then in louder tones he cried, "It's gone!" The wild light no longer shone in his eyes, and he looked unutterably weary but comforted, like a child who has been lost in the dark and suddenly sees the light once more.

"Praise the Lord!" cried Ellie, and others of the group lifted their arms and praised the Lord, aloud or in silence.

Gideon meanwhile was removing the sacred objects from the altar when the sacristy door opened and who should appear but Angela Pritchard and Doris Panella! They froze in the doorway, apparently shocked at seeing the rector and another minister carrying the communion vessels and candles away from the altar. They also saw a group of jean-clad, long-haired young people standing with arms upraised, praising the Lord.

"What in heaven's name—" gasped Angela.

Doris only managed, "Oh my, oh my!"

Gideon's face went red, then white again. "This is my friend, Father Forrester," said Gideon, "rector of the Church of the Nativity in Boston." He was grasping for a straw of respectability, and Paul, recognizing this fact, smiled in courteous amusement.

"We've been having a small healing service," he said gently to the two nonplussed ladies, and added, "That's what the house of God is for, isn't it?"

181

Gideon rallied to Paul's support. "Plenty of people are in trouble nowadays," he said, "and it is good that they can come to God's house for help. And we're grateful too," he added diplomatically, "to you good ladies who keep this altar beautiful."

Angela took the candlesticks out of Gideon's hands. "We came to prepare for tomorrow's communion service," she said in clipped tones.

"Good," said Gideon with a gracious smile, "very good!" Then with a little bow he turned from them.

As the sacristy door closed behind them with more of a bang than was necessary, Paul turned to Gideon. "The Philistines are upon us," he remarked dryly.

"What will I do now?" murmured Jess, as they straggled toward the door. He still looked like a child who has been lost and suddenly is found, and cannot quite comprehend it. "I'm scared to go back in that canyon. I'm scared!"

"Well, you won't be going anywhere tonight anyway," said Beth. "Come on back to the coffeehouse, and we'll fix you up a place to sleep. We've got plenty of pillows, and you won't be the first one to sleep on the floor."

"I've got to do something about those kids up in the canyon," muttered Jess. "Guess I've been leading 'em the wrong way."

"But now you've come back to the right path," said Gideon comfortingly. "Jesus is the way. He said so, and He is. He's the only way. When you get rested and straightened out, you'll have a great time leading your friends back to the right way." Thus Gideon ushered the little band out to the sidewalk and into the cars which had brought them. Behind the first car was one that Gideon recognized, for it belonged to his friend, Stan.

"Hold on, Ellie!" called Stan, as the girl was about to crowd herself among the group from the coffeehouse. "You're not going back with those kooks."

"Where else would I go?" asked Ellie.

"Well, I came to take you out, kind of a date, remember? Get us something to eat and have a chance to talk, without a whole bunch of people howling around and praising Jesus! So you come with me. Don't worry—you'll be okay. I'll take you back there after everybody's settled down."

Ellie looked at Gideon questioningly. He nodded and smiled, her face relaxed, and she drew near to Stan, looking up at him with love in her soft blue eyes. "She'll be all right, Beth," Gideon reassured the matronly lady who was shepherding her flock home. "You folks go on back and take care of Jess, and I'll guarantee that Ellie will be home in good time. Okay?"

"Okay," agreed Beth, and the ancient vehicle churned away, exposing its rear-end sticker with loud red letters on a white background: REPENT NOW. AVOID THE CROWD ON JUDGMENT DAY.

"Repent now," chuckled Paul. "Not a bad idea!"

Stan looked after the car with glowering eyes. "Bunch of nuts," he said, "absolutely a bunch of nuts! Come on, let's get out of here." He bundled Ellie into his car, and they drove away.

"Who is that knight in armor?" asked Paul, gently amused.

"That's my garage man," said Gideon, "you know, the father of the girl who was killed beside the freeway. I guess you might call him my strongest prayer partner."

"Does he come to church?" asked Paul.

"Well, he has once or twice, but he takes rather a dim view

183

of church. I guess it's crazy, or maybe it's like the early Christians in the catacombs—but what happens is that I go down to the garage once in a while. Stan's got the owner, Tom, talked into this, so sometimes after work the three of us sit on a pile of tires, or something, in a little shop back of the garage, and we pray up a storm, believe it or not."

"I believe it," said Paul, and he quoted from the first chapter of I Corinthians: "Not many wise men after the flesh, not many mighty, not many noble, are called. But God hath chosen the foolish things of the world to confound the wise."

"Sorry to have given you such a lively evening," said Gideon, "but I'm certainly glad you were here!"

"Guess I was meant to be," smiled Paul, and they drove back to the rectory, where they regaled Susan with a lively account of the evening's events, and had coffee and cookies with much joy and laughter.

"I can't help laughing and being happy tonight," said Paul. "Nothing makes me more joyful than having a victory over the devil!"

"Do you truly believe it was the devil?" asked Gideon.

"Oh, you can call it other names if you want to, but no matter what you call them, these things don't come from God, and it's quite obvious to me whose they are and whence they come."

Gideon ruminated, "You know, I've always taken a dim view of that kind of praying. You call it exorcism, don't you?"

"Sometimes," said Paul.

"We hear quite a bit about it nowadays," said Gideon, "and it seems that some people run around exorcising everybody, seeing the devil in this one and that one. I've always steered clear of that business."

"That's a good idea," approved Paul. "Steer clear of it as long as you possibly can. Nine tenths of the 'deliverance' or 'exorcism' that people tell about is entirely unnecessary and misdirected."

"I agree," Gideon replied, "but I could see with my own eyes that this one tonight was necessary. It was the only way to save Jess's life."

"That's right," declared Paul. "I knew one other person somewhat like that once, but no one got to him in time, and—"

"What happened?"

"Threw himself out a window. Something like that would probably have happened to your friend Jess, if Stan and those women hadn't brought him to you."

"Explain one thing to me," said Gideon. "How do you know when it really is a devil? And if it isn't, then what do people mean who say they discern the devil here and there? And another thing—Ellie said that the coffeehouse people had tried to help Jess. They had prayed and told the devil to leave him, and it didn't work. Why?"

"Two reasons," said Paul, leaning back on the sofa and putting his weary feet on a hassock. "One could be that those women lost their nerve, which isn't surprising. The other could be that they simply didn't have the power. Remember the story of the seven sons of Sceva?" Grinning, Paul found the passage in Acts 19 and read it aloud, ending in laughter because, as he explained, the story always struck him as being extremely funny: "Jesus I know, and Paul I know, but who are you?"

"You see," Paul went on, closing the Bible with a snap, "a mistake some Pentecostals make is that they assume that as soon as they receive the Baptism in the Spirit, they are instantly, automatically, and fully endowed with the gifts of healing and exorcism—particularly the latter. They greatly enjoy that! But it's not quite that easy. These gifts come not only from the conscious mind, but also the unconscious, through the growth and development within us of the power of the Holy Spirit. Assuming that we instantly have all the gifts is a bit like assuming that a baby can, from the moment of birth, talk, walk, and go to school. He does have the potential within him, but it takes time to bring it forth.

"Another mistake some people make," continued Paul, warming to his subject, "is that they don't understand the difference between temptation and possession. All of us are, from time to time, tempted by the Evil One. We are tempted to do actual sins, and moreover, we are tempted more subtly to lose our spiritual strength by suffering from illness, exhaustion, and depression. None of these things comes from God, but when we do wrong, or suffer from illness, exhaustion, or depression, that doesn't mean that we are possessed. We are merely being attacked from outside, and we are supposed to cope with these attacks of the enemy ourselves, not to run to somebody else and ask him to cast the devil out of us. And if we see that someone else is depressed or sad, we should talk to him alone, find out by gentle sympathy what the trouble is, and pray for him to have strength to resolve it."

"I see what you mean," said Gideon gratefully.

"Well, thank the Lord!" said Susan, bursting into the conversation. "I never understood all that, but now I think I do."

"Yes," said Paul, "a person may be troubled by some old, unconfessed guilt, and what he needs is to make a confession, or to bring it forth into the light and make a right decision concerning it. Or maybe he is just weary and overburdened, and needs rest. It may be, and often is, that he is angry with somebody, and needs to overcome that anger and turn it into love. Of course, it may be that he is or has been tempted by the sins of the flesh, and is doing, or intends to do, things that are wrong, in which case, he not only needs counsel and prayer, but most of all, he needs to make a right decision. Helping such a person by counsel and prayer is not at all the same as praying a prayer of exorcism for one who is truly possessed."

"How can you tell when someone is really and truly possessed?" Susan inquired.

"Gideon, how could you tell that Jess was?" Paul asked.

"Well, he was obviously crazy."

"That's it, " Paul nodded. "Possession is an actual mental illness, a disturbance of the mind. It's very real," he added. "In fact, overenthusiastic people who claim to have the Holy Spirit forget that if they really had the *full* power, they could go into mental institutions and just about clean them out."

"Well, I thank God you were here tonight," said Gideon, not for the first time, "or I don't know what would have happened."

Paul replied mildy, "The Lord does often put us in the right place at the right time, doesn't He?"

"He's pretty good at that," said Susan, rising in her quick, decisive way and carrying the coffeepot back into the kitchen. "But is He going to be any good at handling Angela and Doris?" she called out. "That's what I want to know!"

"Handling them?" inquired Paul quizzically.

Gideon nodded. " 'Handling them' is right," he said. "Before long, the whole parish will know how the rector put the sacred vessels on the altar when they were not even to be used for Communion, and lit the candles, and brought in a horde of hippies from the street— Oh, brother! I'm in enough trouble in the parish now; this will just about fix it!"

"Do you mean they might ask you to leave?" inquired Paul.

"That's just what I mean," said Gideon slowly.

"Don't forget," replied Paul gently, "that no one can force you to leave. You are in authority, and you can simply refuse. Not even the bishop can fire you unless he holds a trial on charges of heresy or immorality, and I doubt if he'd undertake that."

"Oh, I know all that," said Gideon, "but I mean, if the people don't want me, and I'm making them unhappy—"

"You'd turn tail and run?" asked Paul rather sharply. "You're a pastor, a shepherd of the sheep. If your sheep all took a notion to run into a dangerous area full of cliffs and holes, would it be kindness to let them do so?"

"Well, no," grinned Gideon, "but if I stay against their will, it could kill the church. You know that, Paul."

"It could, but it won't," said Paul. Then he inquired, "Who else belongs to your altar guild besides those two doughty females whom I briefly met?"

"No one else," said Gideon. "Those two have always been the altar guild."

"Always?"

"From time immemorial," smiled Gideon, nodding slowly. "I inherited them, and there they are."

"And here you are," declared Paul, "the rector of this parish, the captain of this ship."

"Do you mean I should get rid of them?" asked Gideon, horrified. "That would split the church wide open!"

"That's funny," commented Paul. "It wouldn't split a business wide open if the owner or manager should dismiss two inadequate helpers and hire others."

"But how would I go about it?"

"I'll tell you what I'd do," said Paul. "In my parish, all teenage girls belong to the altar guild. It is just taken for granted, as part of their Christian life and training, and they take turns serving. Two ladies are at the head of the altar guild, and they also take turns, like a revolving vestry, you know. I myself send out the notices, telling the girls when it's their turn to serve on Saturday morning—arranging flowers, polishing brass, cleaning the chancel—and I meet with them. Nothing is so important for my Saturday morning as this—nothing! We go into the church together. The girls kneel at the rail, and I stand at the altar and pray for them, for their work, and for the house of the Lord to be filled with His love and power. Then I leave, but it is understood that while they perform their sacred services, they meditate in silence—no chattering, and therefore no bickering."

"That's wonderful," sighed Gideon. "I never heard of anything like that."

"I do much the same with the acolytes," continued Paul. "Every youth in the parish belongs to the servers' guild, and I myself make up the schedule for two to be on duty each Sunday. I send out the notices, call them on the telephone and remind them, and check that they'll really be there. If the mother says that she'll give her son the message, I say, 'No thanks, I prefer to speak to him myself.' Thus we work together, man to man, and they like it. Then, as they get a

189

bit older, they take their turn in receiving the offering and acting as ushers. At each service, two vestrymen and two young fellows are on duty. In other words, I always treat the young people as full members of the church."

"But don't you have a youth group, and special youth activities? Don't you have to?" asked Gideon, greatly interested.

"Why should I?" said Paul. "They think up plenty of youth activities for themselves. It's all right if people have that calling and want to do it, but I don't, and I don't want to distract the youngsters from their normal duties to the church. They are treated like anybody else. Moreover," Paul grinned delightedly, "I have a children's choir of the littler ones, and they sing every Sunday evening. Many of them come early and find me in my study, and I tell them stories to keep them amused until time for church. Then they take the greatest pride in dressing up in their little white cottas and big black ties and processing into church singing. We have no sermon, just a short service of hymns, Bible reading, and prayers.

"You know, those prayers are effective! A little girl came to me once and asked me to pray for her friend during the evening service, and I said of course I would, but why didn't she ask her own pastor to pray for him? You see, ours is the only evening service in our area, so we have many children from other churches, and many also who have no church. The child said, 'Well, I will ask my pastor, but the thing is, the people you pray for get well.' "

"I see," said Gideon thoughtfully, and again, "I see!" He looked up and away at this picture of a church full of prayer, as one might look up and away at a towering mountain, steep and trackless. "How long did it take you to build up a church like this?"

"Many years," said Paul gently, "and I didn't exactly build it. It just grew. Jesus is the one who really does it. Every Saturday night I go into the church and rehearse the whole service aloud. Maybe it's childish, but then I walk about the church and lay my hands in blessing on every pew, praying for the presence of God to be in that pew and in the whole church."

"And you can really tell that it has made a difference?"

"Something has made a difference," nodded Paul, his eyes far away. "Many people even see a light shining around the cross on the altar. I don't, not being very good at that sort of thing, but I can feel the power, and miracles often happen, just by the presence of God in His tabernacle."

Chapter Fourteen

Next morning, Gideon drove Paul to the airport. The wrench of goodbye as they drew up to the sidewalk—traffic swirling beside them, and a metal voice proclaiming, "This area is for loading and unloading only"—was as the wrench of brothers parting. Indeed, in one short week they had become closer than brothers, drawn together by the mysterious bond of Christ's love, and even after Paul had left, the joy of this brotherhood remained with Gideon as he drove home.

On the pretext of needing gas, he stopped at the garage. Before going back to the dubious welcome of the parish house, where sooner or later Reginald Crabtree would certainly demand to know what he was doing in the church last evening with a bunch of hoodlums, Gideon felt the need of seeing Stan.

How strange, he thought, but the ways of God were often strange, even laughable. Here was Stan, rough and ignorant, yet somehow with a more solidly based faith than anyone at the church. Even his curate, Leslie, continually needed to be fortified by all kinds of groups, but Stan stood firmly on his own feet, and Gideon could not even imagine him at any of those gatherings. His lips spread in a little smile as he thought of it. Stan would roar through an encounter group like an express train!

He came from behind the garage, wiping his hands on an old rag. "I'll take care of the Rev," said he to the boy, and he did so, briskly cleaning the windshield while the tank filled. "Okay under the hood?" he asked.

"Okay," said Gideon, stepping out of the car the better to talk with him. "What did you think of that shindig in the church last night, Stan?" he demanded.

Stan grinned from ear to ear. "Good show!" he said. "But what your congregation will do when they hear about it, I don't know! But you can bet I'll say a prayer for you. You going over there now?"

Gideon laughed. "Yes, so start praying," and he paid and departed.

The moment Gideon stepped into his study, the telephone rang. He answered the call and heard Susan's voice, which sounded strained and strange, as he had never before heard it.

"Gideon, come home!" she said. "Come home, come home right away!"

"What's the matter?" asked Gideon, cold fear clutching his heart. "Anybody—anybody sick, or anything? Accident?"

"No," said Susan excitedly, "no. It's—it's all right, really. At least, I guess it is, but oh Gideon, come home!"

As fast as possible, Gideon drove back through Pasadena, toward the mountains, and into the little street where they lived. In three bounds he was out of the car and in the front door. There stood Susan, every nerve taut. And there, seated in a big chair with a small boy upon her lap, was a strange young woman. She looked up at him pleadingly from her childlike, freckled face, but even though there was anxiety in her eyes, there was a certain composure, a center of quietness, as though she lived in her own oasis in the whirling world.

"This is Donna," said Susan in a strangled voice, "and—and she says she's—Bob's wife. And this is—" with a short sound, almost a laugh, "our grandson—so she says."

Gideon dropped down upon the sofa opposite the young woman, his knees too weak to stand. "Where's Bob?" he asked.

"He's coming," said Donna in a small, quiet voice.

"Then—then why are you here first? I mean, if you really are—"

"I think I am," the girl replied with unshakable honesty.

"Think you are what?" asked Susan, still standing, and trembling visibly.

"Bob's wife," the girl replied innocently.

"Don't you know?" asked Gideon.

"Well, I wasn't exactly, not for quite a while, because, you see, there wasn't anybody on the beach to marry us. And then, you know, the baby came, so Bob thought it would be a good idea if we found somebody. So, it was a little Japanese man that he brought, but I think he really married us, though he couldn't speak English very well. Anyway, it doesn't matter very much, does it, because here we are!"

"Good Lord!" ejaculated Gideon under his breath. "Where is Bob now?"

"Oh, he's on the way," said Donna. "You see, at first we didn't have any money."

"And what did you live on?" demanded Susan, sitting on a straight chair, and inching it unconsciously a little closer to the serene girl, the only one of the three who was not in any way discomposed. She simply sat there, her little boy cuddled in her arms.

"Well, you see, we just lived on the beach," said the girl, "and we didn't need much to eat, because we didn't do much. We fasted a lot, and—and we meditated. Oh, we did a lot of meditating. And about once a week we'd go out and gather fruit, and things like that."

Gideon forebore to ask whose fruit they gathered. "And that was all you ate?"

"Well, of course, we don't eat meat," said the girl. "None of us do—and, yes, that was about all we ate, and we got along all right. All the kids did."

"Who do you mean by all the kids?" demanded Susan.

"Oh, about fifty of us were living on the beach. Some of the others had babies, too."

"And what about the baby," Susan almost cried, her eyes resting on him, "what did he eat?"

"I nursed him," said the girl simply, "and if he wanted anything else, why we found there's a coconut that you can get when it's still kind of green, and it has a nice creamy pulp. He liked that very much."

"Oh!" Susan moaned, passing one trembling hand over her perspiring forehead.

"Tell me," said Gideon insistently, "where is Bob? You said he's on the way. Why are you here when he isn't?"

"Oh, I forgot," Donna said. "Well, you see, after a while we thought we'd better get welfare. You know, everybody gets welfare in Hawaii. So we did, and we saved it up and got enough for my fare home, and you know it doesn't cost anything to bring the baby. Isn't that neat? But we didn't get enough for Bob, so he's working his way over on a ship. They needed an extra deckhand, because two or three of them skipped, so he's working on the ship."

"When will he get here?" demanded Gideon hoarsely.

"Oh, I don't know," said Donna, as though it really didn't matter. "I should think maybe in two or three days. The ship doesn't land here," she added. "It lands in San Francisco—at least, that's where I think it's going."

"How will he get home?" wailed Susan.

"Oh, he'll hitchhike," Donna replied. "That's what we all do. Of course, with Westwind it's easier. Somebody's sure to pick up a girl with a baby."

Gideon turned his horrified gaze upon the little boy, who hid his face in his mother's bosom for a moment and then wriggled out of her arms and stood erect on his spindly legs, his blonde head bent down and his little thumb in his mouth.

"Westwind?" asked Susan feebly. She looked at the child who, thinking she had called him, promptly looked up with blue eyes so like Gideon's that it made her gasp.

"Me big boy," he said, in a little voice that wrung her heart, reminding her as it did of her own babies, their voices as happy as small birds.

"Yes, you are a big boy, aren't you, Westwind?" asked his mother.

"But is that all the name he's got—Westwind?" inquired Susan carefully, her heart turning over within her as she unconsciously stretched out a hand to the little fellow standing so sturdily before her.

"Oh, no," said Donna innocently. "His whole name is

196

Clear Sky Westwind, but we call him Westwind for short."

"Why didn't you write to us?" asked Gideon. "All these months we didn't know anything. Why didn't you write?"

"We couldn't," said Donna. "We didn't have any paper or pen or stamps. You know, we didn't have anything. We were just living on the beach."

"What do you really mean, you didn't have anything?" asked Susan, leaning forward.

"Well, when we went there," said the girl, "when Bob first took me there—he found me, you see, by the side of the road, and the other boy had gone off. I didn't know where he went, and I didn't have anywhere to go—not anywhere. So Bob said to come on, and he put me on the bicycle and he pushed it, and after a while a truck driver came along and picked us up. We didn't have anything—except, I had a knapsack, you know, with a couple of things in it. Of course, I didn't have the baby then. And Bob, he just had some sort of pack on his back, with one or two clothes, and that's all we had."

"Where did you sleep?" asked Susan.

"On the beach," replied the girl. "You know, it doesn't get very cold, and we went to the Salvation Army and got a couple of old blankets, and we didn't need anything else."

"But when the baby came?" asked his grandmother, agony in her voice. Westwind stood before her and looked up at her eagerly.

"Baby come," he said.

Susan again stretched out a hand toward him, her heart warming with a choking tenderness, but the little fellow backed away. "When the baby came," she asked Donna, "what did you do?"

"Well, he just came," said Donna.

"Right there on the beach?"

197

"Yes, it wasn't very hard," the girl replied. "You know, some of the other girls had babies, and Bob was there, and—he just came."

"Good heavens!" Susan moaned. "But then didn't you have to get diapers, and clothes, and things for the baby?"

The girl shook her head, smiling gently. "No, he didn't need anything," she said. "You see, we just lived on the beach, and he didn't wear anything."

Gideon could sit quiet no longer and arose and strode back and forth. "You didn't have a doctor?" he inquired.

"We didn't need a doctor," said the girl. "You see, he wasn't sick, and I wasn't sick. I was just having a baby, that's all, and the other girls kind of taught me how."

"Then this child," reasoned Gideon aloud, "has no birth certificate!"

"What's that?" asked Donna naïvely.

Gideon dropped down again onto the sofa, his hand over his eyes. "But when you got to—where did you get to?"

"Los Angeles," the girl replied.

"When you got to Los Angeles, why didn't you telephone us?"

"Why?" asked Donna. "I mean, you see, on the beach we don't have telephones, or anything like that, and you just kind of forget. If you're going some place, you just go." And she added with a tiny smile, that was not quite a smile, "I—I'm here, aren't I?"

The little boy began tugging at his pantaloons, as though they irritated him. His mother watched placidly, explaining to his grandparents, "He doesn't like them." She made no offer to help, and the child finally worried them down past his round stomach, sat on his haunches, and pulled them off his little skinny legs.

"Off!" said he triumphantly, looking up at his mother with a proud smile. Then he began tugging and pulling at his little sweatshirt.

"He can't quite manage that," said his mother calmly. "Come here, Westwind," and drawing him toward her, she serenely slipped the shirt over his upraised arms. There he stood, as naked as the day he was born.

"Westwind!" proclaimed he, patting his own chest and evidently indicating that without the hampering effect of garments, his personality was now complete.

"Good heavens!" gasped Susan. "Doesn't the child wear clothes?"

"He never did until we came on this trip," explained Donna, as one might speak to a child who lacked under-standing. "Traveling, you know, and all that, we kind of felt it would be better. But now that he's here," she added serenely, "he won't have to wear them."

"Oh, *won't* he!" said Susan, and rose and advanced toward him. However, before she got any further, there was a knock on the door and, without waiting for an invitation, in popped Leslie Ainsworth, followed by his wife, Lisa. They stopped in the doorway, frozen with amazement.

Gideon felt the blood rush to his face as he stood to greet them. "This is —Donna," he said, indicating the young woman who sat in her comfortable chair, not offering to move. "Uh—she's just arrived."

"From Maui," said Donna, who was not in the least shy, although in her serenity she might appear to be. "And this," added Donna, "is Westwind."

"Me!" said Westwind, prancing up to the newcomers, and smiling from ear to ear.

Susan arose, grim-faced and furious. She snatched up the

discarded little garments from the floor, and advanced toward the small boy to put them on him. "No!" said he, definitely.

Donna therefore explained, looking up into the amazed faces of the tall curate and his slender wife, "He doesn't like clothes."

"Sit down," said Gideon rather abruptly. "We'll get some coffee."

"Something stronger would be better," muttered Leslie. "Who in heaven's name *is* Donna?" and he looked at the young woman clad in jeans and some doll-like garment above them, her blond hair parted in the middle and combed straight back, falling limply over her shoulders. She was completely free, apparently, of any embarrassment. Either she was so secure within herself as not to care, or, thought Gideon, she was a bit lacking in the upper story, and did not realize what was going on around her.

Susan meanwhile, holding the little garments in her hand, made for Westwind who with a merry laugh darted through the open door into the bedroom. There was the sound of a small scuffle, a few sharp commands, one tiny wimper, and then quite surprisingly, another laugh, for to Westwind all life was a game. If someone else won a turn, that was nothing to be upset about. Susan picked him up in her arms to carry him back into the living room, and Westwind patted her cheek, smiling his funny little lopsided smile. "Nice lady," he murmured, and at this moment Susan's heart turned over within her. Clothes or no clothes, this child was hers!

She carried him back into the living room, making a detour by the kitchen and putting a cookie into his hand. She then sat down, holding him on her knees so that he would

not again cast off his clothes. He sat there quite complacently, chewing the cookie and looking serenely around at
these new people.

"Who is this child?" Leslie persisted.

Gideon, his lips tight and a nerve jumping in his cheek,
responded grimly, "This is my grandson—or so I am led to
believe."

"Oh my," breathed Lisa. "Oh—are they going to live
here?"

Gideon eyed his wife dubiously, but holding the little boy
tightly to her, Susan proclaimed, "Yes, of course—that is,
until Bob comes. Then we'll see what he wants to do."

"You see," explained Donna, as though it were the simplest matter in the world, "Bob says he's been away long
enough, and he wanted to come home."

"So—Bob's on the way," murmured Gideon, and suddenly
recovering from his state of shock, he felt a surge of joy in
his heart. His son was on the way home! His prayer project!
For this he had prayed day and night, and Paul Forrester
had told him that one must be willing to accept the answer
when it comes, no matter what complications come with
it. So here it was, and he would accept it.

"What's Josie going to think?" queried Lisa, sinking into
a deep chair.

"This may cause Josie to really think," said her father.
"I hope so."

"I like Josie," said Donna simply.

"How can you?" said Gideon. "You've never seen her."

"No, but Bob's told me about her, and I like her. But
then," she added innocently, "I like everybody, don't you?"

Gideon made no reply, but Leslie said with a short laugh,
"Apparently he does. I hear strange things about his new

201

friends. Where in the world—" he went on, "this is what I came to ask you, Gideon—where in the world did you get that motley crew that you had in the church last night?"

"Who told you about them?" asked Gideon. But he knew.

"Oh, Angela and Doris. They're telling everybody how they went into the church to fix the altar—"

"It wasn't the time for them to prepare the altar," snapped Gideon.

"Well, they did anyway, and they said how could you ever let those long-haired, barefooted kids in there?" Leslie looked at Gideon wonderingly and went on, "You're getting farther out than I've ever been. You used to land on me for my encounter groups, and for heaven's sake, look at you! What you had in the church last night was a group to end all groups, if you ask me!"

Gideon grinned crookedly. "It sure was," he said.

"Now really, what were you doing?" asked his assistant point-blank, while Donna, Susan, Lisa, and the little boy listened in silence.

"I was casting out the devil from a troubled young man."

"You were doing *what?*"

"Exorcism," explained Gideon. "Haven't you ever heard of it?"

"Sure, in the Bible."

"It happens today, too," said Gideon. "Wise up, young man, wise up!"

"Did it work?"

"Sure it worked."

"But," Leslie remonstrated, "right there in the church, where anybody might come in and see—"

"That's what a church is for," Gideon declared firmly, "and as long as I'm rector—"

"I don't know how long that will be." Leslie shook his head doubtfully. "Next thing we know," he blurted, "you'll be speaking in tongues."

The fat was already in the fire, so Gideon simply replied, "I already do."

Chapter Fifteen

"Mom?" called Josie, dashing into the house. "Hey, Mom!" There was no answer. Charging across the living room, she stopped in amazement. For there, in the middle of the floor, lay a small, somewhat dingy pair of pants—a *very* small pair. "What in the world?" muttered Josie. She went through the kitchen and onto the back porch, still calling in the timeless way of children coming home from school, "Mom?"

Halfway down the back steps she stood stock still. Sitting in a garden chair, doing absolutely nothing, was a fair girl, or it might have been a young woman, and running around the yard naked was a very small boy. "Good grief!" exclaimed Josie.

The girl got up and came toward her, a gentle smile on her round, freckled face. "You must be Josie," she said, holding out her hand. Then, since Josie still stood frozen to the spot, she withdrew it again and seemed to shrink back into herself.

Josie came down the last step and advanced toward her.

"Uh—who are you?" she asked, and motioning to the tiny boy, now peeking timidly from behind his mother's legs, "And who in the world is that?"

"Westwind," said the little boy distinctly, taking his thumb out of his mouth and then putting it back.

"I'm Donna," said the girl. "I'm Bob's wife."

"Bob!" shrieked Josie. "Where is he?" She whirled about to dash into the house looking for him.

"Oh, Bob—he hasn't gotten here yet," said Donna. "You see, we didn't have money enough for all of us to fly from Hawaii, so I flew, and he's coming."

"How?" demanded Josie caustically. "Swimming?"

"No," said Donna quite seriously, "he's working on a—on a ship."

"And—this?" asked Josie, incoherently struggling for a moment between laughter and tears, "What's this?" She looked down at the little boy hiding behind his mother. His little potbelly and skinny legs were a bit dirty and grass-stained, but there he stood, apparently quite unconscious of his condition.

"That's Westwind," said Donna. "He's—I guess he's your nephew."

At this Josie collapsed into one of the battered backyard chairs. "Oh, wow!"

"Westwind play," said the little boy, and he trotted off, picked up the hose which was busily running, and squirted it around, not in any spirit of mirthful glee but most solemnly, as though he were doing a noble service to the backyard.

"He's never seen a hose before," said Donna simply.

"Never seen a hose?" Bereft of words, Josie looked again at the little boy who had left the hose running and had

picked up a small stick that he trundled on the ground behind him as he trotted to and fro. "Doesn't he have any
toys?" asked Josie, not knowing what else to say.

Donna shook her head. "We don't believe in toys," said
she.

Josie gulped and managed to inquire weakly, "Who in
the world is *we*?"

"Oh, all us New Age kids, you know, living on the beach
and everywhere. A child doesn't need toys," she explained
gravely. "There are shells and coconuts and coral and, you
know, he can find lots to play with."

Josie swallowed hard. "Living on what beach?" Whereupon Donna placidly told her about the hippie colony on
Jefferson Beach, Maui. "Don't you think," said Josie uneasily, "he'd better turn off that hose? You know, water's
expensive, kind of," she added feebly, for some reason feeling apologetic at this quite sensible suggestion.

Donna did not move. She only glanced at the hose, spurt-
ing precious water over the lawn, and made no move to rise,
so Josie herself got up and turned it off. Then, not knowing
what else to say or do, she sat down again and waited to
see what would happen next.

What happened next was David bursting out of the house,
galloping down the back steps on an imaginary steed, slap-
ping his thighs and shouting, "Bang, bang!" with outstretched finger. Westwind pressed close to his mother's
knees, peeped out shyly, and murmured, "Wide horsie!"

"Hey, what goes on here?" shouted David. "What is this,
a nudist colony or something?"

"You're David," announced Donna serenely.

"Yeah, but who's that?" said David, pointing to the little
boy who smiled broadly and wriggled with delight, recognizing a kindred spirit.

"That," said Josie, "is your—nephew!" She flung back her dark head and laughed delightedly.

David abruptly ceased riding a horse. "Nephew?" he demanded, and amid howls of laughter Josie told him, "Yes, nephew. He's Bob's kid."

"Bob! Oh, wow, where is he?" cried David, looking around eagerly.

"Hold everything," said Josie. "Sit down and catch your breath. Bob hasn't come yet, but this—" and she pointed to Donna, who sat as though nothing unusual was happening "this is his—wife, I guess."

"I think so," said Donna quite seriously, whereupon David did sit down. He collapsed upon the grass, gazing with amazement at this strange person, apparently dropped from the skies.

Westwind, meanwhile, had retrieved his stick, once used for tying up chrysanthemums, straddled it, and galloped around the yard beaming delightedly and saying, "Horsie, horsie!" his small behind shining in the afternoon sun.

David burst into laughter. "Gosh, he's cute!" said he. "I don't know where you got him, but he sure is cute!"

At this moment, Susan returned from the store and stood in the back doorway, her arms full of groceries. "Mom, hey Mom!" cried David scrambling up from the grass when he caught sight of her. "Is Bob really coming back? When's he coming?"

"Yes, he's coming back," said Susan a bit grimly, "having apparently sent his wife and child before him. Sort of like Jacob," she muttered low, an allusion which the young people did not grasp. "Donna," she said, "I think you'd better bring Westwind in now, and put some clothes on him."

207

"You're probably right," said Donna mildly, arising and holding out her hand to her tiny son. "It's getting a bit chilly, isn't it?"

"I wasn't thinking about the weather," Susan went on firmly. "Now that you're here with us, Donna, you're going to have to be considerate of our customs."

"Oh," said Donna vaguely. "Well, all right." With her usual placidity she led the little boy into the house to hunt for his pants.

David was less concerned about pants than about other matters. "That little guy doesn't have any toys," he said. "He doesn't have anything to play with. Look at the way he was running around on that stick. Mom, he's awful cute; gee, he really is! Let me take him to the five and dime and get him a couple of things to play with—okay?"

"*When* he has clothes on," Susan said.

Meanwhile, Gideon had gathered himself together and gone back to the office, his mind torn between joy and horror. He had intended to spend the afternoon making hospital calls, bringing light and cheer to those in distress, but there was no light and cheer in him. Rather, there were wild flashes of light, and thundering clouds of darkness, and he did not trust himself to talk to anyone.

He strode into his office and got out the church ledgers, planning to go over them. Any mistakes he made there did not matter; they could be corrected. However, if he made mistakes in speaking to people about the alarming and yet glorious changes in his life, it might not be possible to correct them.

The telephone rang, yet he was not interrupted, for he realized that he was sitting, pencil in hand, gazing out the window, paying no attention whatever to the accounts. It was Susan on the line.

"Gideon, what'll I do?" she said between laughter and tears. "This girl, this Donna—here I am cooking supper, and she tells me she doesn't eat meat, because they—Gideon, who's *they?* I don't know. Anyway, they don't believe in eating meat, and she won't eat white bread, and she doesn't like potatoes, and she wants organic food, and—Gideon, I hate to call you away from your work again, but you'd better come home and help me straighten things out! And the little boy, he won't keep his pants on—oh, Gideon, come home!"

Gideon therefore returned home and coped with the situation by taking Donna to the health food store, where she bought a particularly forbidding loaf of dark bread as well as various seeds, essences, and ominous looking liquids. "Lettuce," she murmured, "you do have that?"

"We do," said Gideon, wondering what his congregation would think if they could see him in the health food store waiting for a bedraggled young woman to fill her bag with anomalous articles. At last they returned home and soon came to the supper table. Westwind sat somewhat unwillingly, wearing clothes, upon a Webster's unabridged dictionary on a dining room chair.

"We need to get him a high chair," said David, who had evidently taken the little one in tow. "Wow, Dad, he's the cutest thing! I put him in back of me on my bike, and he held on for dear life, when we went to the five and dime, see? He's never had anything to play with—boy, he didn't have a thing! So I got him a little car, and a toy spade and rake, and some things like that. Then I was looking at something else, and I turned around and he was gone! I couldn't find that kid! So finally I looked under the counter, and guess what, Dad. There he was, holding a little wooden cow, of all things! When he pushed it the right way, it made a noise, see? And he says, 'I have it!' So I told him to come out of there, but he wouldn't. He just kept on hugging that little cow. 'I have it,' he says over and over. Mom had given me money and—well, you know, that kid is so darn cute! I guess I'm silly, but I bought him that little cow. See, he's got it now; he's feeding it bread! Oh gosh, he's too much!"

Donna placed before Westwind a chunk of health bread covered with some kind of cream sauce, and the little boy patiently dug into it, using most of his fingers. He did succeed in getting a great deal inside him, though a considerable amount was also spread upon his face. Josie was gazing at him in horror.

"Don't you think," said Susan in clipped tones, "that it would be best for Westwind to have his meals in the kitchen until he learns how to eat?"

Donna vaguely replied, "Oh, no, we always eat together, and I think he's the best judge of how to eat, don't you?"

"I do not," said Susan, and she arose, darted to the kitchen, came back with a damp dishcloth, and cleaned up the little boy's face. "Is that all he's going to eat?" she asked. "What about milk?"

"He doesn't like milk," explained Donna.

"And he eats only what he likes?"

Donna looked up, surprised. "Of course," she said.

"No meat?" asked Gideon.

"Oh, no," said Donna. "We think it's wrong to eat meat."

Gideon's lips tightened. "Jesus did," he said.

Donna replied mildly but definitely, "Well, Buddha didn't, and gurus don't."

"I was taught," snapped Josie, her hazel eyes flashing green fire, "that when you go to somebody else's house, you eat what is put before you."

"Oh," said Donna unimpressed, and Josie flung down her knife and fork and made as if she would leave the table.

"Sit it out, Josie," said Gideon with a strained smile. "That's all we can do—sit it out until Bob comes."

At this point, Westwind entered the conversation. "Westwind wear pants," he elucidated, smiling quaintly beneath his little turned-up nose, his blue eyes twinkling. "Big boy, pants!" said he proudly.

"That's right," said David solemnly. "Big boys wear pants. Westy's a big boy now!"

"Big boy!" repeated Westy, shoving another gobbet of bread into his mouth.

Thus the care and training of Westwind was largely taken over by the youngest member of the family, who carried it on briskly and in a spirit of huge glee. "Is he going to Sunday school?" asked David, grinning delightedly at the prospect.

"What's that?" asked Donna.

"You know, Sunday school—what they have for the children while the grown-ups go to church."

"Church?" asked Donna.

"Haven't you ever been to church?" David demanded.

"Well," said Donna vaguely, "no, I don't think so, not exactly."

"I bet you go here," remarked David. "Dad says that anybody staying in his house has to go to church."

"But not," amended Susan, "unless they are suitably dressed." She finished meditatively, "Donna and I had better go downtown."

At this, Donna looked as alarmed as her vague expression permitted, but Westwind took over the conversation. "Go church," said he, looking up at his idol, David. "Westy, church. Wear pants!" he concluded on an enthusiastic note.

"You bet!" said David delightedly, "Did you ever in your life see a smarter kid?"

On Sunday, therefore, Gideon entered the pulpit to preach, and looked down on Donna sitting beside Josie, and clad in one of her discarded dresses. Their faces, thought Gideon fleetingly, were a study to behold—Donna with only a bit of bewilderment added to her usually blank look, and Josie tensely wondering, Gideon knew, how to introduce Donna after church and what people would think.

Westy was nowhere to be seen. He must be in the kindergarten, thought Gideon, with David checking to make sure he kept his pants on. With an effort Gideon tore his mind away from these three, glanced as if for support across to the alto section of the choir where Susan sat, and then began his sermon.

His subject was the impromptu service of exorcism that he had held in the church a few evenings previously. There was no keeping it secret, Angela and Doris having seen and duly reported it everywhere. Therefore some explanation was necessary. "And yet," said Gideon, after a rather stumbling introduction, "why should there need to be any explanation?

"When Jesus was on earth, they brought publicans and sinners to Him; they brought those who were sick and those troubled with demons, and He healed the sick and cast out the demons. Nowadays I know," he went on, "it is fashionable to believe that there is no devil, and the very fact that we don't believe he's real puts us in his power. You may not believe in tigers," he told the congregation with a grin, "but if a tiger should escape from a zoo and stand in your front hall, there would be no use in your not believing in tigers. It would be a tiger just the same, and there you would be, at his mercy.

"I'll admit that in seminary I was definitely given to understand that ideas of the devil were archaic, outmoded, and at the very best, symbolic. I have learned better—or worse. I have learned that what the Bible says is absolutely true: there is a devil. How he got here, I don't quite understand, but I still haven't heard any better explanation than that given in the Bible—namely, that he was at one time an archangel who rebelled against God, lost his high place in the heavens, and landed upon this earth. If you can think of a better explanation, go to it," he added, with a whimsical twist to his mouth. "And indeed, if you can think of a better explanation for the terrible things that happen on this earth, fine! To say that they are God's will, however, is totally impossible. If He is a God of love and goodness, it cannot possibly be His will that a person should be in torment and agony, like the young man who was brought to me here the other evening.

"In modern parlance, one might call him schizophrenic, insane because of a divided personality. It did seem that another personality, not himself at all, was in him, and most certainly, he was not in his right mind.

"Isn't it wonderful that a group of his friends, whom you might call Jesus People, brought him to this church! I see that none of them is here this morning," Gideon said, looking over the congregation. "They are doubtless worshiping in their own way, so I can speak freely. They were in over their heads, and they knew it, so they came to the church, the house of God.

"To tell you the truth," and again Gideon looked at his congregation a bit humorously, and with that confiding look that won their hearts, "to tell the truth, at first I was scared to death! But here they were, and I had to pray. By the grace of God, Dr. Paul Forrester, a leader in the School of Pastoral Care where I have just been, was here with me. So we had the young man kneel at the altar rail, and we simply called upon the power of Jesus Christ—who is still living, you know, and not dead—to come and drive out any dark or evil thing that might be in him. And it worked," he proclaimed. "It happened!

"Most of you know," he went on, "of the time when I myself was in bad trouble. My trouble, however, was different. That was the darkness of depression. It was not really possession, although of course the devil had a finger in the pie, as he always does. To be possessed by the devil is very unusual, while to be tempted or troubled by the power of evil is, unfortunately, common. I have told you how some of these very same young people who brought their suffering friend here the other night happened to find me when I was in trouble. I know that it only happened because God directed it. In their simplicity and goodness, they prayed for Jesus to come in and give me His life. And that worked, as I think you know.

"Now who is this Jesus, and where is He? He is the Son of God. No one but the Son of God could do these things. Where is He? Apparently He is available anywhere on this earth. Why He should love this little mud ball that we live on, I do not know, and why He should care for us infinitesimal creatures inhabiting it, I know even less. But He is here, and He does care!

"Obviously Jesus cannot be everywhere at once in the same body of flesh. Therefore, He is now here in a different way, not in a fleshly but in a spiritual body that we call His Holy Spirit. He is just as eager to heal and to save as He ever was. He yearns over us, broods over us, but He usually

214

has to heal and save us through one another. That is why we are told in the Bible to pray one for another, that we may be healed.

"I should have known all this long ago. In fact, possibly I did know it, or at least glimpse it, when I was a child—something beyond words, some kind of power, some kind of love. It must have been such a knowing that caused me to go into the ministry. Very likely it was the confusion of not knowing how to receive this very power, and how to use it, that led me into depression.

"So now I confess to you that I am just beginning to walk in the way that Jesus, my Lord, called me to walk in. I rejoice that all you good friends are here with me. I rejoice in you, that you will bear with me and be patient as I try to learn. I rejoice in you, believing that when the young, the lost, perhaps what you would consider the modern equivalent of publicans and sinners, come into the church, you will bear with them. I ask just this one simple thing of you—smile at them! Anybody can smile. If you don't know what to think of them, wait until you do, but meanwhile, my dear friends, for Jesus' sake who loves us and who smiles upon us still, in ways that we cannot see with our eyes but can feel with our hearts—for His sake, I say, look upon them with His kindness, and smile!" So Gideon concluded his sermon.

"Do you really want the church filled with hippies and people like that?" Susan asked Gideon, not unkindly, as they lay in bed that night reviewing the events of the day.

"When Bob comes home," said Gideon, "very likely he'll be one of them—bedraggled, unshaven, barefooted. Have you thought of that?"

Susan moaned, "Yes, I have."

215

"Then if we want people to take him in, we'd better look after other people's lost sons and daughters the best way we can."

"Yes, I see," agreed Susan, "if it will hasten Bob's coming. Oh, Gideon, I don't know how I can stand this waiting! Why doesn't he send us some kind of message? Do you suppose he's landed yet?"

"I don't know," Gideon rejoined. "These young ones seem to live in another world. Well, the Lord will see us through this. I asked Him about it in my meditation this morning, after praying in tongues for a while. Somehow I always feel better when I do that."

"So do I," sighed Susan.

"The Lord seemed to be saying to me, 'I will take care of Bob.' I don't know whether it was interpretation, or a message, or just a change in my own feelings, but somehow I know it's true. So—hold everything, dear. It can't be long now!"

"It can't be long now," echoed Susan.

Since the young people of whom Gideon had spoken had not come to church, and there was no word from them, they lay heavily on his heart, and at the first opportunity, he went to the coffeehouse. There was Jess, looking like a new man, his hair smooth and even his straggling beard and moustache neatly combed. There was light in his eyes and a smile on his face.

"Hi, Preacher!" he greeted Gideon, coming to the door and actually throwing his arms around him. "Wow, you sure did a good job! Oh boy, oh praise the Lord, it's wonderful!"

Amid other murmurs of, "Praise the Lord," and, "Thank You, Jesus," Gideon joined their little group. Ellie sat on the floor close to his knees, looked up at him, and several of the

216

others, whose names he did not know, gathered around.

"Hey, what is it about your church?" asked one. "I mean, I don't dig it!"

"What don't you dig?" asked Gideon with a twinkle in his eye.

"Well, there's something there, something different from what we have here, for instance."

"The power of the Lord naturally builds up in a place where He has been worshiped for many years," said Gideon. "That must be what you feel."

"Yes," said Ellie, looking up at him with puzzled eyes, "but, you know, we've got that power too. Remember when we found you on the mountain? The power came through us kids then! But still there's something different in the church. It's a different kind of power!"

"What do you do there anyway, besides just sing and read out of the book?" inquired one of the other girls, with unconscious rudeness.

"There's one thing we do that's different and very, very special," said Gideon slowly. "Every Sunday morning at eight o'clock, and at other times too, we serve Holy Communion."

"Well, we know about that," said one of the young men, meditatively chewing gum. "We've done it ourselves."

"Do you really believe all that about the bread and wine being His body and blood?" broke in one of the young men.

Gideon thought a moment before answering. "I do believe that the energy of His lifeblood that was literally shed on this earth, somehow or other is still here and keeps on increasing. That went into the wine. But, you know, Jesus' body didn't stay on this earth. His body was resurrected and came back to life. Now, I'm not asking you to believe this, but I'm just saying that this is the idea."

"Get back to the bread," said Jess seriously. "What happened to the bread?"

"You see, the body of Jesus was resurrected into a different kind of body. So when He said in the sixth chapter of John's gospel, 'The bread that I will give is my flesh, which I will give for the life of the world,' that must mean some kind of energy or life out of His resurrected body, His spiritual body, don't you think?"

"Wouldn't that be the same as the Holy Spirit?" asked Ellie softly.

"It probably would," said Gideon. "Somehow I never thought of it like that before, but it probably would."

"But we can get the Holy Spirit without that," said Ellie. "You know, sometimes we speak in tongues here. Yeah, we do," she added, addressing one of the men who was looking at her questioningly. "Some of you newer guys don't know it, but we do."

"Yes, but having the Holy Spirit means a lot more than speaking in tongues," said Gideon. "I mean, that's fine, but there's a lot more to it than that."

"Exactly what does having the Holy Spirit mean, then?" asked one of the young men.

Praying hard, Gideon replied, "It means more than we can say. It means the life of Jesus, His Spirit, coming into our spirits and minds, and even into our bodies. You know," he explained, "nowadays scientists say that every cell in the body has a bit of intelligence. So having the Holy Spirit means that His life comes even into the cells of the body, fills the whole thing, floods the whole thing, and sort of transforms us more and more, until one of these days—not in this life, I guess, but somewhere in the life that we can't yet see—one of these days we become like Him."

"Wow!" breathed one of the youths sitting on the floor. "That's cool!"

And Gideon responded from the very depths of his heart, "Yes, it surely is cool!"

Chapter Sixteen

Two days later, Gideon sat in his study endeavoring to compose a sermon. He bit his lips and tried with all his will-power to write those sonorous and meaningful words which he hoped would roll forth on Sunday morning. This was the day of the week when he always wrote his sermon. He had trained himself to it, but today no training availed. Nothing came.

In fact, Gideon soon found that he could not sit still. Something seemed to be pulling him out of his chair. "What is it, Lord?" he finally asked aloud. He did not hear an answer, but he did distinctly feel that there was something that he must do now, at this moment. He flung himself out of his study, and into the church, where he sat in a back pew, grateful that no vacuum cleaner or practicing organist was disturbing the quiet.

"What is it, Lord?" he said again, and there came the gentle impulse to pray in the Spirit. He did so, murmuring under his breath words that he did not understand. As always when prayed thus, quiet and peace enveloped him. Then spontaneously, he paused and listened, as Ellie had taught him.

"After you pray in tongues, listen awhile," she had said, "so God can answer you."

As Gideon listened, he heard within his mind, quite distinctly, the words, "Bob is coming today, soon now."

So that was it! Donna had casually figured that he could not come for several more days, so she and Westwind had gone shopping with Susan for garments that Susan deemed absolutely necessary. Josie and David were in school, so the house was empty.

Gideon hurried to his car, and headed home. Sure enough, the house was empty. Pray God, he thought, that Bob had not already come. But no, he knew that he had not. Gideon therefore picked up Westwind's little shirt from the floor, where he continually dropped it, and cups and dishes from tables and counters, unconsciously making things straight. As he did so, there were steps on the porch, heavy yet hesitant steps. The knob turned, the door opened softly, and in came Bob—bearded, lank of hair, bedraggled of clothes, yet undoubtedly Bob!

He stood hesitating in the hall, and Gideon ran and threw his arms around him. "Oh, Bob, Bob!" he cried. In spite of himself, tears came.

"Dad!" choked Bob, his head hidden on Gideon's shoulder. There they stood, not knowing how long, but by the time Susan, Donna, and Westy returned, they were at the kitchen table having coffee.

Gideon stiffened as he heard the family on the front porch, and Bob leaped to his feet. The door opened, and in they came. "Oh, Bob!" cried Donna, with the first enthusiasm

221

she had shown since being there. She tripped toward him and threw her arms around him. "Oh, Bob! Oh, wow! I didn't figure you'd come so soon. Oh, wow!" Her incoherent exclamations continued, as Bob kissed her tenderly and then lifted his little boy in his arms.

"Daddy!" said Westwind, and added portentously, "Westwind got car!" Then he scrambled out of Bob's arms, trotted to the bedroom, and came back with a tiny car. This he rolled up and down the floor, making engine noises in happy concentration.

Meanwhile, Susan, at first frozen into immobility with the suddenness of this long-hoped-for return, found herself gathered into her son's arms, shedding tears of joy even while she noted that his clothing needed laundering and his hair a shampoo. Here he was! He was dirty, and he smelled, but he was her son, and she loved him!

Gideon watched with his broadest, happiest smile. Then Bob's eyes turned back to his father, and in a questioning voice he said, "Dad?"

"Yes, son," said Gideon, "what is it?"

But Bob could not speak, for the three voices chattering around him, for the tugging at his jacket of little clinging hands, for the pattering about of his wife, urging him to sit down and rest, and for the deep, quiet words of his mother. "We've been praying," she said. "We've been praying." She wiped her eyes, and smiled through her tears.

Again in that inquiring voice, Bob said, "Dad?" and Gideon knew that it was he whom the young man needed now, his father.

"Yes, son," he said. "Tell you what: you stay here awhile. Your mother and your—wife will have fits if I lug you off, so I'll go to the church and do a few things. Then, as soon as you can, you come and see me there, okay? We'll have a good talk."

"There are some things I've got to—got to decide," said Bob uncertainly.

His father said, "Sure there are—sure! I'll be waiting for you. You come as soon as the gang will let you. Right?" He turned his back and went away. He could no longer restrain his tears, and when he got to his car, they fell unheeded. The mountains shone dimly in the softly veiled sky. The new spring trees gleamed with leaves unbelievably green. Roses and geraniums and screaming scarlet and orange ice plant grew by the sidewalks. The whole earth sang, danced, and was alive with beauty, but Gideon saw only a tall young man, tired and dirty, with a haunted look in his eyes and a questioning voice that said, "Dad?" He must pull himself together, Gideon thought, to be the father that his son needed. He must quiet himself and ask God what he should say.

Susan was taking charge of affairs at home. "You need a bath," she announced in tones that she trusted were sympathetic rather than critical.

Bob grinned. "Sure do," said he. "Can't bathe very well on a freighter or hitchhiking—that's the trouble."

"Why didn't you call us?" said Susan. "We'd have come to get you, or sent you money for a plane ticket, or something."

"Never thought of it," said Bob, with his faltering grin. "You sort of forget about things like that living on the beach."

"That's what Donna said," commented Susan.

"Where is Donna?" asked Bob, sitting rather helplessly on the edge of his bed while Susan rummaged in the closet and bureau looking for clothes he had left behind three years and more ago.

"She's feeding Westy, and then she'll put him to bed for a nap."

"A nap?" inquired Bob with a short laugh. "Westy was never put to bed for a nap in his life."

"How did he manage?" snapped Susan a bit sharply.

"Oh, like all of us, I guess. When he got sleepy, he'd just sort of sleep where he was."

"Well, he's being put to bed now for a nap," announced Susan. "He'll be a lot better off with some regular habits. And," she added, with a mother's glance at her son, "probably you will, too."

"Is Donna—?" asked Bob.

"Donna!" exclaimed Susan. "I don't know. She—I don't understand Donna. She sort of drifts around. I wonder if she even realizes she's not on the beach anymore."

"Yeah, she's like that," Bob admitted, taking off his shoes and wriggling his tired feet.

"You better get into the shower pretty soon," his mother advised, but then she sat down beside him without waiting for him to get clean. "Oh, Bob," she said, taking his grimy hand and holding it to her cheek, "Bob, tell me, do you love Donna?"

"I—I guess so. Why, sure!" said Bob stoutly.

"I just wondered. Tell me, where did you find her?"

Bob's mind went back to that day on Maui, more than three years ago, when for lack of anything better to do, he was riding his bicycle up the steep, winding road on Mount Haleakala. He did not expect to reach the ten thousand foot summit which split the sky in a frightening wedge, blue black against the blue sky, and where there was nothing but lava which had spouted forth for millions of years building the island. He was just riding.

While he toiled upward on his decrepit bicycle, Bob's eyes fell on a young girl seated in the deep grass at the edge of the road, little blue flowers growing around her. When she lifted her eyes to his, Bob saw that they were as blue as the flowers. He descended from his bicycle, pushed it to the edge of the road, and sat down beside her. "Hi," he said.

The girl answered in a voice that was almost a whisper, "Hi."

"What're you doing here?" asked Bob.

"I—don't know," she answered. "I'm just sort of waiting, I guess."

"What for?"

"Well, I don't know where to go," said the child, for she seemed little more than that. Her small round face was freckled, like a little girl's, her long hair was drawn back, and the doll-like placidity of her face was troubled by a look of uncertainty and fear.

"How'd you get here?" Bob asked, chewing a blade of grass.

"There was a boy—"

"Yup," thought Bob, "there would be a boy."

"You see, I—I sort of ran away with him, because I didn't know where else to go."

"Don't you have a home?" asked Bob.

The girl shook her head. "Not really," she said. "You see, my father and mother were divorced, and my father married again—oh, a long time ago—and his new wife, well, she just can't stand me, so she told me I couldn't stay there any more. She told me not to tell my dad or she'd beat me, but I had to go. So, there was this boy—"

"Did you love him?" asked Bob abruptly.

"No, not really," said the girl, "but, you see, I didn't have any place to go, and he said anybody could go to Hawaii, and—and they could get welfare, and they could just sort of pick fruit from the trees, and dig up things from the ground, and it was so warm they wouldn't need a house to live in. So I came and, you know, I thought he'd take care of me," she ended, "because he said he would."

"Like hell he did!" muttered Bob under his breath. "So then what?"

"Then he met another girl and, oh boy, she's beautiful! I mean, she's something! And, you know, well, he went off with her."

"What did he say when he went off?" demanded Bob angrily.

"He just said, 'Well, so long, kid. I got you this far; now you're on your own. You'll be okay.' That's what he said. So now—" and she looked wistfully at the road winding up the mountainside, "I don't know where to go."

"Hmmm," said Bob, who did not know either. He looked away from her, up at towering Haleakala. Clouds were gathering about its middle, forming and dissolving again, so that one could see through them to the solemn, glittering peak lit by sunlight.

"Somebody said you could sleep on the mountain, and nobody would bother you," said the girl.

"What's your name?" asked Bob.

"Donna."

"Don't you have any other name?"

The girl shook her head, and although slow tears came into her eyes, her face was expressionless.

"Oh, the mountain's no good for sleeping," said Bob.

"That's idiotic. Anyway, it's too rough. But—some of us kids have been hanging out on the beach. You know, it's part of the shore where nobody bothers us. It's always warm there, and there's a spring a little way back, and a brook and—well, we just kind of stay there. It smells good," he added abruptly, "you know, all salty and wild and faraway-like."

"Here smells good, too," murmured Donna, and indeed the tropical air was delightfully scented with frangipani and wild ginger and other blossoms swinging half-seen between them and the warm blue sky. "You mean, you can just sort of live on the beach?" asked Donna after a pause.

Bob nodded a bit grimly. "Just sort of live," he said.

"What do you—eat?"

Bob looked at her and suddenly realized that she must be hungry. "When did you last eat?"

"I don't know," she answered. "Yesterday, sometime."

"Oh, for Pete's sake!"

"Oh, I—I found a coconut. You know, it was just lying by the road." She lifted up the heavy brown thing to show him. "But I don't know how to open it."

Bob found a sharp rock and opened the coconut, and searching through his own pack, located a bit of stale bread and some cheese, only slightly moldy. The girl ate, and color came back into her cheeks. Then, at Bob's command, she climbed behind him on the bicycle and held on precariously while they coasted down the mountain and started on the winding road through pineapples and sugarcane to Jefferson Beach on the other side of the island.

"Donna and I started staying together—" Bob resumed the narrative to his mother.

"You weren't—married?" she asked, a catch in her voice.

227

"Oh, Mom," said Bob with a shade of impatience, "I guess you're too old to understand things like that. You know, they just happen."

"I do understand," Susan smiled faintly. "They happen, but are you married now? I asked Donna, and she said she wasn't quite sure."

"I think so. I scouted around and found a little Japanese minister—a good little guy, too."

"Have you got a marriage certificate?" inquired his mother.

"What's that?" asked Bob vaguely. "Oh, yeah, I guess he did write something on a piece of paper. I don't know where it is, though."

He hasn't quite got his feet on the ground, thought Susan. "Well," she said aloud, "never mind. You go take your bath now, and here are some clothes that I think you can still get into. We'll go downtown after a while and find you some more." Thus she spoke, forgetting that he was no longer a little boy.

Bob smiled, patted her hand, and ambled into the bathroom. Susan stood still for a moment in the middle of the bedroom, looking at the closed bathroom door and wondering. Were these young people on drugs, that they should be so vague, so totally disoriented? In some fashion they were disconnected from real life. She had asked Donna if she was on drugs, and she had replied, "No, I don't think so—not really. You know, a little grass now and then—"

"Then," Susan persisted, "what makes you so—kind of different, as if you didn't care about anything?"

"We learn," said Donna softly, "not to care about anything." Susan was utterly nonplussed as Donna continued gravely, "Yes, that's part of meditation, you know, kind of living the spiritual life. You sit quiet and meditate, and you just sort of let yourself go way off, and you don't care about anything."

"Not—ever?"

"Just one day at a time," said Donna, "one day at a time."

"So you never worry about your future? Here you are, you and little Westy, and Bob is coming," Susan had exclaimed, "and you don't worry about the years ahead?"

"Oh, no," Donna replied. "We learn not to worry."

It was, thought Susan, as though these young people stepped out of real life into a dim world, slightly out of focus, and who their guides were in this unreality—whether people or ideas—Susan could not imagine.

Nevertheless, Bob had come home in answer to Gideon's and her prayers, and although this was only the first step, Susan knew that others would follow. As she turned and went out of the bedroom, Susan whispered to herself, "Bob will never be the same again—never again."

At church, Gideon reached the refuge of his study and sank down at the desk, his heart pounding. Here was Bob, his son and yet not his son, his son and yet a stranger, dirty, ragged, unkempt, and yet his son. He loved him with his whole heart, but he was afraid. What should he do with this young stranger? Would Bob be willing to work, and could he get a job? What would the church people think of him, not to mention his wife and child? If Gideon insisted that he cut his hair and shave and look decent, would he run away again? Like as not, he would! Gideon hid his face in his hands, torn wildly between fear of the unknown and unbelievable relief.

Then a thought came to him, whether from God or from himself he did not know; and it didn't matter, for Gideon was beginning to understand that the life of God was in him, and a certain ephemeral part of himself was in God. The thought was, quite simply: call Paul Forrester.

"Oh Lord, let him be there!" Gideon prayed as he dialed long distance. By the mercy of God, Paul was in his office, and alone. "Paul? Gideon. It's happened! Bob's come home!"

"Praise the Lord!" said Paul.

"Yes, praise the Lord, but—what shall I do with him, for him? Whatever shall I do?" The words tumbled from Gideon. "You know, Paul, I couldn't have handled praying for Jess if you hadn't been with me, and now—"

"I'm with you!" cut in the warm voice at the other end of the line, and in his mind, Gideon could see Paul Forrester's face with the light in the dark eyes that somehow conveyed the love of God.

"Then what do I do?" asked Gideon.

"Remember the Prodigal Son?" Paul replied. "What did the father do?"

"Ran and fell on his neck and kissed him," said Gideon. "I guess I did that in my own clumsy fashion."

"All right, what did the father do next?"

"Well, he got his servants to clean the boy up, and he put a fine robe on him, and a ring on his hand, and shoes on his feet, and he threw a huge party."

"Okay, why don't you do just that?"

"What!" exclaimed Gideon, and then as he thought about it he began to laugh. "You know, I think I will!" he said.

So when Bob appeared at the study door, clean and combed but still unkempt, his father said with a broad grin, "Bob, sit down. I'm going to give a party for you!"

Bob dropped into the big leather chair, resting his head

and stretching forth his weary legs. "Never mind any party," said he rather grimly, and then went on with a sigh, "Dad, I'm sorry I hurt you by running away. I had to, though. I just couldn't—" Gideon made an involuntary sound, as though he would speak, but Bob hurried on, unwilling to be interrupted in what he needed to say.

"Dad, when I left, everything around here was making me sick. I thought you and Mom were too tough on me, not letting me have a car, and all that. I hated going to church, and thought they were all a bunch of phonies. You, too, Dad." Bob looked up at his father, with a shamefaced grin. "I couldn't see why you wanted to be a minister, and it sure made it tough for me with the kids at school. I didn't see where any more school would help me. Look at all the educated creeps we've got in Washington, messing everything up. Dad, I wasn't really mad at you or the family, but I couldn't talk to you, and I just couldn't stay around. I had to split. Can you understand, Dad?" Bob concluded, wistful appeal in his voice.

Gideon drew in his breath. "Son, I'm beginning to understand. Please forgive me for not being a better father to you back when you were in high school. When you were little, I think I did all right," he grinned, happy memories crowding into his mind, and apparently they were in Bob's mind, too, because he grinned in response. Gideon went on. "I do understand your disillusionment with people, Bob. I had a bout with it myself. Sometime I'll tell you about it, but now we'll just talk about you. I suppose you might say you're down on the way the whole world is being run, is that it?"

Light broke over Bob's face. "Gee, Dad, I guess you almost do understand!" he exclaimed.

"Well," said Gideon, "let's think it out further. What

231

needs healing in the world is selfishness and hate, isn't it?" Bob nodded. "So what's the opposite of that?"

"Love, I suppose," said Bob, shrugging his shoulders and pulling down his lips.

"Well, then—" Gideon was about to go on, but Bob broke in with his views.

"That's just what we New Age kids do," he said, "love everybody."

"Does it work?"

"Well, where there's a bunch of us together, it does."

"For very long?"

"Until the grass runs out, or it gets cold, or there isn't enough food. Then it gets pretty heavy."

Gideon nodded. "You mean, people begin behaving the way they used to?"

"Yeah, only worse, because they're bitter that it didn't work. Even before we left, things were beginning to go sour on the beach. In fact, it got so bad, the police were about to close it entirely."

Bob looked around the familiar study and shook his head.

"So," Gideon concluded, "your love never really changed anything, not even yourselves." He paused and looked at Bob. "You know, that's kind of sad, because you kids are right: love *is* the answer. But not man's love. The spirit of love that comes from Jesus Christ—the Holy Spirit."

"The Holy what?" asked Bob.

"You know, the Holy Ghost," his father answered.

"Don't know Him," Bob declared.

Gideon remembered Bob as an acolyte, carrying the cross, saying the creed, as he himself had often said, "I believe in the Holy Ghost." Bob had not understood, and after all, he, Gideon, the priest for years and years had said the words and not understood either.

232

"Look," he said earnestly to his son, "I should have taught you this long ago, but to tell the truth, I didn't understand it myself." He paused, floundering, and then said abruptly, "I guess I will tell you about what I did while you were away. It was worse than anything you did, son. You copped out of school and church and growing up, for a while, but I copped out of life, or tried to, you know."

"Yup," said Bob. "I heard a little from Mom. And a bunch of Jesus People found you, so now I guess you're one of them, huh?"

"I'm not," Gideon replied a bit stiffly. "But these kids do know the power of the Holy Spirit. They prayed for me, and I got well, which the doctors said I couldn't. This wasn't all. I asked them what this power was. I—a minister—had to ask kids, about your age, Bob! There was a girl," he added, "not much older than your Donna, I guess, but she knew. She couldn't explain it, just as I can't really explain it to you now, but she knew that there is a power beyond man, the love-power of God, and that somehow it comes through Jesus. It is His gift. We call upon Him, and He gives it to us."

"I don't dig it," said Bob.

Gideon tried again. "You see," he said, "we're not just what we think we are. We've got more in us. We've got more than a mind and a body. There's something else in us, called the spirit—sort of the breath of God, that God breathed into man at the beginning." Gideon reached for his Bible, but his son said abruptly, "Can it! No time for the Bible now!"

"Okay," said Gideon meekly. "Anyway, we're created that way. It's a sort of reserve available to anyone who knows that Jesus is alive and wants to live for Him. We use only about two-thirds of our natural energy. We use the strength of the body and the mind, and we don't realize that we also have the strength of the spirit, like a car with six cylinders, only running on four. Then somebody tells us we've got two more cylinders, so why not use them?"

Bob looked at his father with suspicion, but also with dawning interest. "That's what the girl told you?" he asked.

"She didn't use those words, but that was the idea. Of course, I said I didn't know how to use the strength of the spirit, and she said she didn't know how to tell me, but she'd pray for me. So, just as simply as she had prayed for the healing of my body, she prayed for the awakening of the spirit. And something happened!"

"What?" demanded Bob.

"I don't exactly know, but ever since, there's been more power available. Remember, we were talking about how we can change people, and make a better government and nation? Well, the only way is by this invisible energy, this tremendous flow of God's love, greater than any power of hate and selfishness. We can project it to people, and they change! We can do miracles with it—you know, healings and things like that."

"Have you done any?" asked Bob.

"Yes, I have," said Gideon, and he told briefly about Sammy Bernstein in the hospital. "And you know," he added in tones of deep tenderness, "last week I got an invitation to his Bar Mitzvah."

"Are you going?" asked Bob with a grin.

Gideon had not yet made the decision, but at this moment he made it. "Yes, I am." he said, lifting his head.

"What'll the church people think?"

"I don't care," said Gideon, laughing briefly. "I'm going."

"That's kind of cool," opined Bob, and he added, "do you

234

teach your gang at church what you've just been telling me?"

Gideon started, stiffening slightly. "Well, no," he said, "not all of it, not all of them."

"Any of them?"

"Well—" Gideon temporized, scratching the back of his head.

"Come on, Dad," said his son. "Any of them?"

"I've taught it to my garage mechanic and his boss," said Gideon. "I go down to the garage and pray with them. Let me tell you, when we three get together and pray, things happen!"

"Okay, but not your congregation, huh?" said Bob. "That's really weird! If this Holy Spirit thing is true, and if you believe it, why don't you tell your congregation?"

"Because they wouldn't accept it," said Gideon. "I'm hoping that one day they will, but right now—"

"You're afraid they'll kick you out, huh? But look, Dad, if all this that you told me about the power of God's love and the Holy Spirit is really true, then why don't you get brave and tell those people in the church just what you've told me, and of course, a whole lot more, like what the Bible says about it, and maybe start a class?"

Gideon, accepting his son's challenge, replied simply, "I will."

With a sense of high adventure, and in tune with one another as never before, the two of them went home to the family. Bob endured Josie's hugs and tears, and David's awestruck exclamations, "Oh, Bob! Gee! Oh, wow! You know, Bob—" in the incoherent manner of his peers.

"Bob's home again, and it's wonderful!" Susan whispered tremblingly, when she and Gideon finally gained the privacy of their bedroom. "But, oh, what do we do next, Gideon? I mean, he looks like a wild man! What are we going to do?"

"We're going to throw a huge party for him, that's what!" declared her husband, laughing heartily.

"Gideon!"

"Don't you see how much better that will be," he declared, "than sneaking around and acting as though we're ashamed of him?"

"But, Gideon, we *are* just a little bit ashamed of him, aren't we?" faltered Susan.

"No," said Gideon firmly, "we're not. What we're going to do right now is to make in our minds a picture of our son as he really is, and as he's going to be. We see him tall and straight—and neat," he added with a short laugh, "and beautiful, with light in his eyes, and power in his voice. And we rejoice!"

"But this party— How are you going to do it?"

"I'm simply going to make it a church affair," said Gideon. "Open house for the whole parish. What about a week from Saturday evening? Think that'll be okay? I'll get hold of Angela and Doris, and they'll love it—I hope!"

"But, his clothes—" asked Susan.

"I'm getting an inspiration about that," said Gideon. "You pray and leave it to me, and we'll see!"

"The first thing," said Gideon to Bob the next morning, "is to plan the party. Later on, we can talk about what you want to do next—a job, more school, or what—but for now, all I've got on my mind is making this the best party that ever was! I'm going to act dumb with the church ladies, and throw all the details into their hands, and if it works the way I think it will, they'll come up with flowers and decorations and refreshments, and it'll be first class!" Gideon concluded, praying silently that it really would.

"But you can't go to a party looking like that!" David spoke solemnly to his big brother.

"Of course he's not going to," said Gideon heartily, smiling at Bob as he continued. "Around the house, you can look any way you please. But for the party, come on, Bob, let's blow a big wad! I'm setting you up to this, so humor your old man! Let's go downtown, and let's see what we can find!"

To the amazement of the whole family, Gideon succeeded in taking Bob to a clothing store, where the wise clerk advised him on changes in style, and sold him a suit of elegant yet very modern cut that would make him, he said, way out, and indeed, in advance of the times. Moreover, once the salesman had his confidence, he suggested that the suit would become him better if his hair were trimmed in the latest style. "And I wonder if you'd consider taking off the beard?" he finally said. "Keep the moustache and sideburns—just trim them a bit—and your hair is great, just great. Might shorten it a little—yes, I would think you'd want to shorten it some, you know, just to catch up with the times. It's not worn as long as it used to be, you know. How about it?"

With a sheepish grin, Bob consented. "Now," said his father, "we want to put new shoes on your feet." Bob, not recognizing the biblical allusion, bought new shoes. Finally his father came to him with a gold ring and said, "Look, Bob, here's an old family ring. I don't wear it around the church, because it hardly seems suitable. Here!" He put it upon his's son's hand and turned away before he should laugh—or cry.

237

Chapter Seventeen

"Hi! How's Jess?" Stan greeted Ellie, as she eased the coffeehouse's old car up to the cheaper pump.

"Well, he was doing fine until all of a sudden he started up with that God-had-ordained-that-I-should-marry-him business again. We tried to straighten him out, but he's convinced he's got a straight-through pipeline to God, and so he split, madder than ever. I doubt very much we'll ever see him again."

Stan stopped polishing the windshield and stood between Ellie and the pump. "Look," he said, "why don't you get out of all this monkey business and marry *me*?"

It was an odd place for a proposal, but this was not exactly a proposal. Stan had made this suggestion before. "I've already told you, Stan," said Ellie gently, "I just don't think Jesus would want me to."

"Well, suppose you tell me again—why?"

"I don't think He would," persisted Ellie, "because you see, you don't—well, you don't exactly believe in Him, do you?"

238

"That's my business," growled Stan. Somehow he had not wanted to tell Ellie about this, the prayer sessions in the little shop room, lest she think he was joining the Jesus people. Stan's spirit recoiled against those young people running in droves, shouting, "Praise Jesus!" and "Bless you good!"

"Maybe I do," he said, conceding that much. "Maybe, in my own way, I do."

"Anyway," said Ellie, "Jesus is coming back soon, you know. It might be next week. So what's the use?"

"Waiting for the rapture, huh?" muttered Stan sourly.

"Waiting for Jesus," said Ellie, "and, you know, Paul said that if you could get along without marrying, it was better."

"Yeah? Why did he come out with that crack?"

"He said, because Jesus was returning soon."

"And wasn't that two thousand years ago?" challenged Stan. Ellie nodded. "And He hasn't come yet," Stan went on. "You dumb kids, you're still waiting!"

Quick tears came into Ellie's eyes, misting them with a gentle veil. Stan stalked around and pulled out the gas hose, which had long since clicked off, while Ellie got back into the car.

"Three seventy-five," said Stan. "Want stamps?" Without a word Ellie nodded, and without a word, Stan gave her the stamps and her change. Lifting one hand in a bit of a salute, he turned and strode back to a car he had on the rack.

Before Stan finished greasing and checking that car, Gideon appeared, leaving his car at the pump, and coming around to find his friend. "You know what Bob suggested?" he beamed. "He said why didn't I have a class? Anybody could come. Teach them about the Holy Spirit, and things like that. What do you think, Stan?"

Stan emerged from under the car, his face brightening. "Neat idea!" he said. "Why not?"

"If I do have a class, you know, some week night, could you come?" Gideon asked. "Would you?"

Stan scratched his head, tightening his lips as he thought about it. "Might as well," and he added with his quick grin, "I can always quit if I don't like it!"

"Another thing I'm thinking of," said Gideon, "you know, now that Bob's home, prodigal son and all that, I'm thinking of throwing a party for him—sort of a parish party."

"Oh yeah," said Stan. "Fatted calf, and all that jazz! Well, might as well see what happens."

"Would you come?" asked Gideon.

"No way!" said Stan instantly. "No point in making more trouble than you've got. Uh huh!" He shook his head. "Now listen to me, Rev. If it's a parish party, you keep it a parish party, see? Never mind inviting us outsiders."

"Well," said Gideon thoughtfully, "you may be right, but I'm glad you'll come to the class—if I have it," he added, starting up the car.

There was trouble on the home front when Gideon returned to the rectory. Josie was waiting for him. "How long are you going to put up with that Donna, Dad?" she asked furiously. "She just sits around all day. I really don't believe the girl's got any brains! She won't eat with the rest of us. She has to eat that silly stuff she gets at the health-food store. And Westy, you know she doesn't give him enough to eat! She thinks breakfast isn't good for him—only some darn fool apricot juice, or something. The poor little guy's as skinny as a runt. And this party—what's the sense of giving them a party, for Pete's sake? I've been round here all this time, and you've never given me a party. Bob hasn't been doing anything except goofing off, and picking up this Donna. What's the idea of giving them a party?"

The elder brother to a T, Gideon thought, and remembering what that father said, he replied warmly, "Josie, you can have a party any time you want. You're my only daughter, and you know very well that neither Donna nor anyone else will take your place. But, you see, Bob—" Smiling a little, Gideon quoted Scripture. "Bob was dead and he's alive again, he was lost and is found. It's like that, Josie." She flounced out of the room, her head in the air.

Gideon remembered this when he entered the guild room to meet with representatives of all the women's work of the church.

"Now what about that party you announced Sunday?" Angela demanded, her chin stuck out ominously.

Gideon's heart failed as he looked upon the grim faces. He was not putting on an act when he threw out his hands in a gesture of helplessness, and said, "Ladies, I don't know! It was my idea, and it seemed to come from the Lord. My son had run away and come back again, and I forgave him, and I hoped that my friends would forgive him, too. That was my idea," he said, "but to tell the truth, now I'm scared! I'm stuck with it. Maybe I was over-excited when Bob came home, I don't know. But, ladies, you're the auxiliary, and that means the helpers. If you can help me now, I sure would be grateful. What do you think I ought to do?"

An audible sigh swept over the room. The ladies shifted in their chairs, cleared their throats, gathered themselves together, and prepared to act. "It is clear," proclaimed Angela, "that you're just not up to it, Father Bruce—and what man would be? So I guess we'd better take over!"

241

"Why not make it a potluck supper?" said Doris, beaming. "I mean, everybody bring something, and make it a real meal. Father couldn't afford to feed everybody, and good food makes a party."

Gideon thought that without a raise in salary, he couldn't afford much of anything. Aloud, he said, "Oh, that would be wonderful, just wonderful! I knew I could count on you ladies. When I get in a jam, you always pull me out! But look, I want to do something myself, because after all, this is kind of my party. What do you think I should do?"

A half-hour of lively discussion followed, out of which came the suggestion that Gideon himself provide ice cream and a big cake, and perhaps something for decoration. This latter was left vague, however, because the ladies would see what they could find in their own gardens, or borrow from friends. All together, they would put on a parish celebration to end all celebrations.

"Ladies, thank you," said Gideon, his voice vibrant with gratitude. "I don't know what I'd do without you. Every one of you is wonderful!" Upon this joyous note, they went home, aglow with satisfaction.

Before going to his study the next morning, Gideon slipped into the church, a recent habit without which he could hardly face the day's work. He sat down in a pew, lifted up his soul to the Lord, and permitted himself to murmur in a language he did not know, and then entered the silence that always followed this excursion into the spiritual kingdom. The thought came to him: At the party, tell them about the class Bob suggested. He had better wait until Lent to start that, thought Gideon, but then the other one of him said within his mind, No, start it now.

Still pondering this unsettling prospect, which might add

problems and rush the parish into too many things at once, Gideon entered his office to find the telephone ringing. "Trinity Church," he answered.

The voice on the other end said, "Gideon, it's Paul."

"Praise the Lord! How did you know I was thinking of calling you?"

Paul laughed. "Oh, I could sort of feel you worrying—what about? What is it?"

"Well," said Gideon, "I stuck out my chin, and did what you suggested. Last Sunday, before I had time to change my mind, I invited the whole parish to a party for Bob this coming Saturday, and now I don't know what to do with them—if they come. Meanwhile, there's something else: Bob, of all people, suggested that I teach a class on the Holy Spirit, right here in the church!"

"Does he know anything about the Holy Spirit?"

"No, but he claims he'd like to, so he said why didn't I teach a class for anybody who wanted to come, and sort of tell them what's happened to me, and how the church can change, and all the rest of it. But you said, Paul, to keep quiet about it. You said these people are the sheep of my pasture, and I am their shepherd, and must take care of them, and not frighten them."

Paul Forrester meditated at the other end of the line for a moment. "Sheep don't change," he said at last, "they're always sheep—but people change. First, they're the sheep of your pasture, but they have it in them to become no longer sheep but the children of God. John 1," he added unnecessarily.

"Yes, I know," said Gideon, the familiar words running through his mind: "But as many as received Him, to them gave He power to become the sons of God."

"It's a matter of timing," said Paul, and then he laughed, "and after the fire, a still, small voice."

"What?" Gideon inquired.

"Well," laughed Paul, "I remember how for a while you ran away from life, like Elijah, and sat under a juniper tree and told the Lord, 'It is enough; let me die.' The Lord didn't let the first Elijah die, of course, but sent him forth, and it stirred up a great wind that rent the mountains and broke the rocks in pieces. That wind's begun blowing in your parish, though not quite as violently as in First Kings, 19.

"But remember, the Lord wasn't in the wind. After the wind came an earthquake, and something seems to be shaking your parish, but the Lord's not in the earthquake. After the earthquake came a fire, and after the fire the still, small voice. The funny thing is that the still, small voice telling you to go ahead and start a class came from your own son, of all people! That's the holy humor of the Lord— out of the mouth of your son! But anyway," Paul concluded, "go ahead and do it, and God be with you!"

Gideon awoke the next morning with the welcoming party heavy on his mind. "Why in the world did I ever start such a thing?" he moaned. Then he recalled a recent book concerning the value of praise. "Might as well try it," said he, and so he began, "Thank You, Lord, for this party we're going to have. Thank You, Lord, for the parish, and for the way they're going to enter in and help, with joy and thanksgiving." Oh, yeah! said Gideon to himself, as he began this exercise of praise, but every time the party came to his mind, he once more thanked the Lord for it. To his amazement, ideas began coming to him, as if out of the blue, and he found himself looking forward to the party as a great adventure.

The senior warden came to mind, and he chuckled. Why not go to Reginald Crabtree, be quite frank about his own uncertainty, and ask for his help? Furthermore—and at this, Gideon's hair practically stood on end—he should ask Mrs. Crabtree to sing a solo! This she loved to do, being wont to rise on the slightest provocation, in the choir or elsewhere, and bellow loud and unintelligibly, thus making herself exceedingly happy. And after all, thought Gideon, it did no harm. He would ask her!

Therefore, that night after dinner, he called upon the Crabtrees. Until recently, Gideon had all but given up making parish calls, finding life too full, but now he had come back to the practice, first telephoning to find out when would be a convenient time for him to drop in. If there was a favorite program on TV, for instance, or if they were going out, he would arrange his call for another time. He found this method very valuable. There was freedom and loving-kindness in calling on people in their homes, which was quite different from seeing them at the church.

Gideon called on the Crabtrees, joined them over coffee, and laid before them the projected party for his son. "I'm scared now," he admitted. "Kind of wish I hadn't started it, but I did it because someone reminded me of what the father in the Bible did when the prodigal son came home. He wasn't saying he approved of what the boy had done. All he was saying was—he's home again, and we rejoice!" He paused and looked at Mr. Crabtree. "You're used to dealing with ticklish situations in the business world. Do you suppose you could make a few remarks, and kind of get that idea across? But wait—let me ask you something else first. Mrs. Crabtree, would you be willing to—sing a solo for us? You know, a little music and a little joy to loosen things up?"

"Why I'd be glad to sing!" exclaimed Mrs. Crabtree, her eyes lighting up. Gideon judged from her speculative expression that she was already running through her repertoire to choose the ideal solo.

"Well then," said Mr. Crabtree, only slightly grudgingly, "I'll try to help too. As you say, I'm used to getting things across without seeming to. Yes, yes, I'll say a few words."

So Gideon departed in a mood of deep thanksgiving. Another complication awaited him, however, on his return home. "They say Westwind has to come to the party, too," reported Susan, her lips tense although in spite of herself her eyes were twinkling.

"Well, he never makes any fuss," said Gideon. "I've never heard the child cry—"

"I suggested getting a baby-sitter," said Susan, and at that ominous word, Donna herself appeared in the living room.

"We don't believe in baby-sitters," said she firmly. "We've always done things together as a family, and we always will."

She said this so positively that there seemed little point in arguing. Gideon merely shrugged and said, "Won't he get awfully tired?"

"If he gets tired, he'll lie down and sleep, just as he always does," his mother said serenely.

Gideon grinned, remembering how from time to time he had to step over the small boy as he slumbered on the hearth rug, or even in the middle of the floor. "Okay," he said, "he's your child, and it's up to you. Let him come."

Leslie, Gideon's assistant, supported him heartily in the party venture. "Great idea," he said, "great! How about if I bring my kids' band along?"

"It's pretty noisy," reflected Gideon, and he knew, because occasionally Leslie insisted on having a young people's eucharist at which his youth group twanged guitars and banged various objects, creating what Gideon considered an unholy din.

"Oh no," said Leslie. "They'll have a great time playing, and everybody'll like it. You know, wait until the speeches and stuff are over, and then let the kids turn it on! If anybody wants to dance, let them. If anybody doesn't like dancing, okay, they can go home when they want to." To this, Gideon somewhat dubiously agreed.

On Saturday night, therefore, the three wanderers went with Gideon and the family to the parish party. Bob was shy and embarrassed, but extremely handsome, with his more moderate haircut, resplendent new suit, shining shoes, and the ring upon his hand. His wife, Donna, followed after him in a long dress, suitable for informal evening wear and becoming to her mild, old-fashioned type of beauty. Westy wore a new suit, purchased by his grandmother, but which he privately considered scratchy and uncomfortable. However, after one or two futile attempts to remove it, he sighed and went to the party, sitting on his father's lap in the car and then trotting serenely into the room full of people without quailing or quivering. Westwind was used to taking life as it came.

The long tables set around the parish hall were beautifully decorated by the ladies who bustled back and forth bringing tea and coffee and arranging their casseroles and salads. After everyone had dined bountifully, Gideon arose, thanked them all for coming to welcome his son, and introduced the senior warden who would now say a few words.

The few words were smoothly and successfully said, creating the feeling that with real love they all welcomed the rector's son back into their midst. After this, Mrs. Crabtree arose and, accompanied on the piano by another vigorous member of the parish, sang her solo with verve and enthusiasm. Everyone clapped heartily. Then, after the dessert dishes had been carried out, Gideon rose to make his own little talk.

"I needn't tell you," he said, "what a joy it is that my son has returned home, bringing with him his wife and little boy. Now I want to tell you of a suggestion that Bob himself made to me. He asked me what some of the rest of you have also asked, though perhaps in different words. He said, 'What on earth's happened to you, Dad?'

"Something has happened! All of you have seen it, and many have wondered, knowing the circumstances that brought it about, but not, I think, quite understanding what actually happened. It is, I hope, a change of character that is, I feel, a step toward something greater.

"Now this same step toward something greater—greater joy, greater power, greater freedom—is available to every one of you. My son, Bob, asked me, 'Dad, have you told them?' and to this I replied in the negative. It is a little hard to explain such things. So Bob made a suggestion: 'Dad, why don't you have a class, and teach the things about the Holy Spirit that you've been learning? I'll bet some people would like to know!' I decided this was a good idea, so the first class will meet next Thursday evening from eight to nine o'clock." There was a stir of interest, and he waited before concluding. "Now, thank you, all of you, for coming here and meeting Bob and Donna and—and their son," he finished, hardly daring to say Westwind, and still less his full name, Clear Sky Westwind. "I appreciate it more than I can say, and my heart goes out with gratitude to all of you."

Gideon sat down amid heartfelt applause. Final dishes were cleared away, tables were pushed back, and Leslie assembled his youth band, who thereupon struck up a considerable racket. Under cover of the noise, people gathered to talk in little groups, some of the young people began to dance, and others—only a few—drifted away.

At this point Westwind created somewhat of a diversion. He had slept for a little while, under one of the tables, but when the table was moved, he awakened, rubbed his eyes, and trotted out into the middle of the room, looking about for father or mother quite contentedly, sure that they were present, and there was nothing about which to concern himself. At the same time, he became aware of a very real discomfort, located at the region of his abdomen. He realized it was caused by his new trousers, which seemed a bit tight.

Westwind thought about this a moment and came to the conclusion that the remedy lay in his own hands. He began to remove the offending garments, standing in the middle of the room without self-consciousness.

First to see what was happening was Angela Pritchard, who with a gasp swooped upon the little boy, pulled up his pants over his small, shiny behind, and gathered him into her arms. She may have planned to remove him to a quiet spot and instruct him in the art of living, but Westwind responded to what he thought was her friendly gesture by beaming brightly at her from under his little turned-up nose, patting her on the cheek, and saying in the horrified hush which his action had incurred, his sweet little voice heard by everyone, "Nice lady!"

Angela melted as she hugged the little boy close to her, smiling from ear to ear. The room full of people burst into roars of delighted laughter. The guitars struck up a merry tune. The cymbals clashed with enthusiasm, and the party ended on a note of joyous hilarity.

Chapter Eighteen

The next major project, the party having been so successfully carried out, was Gideon's class on the Holy Spirit,
which held its opening session on the appointed night with
a much larger attendance than anticipated. Even a couple
of vestry members sat inconspicuously at one side, and
Gideon wondered at first if they were there to spy on him.
However, once he launched into his subject, simply describ-
ing his own new understanding of the work of the Spirit,
citing Scripture passages, encouraging comments and
questions from the group, he was so caught up in the joy of
this new dimension of his ministry that all doubts left him.

Near the beginning, he referred to his own rescue from
the mountain and his subsequent miraculous healing. Ellie
and Stan were sitting together near the rear, and a few
others from the coffeehouse were also there, but Gideon
made no direct identification of them, eager that the whole
group, about evenly divided between church people and
those from outside the parish, should blend together in
unity.

When the hour was over, Gideon concluded his teaching and closed with prayer, not from the Prayer Book but from his own heart, that the Holy Spirit should continue to guide and direct each one of them. He also suggested as a sort of afterthought, perhaps the immediate result of his prayer, that each person undertake to pray with faith for the solution of one critical situation during the week, and be willing to report at the next meeting on the effectiveness of the prayer.

"Right on!" said Bob, as he and his father drove home from the class. (Susan would have come, but felt the need to supervise Josie's and David's homework, and Donna had shown no interest.) "It's really heavy," Bob went on. "I mean, it makes sense to teach people about the power of God, and then put them to using it."

"Good!" sighed Gideon. "I'm glad you liked that. Have you—decided what you're going to pray for?"

"Yup," said Bob. "I've been thinking about it ever since I got home, but I was scared, I guess. But, gee, Dad, I've got to have a job, and Donna and Westwind and I have got to have our own place to live!"

"We love having you," said Gideon.

"Oh, come off it, Dad! Maybe you like it all right, but all those women—my gosh! Mom giving Westwind a cookie, and Donna taking it away . . . Josie storming in and stalking out again, her face like thunder. David seems to do okay, and Westy sure likes him. But oh, no, Dad, we've got to get out of there soon. So I'm going to pray for a job."

"Good!" said Gideon, "I'll join you, and you know what? The only real prayer group I've got meets down at Tom's garage. It's just he and Stan and I, whenever we can get together. Want to come and meet with us next time?"

"Okay, I guess," said Bob dubiously, but the next time the little group met, he was there, and on Gideon's suggestion mentioned his need of a job.

"I know a guy," said Tom, shifting a bit on his uneasy perch, "needs a fellow to help in his lumberyard. Suppose you could do that?"

"Don't know why not," said Bob. "Tell me about it." So the details were told, the group prayed, and in due time the job was secured. Bob began rising at six in order to get his breakfast and go to work, and returned home weary at night after loading lumber. Nevertheless, he became a new man. "You know, Dad," he said, "it makes you feel good. I mean, this kind of getting tired changes everything. Gosh, I never would have thought it. I thought work was stupid, but I like it!"

"It does make you feel good," agreed Gideon. "All kinds of work does. When I get tired of people, and worrying about finances and church problems, I like to get out and mend the fence, or mow the lawn or something. It uses different muscles. I suppose the thing is," he explained, "we're made after that pattern. God is a creator, and He made us to be creators. Say, Bob, I never thought of it before, but the ten commandments not only tell us not to work on the sabbath but also give us this command: 'Six days shalt thou labor, and do all thy work.' "

"Just think," said Bob, "for three years I didn't do a thing! I thought I was having a good time, but looking back, I see I was getting like a vegetable, or a jellyfish. You know," he added seriously, "it's no fun to be a jellyfish!"

"I guess the only real fun," said Gideon, "is to be what we're meant to be. We were made to be creators, as a bird is made to fly and a fish to swim. Of course," he added, "we get into trouble if we don't create according to God's plan for us. That sounds kind of stuffy," Gideon added gently to his son, "but you know what I mean, Bob."

"Yeah," replied Bob, "I know what you mean. And I'm not always going to work in a lumberyard," he added. "I don't know yet just what I am going to do. Guess it's kind of up to me to work at some kind of peace-on-earth deal. Sounds sappy, but you know, a guy has kind of got to do something!"

All this, thought Gideon, was too good to be true. Maybe more trouble would come, but meanwhile he would rejoice in seeing the Spirit at work in the parish and, most of all, in his own son Bob.

What happened next began in a small way and grew to alarming proportions. It was simply that Gideon attended the Bar Mitzvah of his young Jewish friend. The lad's father met him at the door, gave him a yarmulke to wear during the ceremony, and thanked him with great solemnity for being there. Gideon was seated with the family, and watched the ceremony with tender curiosity. He was impressed by the solemn vows, the performance of the boy, who recited from memory long passages from the books of Moses, and by the warmth of all these people gathered to help a young lad turn the corner from childhood into manhood.

Before leaving, Gideon asked Mr. Bernstein, "Where is your synagogue?"

"Ah, we have none in this town," said he regretfully. "In our small way, we want to build a temple to the Lord."

"Where do you meet now?" asked Gideon.

"We have no place. A house here, a house there—"

"Look," said Gideon spontaneously, moved with tenderness toward this little man of great faith, "you meet on Saturday, don't you?"

"That is so—the Sabbath."

"Well, all day Saturday, our parish house is practically empty. We'll invite you to use a room there until your synagogue is built."

"Oh, I will talk to our people! May the God of Abraham and Isaac and Jacob bless you!" So cried Mr. Bernstein as he escorted Gideon to his car, and Gideon drove off, touched by warmth not only in his heart but in his whole body.

To his surprise, however, when he mentioned this matter at the next vestry meeting, there was at first a frozen silence and then a wall of subtle opposition—it wasn't convenient, it would influence the atmosphere of the church, nothing like that had ever been done before.

"Let's get down to the question, gentlemen," said Reginald Crabtree when he was sure they were of one accord. "Shall we, or shall we not, permit our parish house to be used on Saturdays by a Jewish congregation?"

"Only until their synagogue is built," interjected Gideon.

"Only," repeated Reginald Crabtree with a hint of sarcasm, "until their synagogue is built. Gentlemen, what is your wish?"

Gideon brought his palm down on the table. "I did not ask you gentlemen what was your wish," he said. "I simply stated that I had made them this offer. Financial and business matters of the church are your responsibility as a vestry, but the use of the buildings for worship is entirely my responsibility as rector." So declared Gideon with all the authority he could muster.

The vestry had to agree that indeed this was so, but their intense disapproval was not altered by all Gideon's persuasion. The basement room which he had offered was never used on Saturdays. "And, as a matter of fact," said Gideon, "I am quite sure that the Jewish congregation would pay for the use of the room."

"Well, in that case—" ruminated Mr. Crabtree, his mind always open to matters of cash, but others around the table murmured continued opposition to having anything to do with Jews. Gideon let them talk on, allowing himself time to utter a fervent prayer of faith within his own mind that God would resolve the matter according to His will, and that right speedily.

When Gideon spoke again, the truculence was gone from his voice. "Gentlemen," he said with a smile, "I don't understand what God has in mind for this strange people of His, but I know one simple thing—that Jesus, our Lord and our friend, told us to be kind to them for His sake. In the matter we're discussing, that is all I had in mind, being kind to them. Perhaps I made the offer hastily, but it never occurred to me that you, who have always been so kind and openhearted, would object."

"Oh well," said Mr. Crabtree, "let them have it, for a little while. But make it clear that it is just temporary, until they can find some more adequate place."

"Very well," said Gideon, deeply relieved. "Thank you for your consideration. I know they and their rabbi will be most grateful."

So it was that on the following Saturday, Trinity parish house echoed to ancient chants which, overheard by Gideon in his study, greatly comforted his heart. After all, he also had been lost, and now was found. His soul had also wandered in a strange land, knowing no home, and the mercy of the Lord had brought him forth into a place of peace.

During the week, however, it became increasingly clear

to Gideon that his arrangement with the Jewish congregation did not please his parish. The senior warden visited the bishop to complain about a rector who encouraged Jews to worship there as well as inviting all kinds of other outsiders to Holy Spirit seminars; who openly admitted that he spoke in tongues, and was in general leading the parish in dangerous directions, very likely explainable by his own mental instability for which he refused treatment. At the next vestry meeting, Mr. Crabtree reported on his conference with Bishop Updyke, but Gideon did not hear the report as he was bidden to wait until they called him into the meeting, a request which could be interpreted only one way. It was with heavy heart, therefore, that he entered when they called for him, and sat down after greeting them briefly.

"Well?" he inquired gravely, looking at the chairman.

"You know, Gideon, that we are very fond of you," began Mr. Crabtree heavily, after which ominous preamble he went on to the inevitable list of grievances. Gideon had perhaps been with them long enough, very likely needing a rest after his unfortunate accident. He was hand in glove with the Jews, was aping the Pentecostals, was getting known as a "miracle worker," which could only cause misunderstanding and disappointment, was neglecting the old-time church people while he consorted with riffraff off the streets—and so on and on. Gideon listened in a daze, trying to pray while keeping his mind on what the men around him were saying.

"I have been to see the bishop this week," Mr. Crabtree was saying. "We feel he is sympathetic with us, but—"

"But unwilling to take action," Gideon finished for him, as Mr. Crabtree's words trailed off.

"Exactly," the senior warden admitted, soon after which

the meeting adjourned inconclusively. No one had heart for considering any other business, and Gideon himself could hardly face the vestry members as they filed out. Nevertheless, as he thought on the way home about the meeting and what he would tell Susan, he found himself with a strange sense of peace, as if he were in the eye of a hurricane.

Chapter Nineteen

"Anyway, they can't make me go," said Gideon, sitting on the sofa and telling Susan about the vestry meeting, his head bowed as he held a cup of coffee and forgot to drink it. "Nobody but the bishop can make me go, and then only on grounds of moral delinquency or heresy."

"Don't be ridiculous!" snapped Susan, sharp-tongued in her perturbation.

"No," said Gideon, "and Bishop Updyke wouldn't be ridiculous. In fact, I think he has been unusually kind to me lately. But if the vestry press him enough—"

"To do what?" asked Josie, erupting out of her bedroom.

"To kick me out," said Gideon, his eyebrows raised.

"You've got to be kidding!" said Josie, dropping on the floor before him. "Why, you're just beginning to really say something when you preach. All the kids think so! I don't quite dig it yet, but—come on, Dad, why don't the vestry want you to stay?"

Gideon looked inquiringly at Susan, but she rose abruptly and went into the kitchen.

"Well, you see," said Gideon to his daughter, "most vestries, and most people, don't like new ideas. So when I talk about healing and the Holy Spirit—"

"I know," said Josie wisely. "And I bet they don't like Bob and Donna and Westy living here either."

"But they have to live here," remonstrated Gideon.

"Why do they, Dad? Donna doesn't like it either, you know."

"Did she say so?"

"Oh, Dad, you know she never says anything! But I asked her, and she said, 'Where can we go? What else can we do?' and she sounded so sad, I really felt sorry for her."

"If she'd only do *something!*" muttered Gideon. "If she'd only help your mother—"

"You hate her, Dad, don't you?" Josie broke in.

Gideon cringed, and tightened his lips. "No, I—"

"Oh, yes you do," interrupted Josie sagely. "You might as well admit it. You know, I understand you, and you might as well start doing what you tell other people to do— Pray about this, Dad. Pray that you can love Donna, and help her!"

So he could, thought Gideon. This little rebel, his daughter, was the nearest to his heart! Josie took his hand and patted it quite as if she were the parent and he the child. "When you hate somebody, the first thing is to admit it," said she solemnly. "We had that in psychology."

"But not to the person you hate," said Gideon, and after a moment's silence he added, "And the next thing is to pray. Look, Josie, where could they go if they didn't live here?"

"You know that little apartment over the Pritchard's garage? It's empty now, and Mrs. Pritchard is crazy about

Westy. Ever since the party, she has been. I'll bet she'd rent it to them cheap!"

"Not a bad idea!" Gideon brightened.

"Just what Donna would like," said Josie. "She could meditate and eat what she liked, and Westy could play in that big yard."

"With clothes on—or else!"

"With clothes on," agreed Josie.

"That just might work out," sighed Gideon, and he smiled as he thought of Westy's conquest of Angela Pritchard and, in fact, of everybody, at the parish party.

A car honked raucously on the street, and Josie leaped up. "That's Mark, or somebody," she said. "Be seeing you!" and she turned toward the door.

"Don't you mean Marcus?" asked Gideon.

"No, this is a different guy. Marcus is—"

"He's what?" insisted Gideon.

"Oh, sort of too far out—he and Florrie both," called Josie over her shoulder, as she banged out and away.

"Well?" asked Susan when Gideon joined her in the kitchen.

"Well, what?" asked Gideon mildly.

"Are you going to let yourself be run out of the church?"

Gideon had forgotten all about the church. "Heavens, no!" he assured her, wondering at his own temerity.

"But the vestry—"

"The vestry," explained Gideon quietly, "have authority over buildings and funds, but none over the minister."

"Who does, then?"

"God!" answered Gideon with a sudden grin. "And if I do my part, I think He'll do His."

During the day, Gideon faced his home situation hon-

260

estly. Yes, he almost did hate Donna. He really was angry with her for having married Bob. It was as simple as that, and until he had overcome his own resentment toward Donna, how could he expect to deal with the anger of the vestry toward him?

He did not approach Donna immediately. First he prayed for guidance, and for the love of God to fill him. The next afternoon, when he returned from hospital calls, Gideon found Donna in the backyard and sat down beside her, dragging a lawn chair next to hers.

"Donna, are you happy here?" he asked her gently.

She turned and looked at him, as though trying to understand what he was asking. Then she replied mildly, "Not very."

"You like sitting out here and looking at the mountains, don't you?" asked Gideon. As she did not answer, he went on, gazing at the towering crags, misty in the golden sunset. "I do. When I look at them, I think of baby coyotes coming out of their caves and blinking in the sunlight, and of the mesquite soaking up the dew, and a hawk flying high and watching, waiting—"

"Waiting for something to die," responded Donna.

"Is that sort of how you feel?"

"I try not to feel anything," answered the young woman softly.

"But why?"

"That's what you do when you meditate—think about nothing."

Again Gideon asked, "But why?"

"To—lean out on the void, to sink yourself into the universe—to attain—"

"Nirvana?"

261

She looked at him with surprise. "You understand about that?" she asked.

With difficulty, Gideon kept his voice gentle. "Of course," he said. "It's an old Eastern doctrine. Supposed to give a person peace."

"Don't you think that's a good idea?"

"Well, I can think of more constructive ones," offered Gideon. "You know, ideas that kind of—make a better world."

"We aren't supposed to do that," said Donna sedately. "You just—you just—"

"Cop out, and let the world go?" suggested Gideon. "Never mind, Donna, I didn't mean to preach. I just want you to be happy, that's all."

"Really?" Donna's voice faltered, and her eyes misted over. "Nobody's ever cared whether I'm happy— except Bob, of course."

"Never? How about when you were little?"

Donna shook her head. "It was grim," said she sadly. "My mom and dad, they fought a lot and—and I used to be so—"

"Scared?" supplied Gideon as she paused, afraid of giving herself away.

Donna nodded. "It's an awful feeling," she managed, "you know, like you shouldn't have been born. That's why I began sort of trying to forget I ever *was* born. I'd look at the mountains, and tell myself stories, and, you know, pretend they were true—"

"I understand," said Gideon. "Trying to escape life even when you were a child."

"Sort of, I guess."

"This is a wonderful place to meditate," pondered Gideon aloud, his eyes still on the mountains, tall yuccas

262

marching up them like exclamation points among the green. "Yet," he spoke directly to Donna, "you're not happy here."

She shifted restlessly, and Westwind left his play in the dirt and came and laid his tousled head in her lap. "I feel so—well, I ought to help Bob's mother cook, and wash dishes, and all that, but when I try, I'm so slow and clumsy, and I hate it, and anyway, we're taught not to do anything we don't really want to, or we might injure our souls, you know—so I just don't do anything."

"Westwind wide horsie," observed the child, and he cantered about the yard astride the stick that was his steed, clad only in tiny shorts, which at any moment he might discard.

How extraordinary, reflected Gideon. Donna did almost nothing and Westwind did exactly what he pleased, to the exasperation of his grandmother, who found almost unendurable his lack of, for instance, bathroom awareness. Yet he was as serene and intelligent as any child Gideon had ever seen. He knew the entire alphabet; he could name any color. Could the way of life that this young woman was seeking possibly have some advantages?

"If it were possible," Gideon asked tentatively, "would you like a little place of your own, off by yourselves?"

Donna, started, and her slight body seemed to freeze. "I might be scared!" she faltered.

"You weren't scared in Hawaii."

"No, but—there were lots of us, and Bob was there, and he didn't have to work—and leave me alone, and—"

"Would you like to go back to Hawaii?" Gideon asked gently.

"Oh, yes! But—Bob wouldn't."

No, thank God, thought Gideon, Bob wouldn't. He had come awake, had roused out of that dream of nothingness. He had found the joy of creativity. If only Donna—

"Anyway they've closed the beach," said Donna wistfully. "Just after Bob left. They won't let the kids live there any more, I don't know why—" she trailed off.

Gideon realized that Donna really didn't know. He could imagine the once beautiful beach inhabited by mindless runaways on an endless marijuana reverie. Donna apparently never saw the squalor and sickness around her, for her gaze had always been out to the far ocean horizon, or up to the gentle heavens.

"I don't know the answers any more than you do." Gideon spoke from the depths of his heart, for as soon as he had started praying for Donna, his feelings had swung around as surely as a ship when the captain turns the rudder. He had deliberately turned the rudder of his mind away from resentment and toward compassion, and now all he felt was compassion. "I do want you to be happy," Gideon said rising and laying his hand lightly upon Donna's head before he went his way.

"Aren't you going to talk with the bishop?" asked Susan, reviving the question of Gideon's rectorship when Gideon and she were alone later that evening.

"Not unless he sends for me," was Gideon's reply.

"Won't the vestry demand that he send you away—"

"If so," Gideon grinned unconcernedly, "Angela and Doris will make up a committee and go and see the bishop, and then the fur will really fly!"

Gideon had taken Paul Forrester's advice about the altar guild. He had diffidently approached the women who had run it for years, asking anxiously whether they felt able to train a group of young girls as their assistants. "It isn't that you need help," he had said, "but it will make the girls feel part of the church. I'm trying to do that more and more with the young people, because either we hold them, or they'll be dashing off to some weird group—" Gideon had paused to give the ladies time to express their opinion of such offbeat groups, while plunking down their vases and dusters with more emphasis than necessary. "I know it will increase your work," he said humbly, "and sort of put you in a position of authority—"

The ladies had beamed with pleasure, and generously consented to the enlargement of the altar guild. Therefore, when they got wind of the vestry's dissatisfaction with the rector, loud were their complaints.

"What's this I hear," boomed Angela, when Gideon stepped into the sacristy where the ladies were ironing vestments, "about the vestry wanting you to leave us?"

"They did say something about it," said Gideon.

"Oh, Father Bruce, dear Father Bruce!" mourned Doris, tears in her eyes.

"Never mind, I haven't gone yet," said Gideon cheerily. "Very likely they'll change their minds."

"They'd better," declared Angela emphatically, adding ominously, "We'll pray, and that'll fix it!"

Gideon had to laugh at her belligerent tone, and then suggested, "Wouldn't it be better to pray that God's will be done, and for Him to take care of the church however He thinks best?"

"No," said Angela positively. "Don't want to give Him that much rope. We're praying that *you* stay right *here,* that's what!"

When Leslie returned from a week's vacation and heard of the vestry's stand, he burst into the rector's study. "What's the big idea of them wanting you to leave?" he demanded. "Here you preach better than you ever did, and you're all over the place praying for people, getting them out of sickbeds, even deathbeds—"

"That's a slight exaggeration!" laughed Gideon. "Sure, when I pay hospital calls, I always pray. Now that I know it's what people want, it seems perfectly natural. In fact, if I didn't pray, I'd feel as if I had invited friends to dinner and hadn't given them any food!"

"But after the deathbed scenes and resurrections," stormed the irrepressible Leslie, "if the vestry don't know you're God's man, what's wrong with them?"

"You're exaggerating. But it is true about the Jewish lad. His healing was almost as wonderful as my own."

"And I just heard about another kid, supposedly dying of an infection in the bloodstream and kidneys and heart, and the miracle drugs weren't doing any good. Then you went and prayed for him—"

Gideon smiled. "Yes, Jimmy was almost the first of our own church people that I prayed for," he said, "and his recovery is quite wonderful."

"Tell everybody about it next Sunday," challenged Leslie. "Come on, stick your chin out, and tell the whole church!"

"Maybe I will," meditated Gideon, "maybe I just will. More and more people are coming to my class on the Holy Spirit, and they don't understand the vestry being so upset, so maybe it is time for me to speak out to the whole church."

The next Sunday morning, therefore, Gideon entered the

pulpit, invoked the Father, the Son, and the Holy Ghost and faced the congregation with a twinkle in his eyes.

"I have been asked to tell you a story this morning," he said, "and I'm having the older Sunday school pupils remain, because children always like a story. It is about a little boy named Jimmy of this very congregation, younger than most of you," and he smiled down on the upturned faces in the first rows.

"Jimmy was in the hospital, very sick, and the doctors didn't know what to do, because none of the medicines seemed to work. He had what we call an infection. That means, he had germs. You know what germs are?" he asked the children, and they nodded. "Yes, everyone knows germs, don't they? They seem to know germs better than they know God," he said, as though under his breath.

"Anyhow, he was in the hospital, and when I went to see him, I thought: I wonder if Jesus could do a miracle and make this child well? Do you think He could?" Gideon asked the children, and they nodded, their faces alight. "Well, you're more sure of it than I was at the time. I knew Jesus could, if He were right here, you know, and we could see Him in a body, but I wasn't sure whether He could do it through me.

"Well, when I went to see this sick little boy, I just said to him, 'Jimmy, you know about Jesus, don't you?' and he said he did. I said, 'You know that Jesus put His hands on sick people and made them well, didn't He?' Jimmy said, 'Uh huh.' So I said, 'Well, shall we try? Will that be okay?' 'Sure,' said Jimmy.

"So I put my hands on him, and I asked Jesus to come into him and fill him with His life, so that all the germs would go away. And, you know, the very next day, his temperature was normal, and the doctors said there were no more germs in the heart or the bloodstream. There were a few still hiding out in the kidneys, so they kept him in the hospital one more day, and then Jimmy went home, as well as anybody!"

"Yeah, I know!" piped a voice, and then a little hand went up over the mouth, a few children tittered, and there was silence.

"I'm glad you know," said Gideon soberly, and then he looked squarely at the rest of the congregation. "I'm glad Ernie knows," he said, "and although I'm a bit frightened at telling all of you that Jesus is alive today and still does miracles, yet I have to tell you right out, because so many people have asked me about it.

"Some people ask how I know that it is Jesus that makes someone well—for instance, Jimmy—and not the doctor's treatments. I don't know; probably it's both, except in Jimmy's case, the treatments weren't working. There are other questions, too," he went on. "Some have asked why everybody we pray for doesn't get well. My only answer is that I don't know. Sometimes, for example, people who are very old can probably get well easier by going to heaven. I would rather do it that way, I think, if I were old. I think it would be more fun, really," and he smiled down at the children who were listening intently.

"But then, there are others who aren't very old, and we pray for them, but they don't get well. All I know is that God's perfect will is not yet done upon this earth, because it is still covered with dark clouds of wickedness, and the power of Satan is very real. When the breath of the Holy Spirit blows away the clouds, then miracles happen, but in other cases there is so much darkness that somehow God's power can't get through. But I don't believe that is the way Jesus wants it." Gideon concluded his sermon with emphasis. "I believe He really wants the kingdom of God to come, and God's will to be done upon this earth as it is in heaven. He must, because He told us to pray for that very thing."

"How'd they like your sermon?" asked Stan the next day, leaning against Gideon's car while the tank was filling. "You know, I was in church."

"Yes, I saw you," smiled Gideon, looking into Stan's blue eyes. "I knew why you came, too."

Stan shrugged. "Got to give you a hand once in a while. It's really a laugh," he added. "A mechanic there to pray for the minister, while all the rest of the congregation grind their teeth!"

"Not quite all," said Gideon mildly.

"Nope," Stan conceded. "You've got a good praying gang, and they were there rooting for you. But the top brass—!"

With a picture in his mind of Reginald Crabtree's lowered brows, Gideon muttered to himself, "I wonder if they'll ever—?" while Stan went to disconnect the hose. Suddenly Gideon looked around to find Westwind gone, that small person having chosen to accompany his grandfather to the garage. "Is Westy all right?" Gideon called.

Stan replied, "Yeah, he's helping me. Hey, Westy," he addressed the tiny child, who stood knee-high to his tall figure, "better lend me a hand with this car!" Gravely he handed the child a rag while he raised the hood to check the oil. "Down a quart," he reported.

Gideon got out and stood beside Stan while he put in

the oil and tested other things, muttering uncomplimentary words about the car's age and condition. "Seen anything of Ellie lately?" Gideon asked him.

"Nope," said Stan, slamming down the hood and starting to clean the windshield.

"Every now and then she asks about you," said Gideon.

"Is she still hanging around with those freaks waiting for Jesus?" demanded Stan.

Gideon nodded. "A lot of people believe that these *are* the latter days, and that His arrival *is* imminent," he said thoughtfully.

"Ellie doesn't want to marry and have children like anybody else," muttered Stan, tight-lipped.

"You asked her?"

"More or less, kind of, but when it looked like I'd have to join that bunch of howling maniacs, I pulled out." He lowered the hood.

"That Ellie —" He paused, looking out over the street.

"You love her, don't you?" asked Gideon gently.

"It's hard not to," muttered Stan, not looking at him. "But I'm not going to quit my job, and live on other people's money, and roam around the city asking people if they're saved. That's not for me."

"Would you have to?"

"Guess so. It's all Ellie thinks of."

At this Westwind trotted up gravely, holding out a very black bit of rag. "Dirty!" said he.

"It sure is," agreed Stan, rising to renew the child's supplies, and laying his big hand for a moment on the little head, where the hair still stuck out in kewpie wisps despite his grandmother's vigorous brushing. "Okay, boy, do a good job!" Stan turned back to Gideon. "Another thing I

270

don't get is all this about the battle of Armageddon. What I want to know is who's going to fight, if all the good guys are floating around in heaven, and the rest of us are toasting in hell?"

"Christians have wondered about that for two thousand years," said Gideon. "Saint Paul thought it was going to happen right away. That's why he said Christians might as well not get married—"

"Some deal," groaned Stan. "And here's Ellie saying the same thing."

Gideon looked at the tall young man with his honest eyes and the look of sorrow about his face, and said compassionately, "I think someday Ellie will grow up and understand a little bit more—or else, Jesus will come and we'll all understand a bit more!"

"It's a long time to wait," said Stan, shaking his head, "a long time to wait."

"But you are still waiting."

"Nothing else to do," said Stan, turning to his work, after first smiling at the sight of his tiny helper who was vigorously polishing the rear bumper. "Don't know how I'd stand it, if it wasn't for—" He looked at Gideon, not knowing how to say what was in his heart.

Gideon knew. "If it wasn't for the magic joy of the Holy Spirit," he said.

Stan nodded, sunlight breaking out on his face. "It's the darnedest thing," he said.

"Like a light inside when there's no light outside," agreed Gideon.

"Yup. Hey, Westy! Time to knock off for lunch!" He turned to Gideon as they strolled toward the car. "Hey, you suppose that's what Jesus meant when He said He was coming again soon? I mean, that light inside?"

271

" 'A little while and ye shall not see me, and again a little while and ye shall see me.' Could be," Gideon mused, "and it could be a lot more than that. Maybe that's the beginning of His coming again, and the end no man has yet seen—or foreseen."

Chapter Twenty

The months passed slowly from blazing summer into a yet more stifling fall. The parched earth cried out for rain, even while unaware citizens prayed complacently for fine weather that they might enjoy the ocean, whose water stayed uncompromisingly cold.

Life at Trinity Church slowed, but did not stop. Gideon's classes ceased for the summer, true, and the church school rested, but the services continued and mysteriously, inconspicuously, the power in them grew. For the moment the vestry were quiescent, having been bidden by the bishop to bear with their rector for a year, and come to him again if they were still displeased. Fair enough, thought Gideon with a smile, thinking ever more gratefully of his bishop.

When Gideon had talked with Bishop Updyke about possibly resigning from the organized church, the bishop had said, "Sure, you can go off and be independent, and have yourself a little group. But what of the vows you made before God when you were ordained? And what of the people who may want fellowship in the Holy Spirit, but also desire and need the sacraments of the church? Would you throw all that away for a few new-old ideas, like speaking in tongues at cottage meetings?"

Gideon had to agree. If only the church, the house of the Lord built on the martyrs' blood and tears and on the visions of the saints, would shake out of its lethargy and come into its full inheritance!

"Lord, show me how to bring this to pass," Gideon prayed one morning as he sat alone in the rear of the church preparing for the day's work. He waited in silence and the response came: "Besides your adult class, you are about to start your fall confirmation class. Teach those young people about My Spirit, and prepare every one of them to receive in full measure when the bishop lays hands on them."

"But, Lord, what if they should break loose there in the service and speak in tongues?"

Almost with heavenly laughter, the voice within Gideon answered, "Leave that to Me."

As Gideon rose and went to his study, another thought came: If only Donna would join the confirmation class! His reason told him that she would not do so. But Gideon had been praying faithfully for Donna ever since Josie had challenged him to face his anger at her. Her mind, he now realized, was almost as childlike as Westwind's. He could not hate a mind like that; he could only brood over her in prayer, longing for her to awake from long slumber. Gideon tried every way he knew, but could stir no response in her. When he spoke of Jesus and the Holy Spirit, she listened—or did she listen?—with a vapid, uncomprehending expression, and finally she asked him not to talk to her that way, as it only confused her.

"You've drawn a blank with Donna, haven't you, Dad?" Josie commented one day. "But at least you don't still hate her, do you?"

"There's really not enough of her to hate," Gideon answered. "Anyway, when you pray for somebody, even if it doesn't do the other person any good, your own feelings always seem to change."

Entering his study, Gideon thought how strange it was that he could now talk so freely to Josie, whereas for a long time they had been practically strangers. Was it because he had confessed to her his own failings and weaknesses? Even Bob refused to discuss his wife's separation from reality, perhaps because he knew nothing to do about it. But Bob himself was now so alight with the unreasonable joy of the Spirit that one would expect Donna to catch it from him.

"Donna just doesn't dig it," Bob had told his father as they worked together on an old car, salvaged practically from a junkyard. Periodically, he took it apart and spread its entrails over the bit of scuffed ground beside the driveway. "Only Himself can reach her now," he said finally.

One October Sunday morning, the air, which had been fairly sparking with dry electricity, was moist and cool after a shower. "The earth can begin to breathe again," Gideon murmured, as he crossed the patio from church to parish house and glanced up at the mountains with compassion, as though understanding their relief. It was strange that, as he grew to love God more, he also felt a deepening love for God's creation—or perhaps it wasn't strange at all.

A group of small boys released from church school burst

out of a classroom, his own eleven-year-old in the lead. "I'm Moses," announced David, cantering around the patio with a gait suggestive of chariots and horses. "Come on, you guys! See the waters of the Red Sea piled up there; they won't hurt you! And old Pharaoh's way behind! Shake a leg, you guys!"

"That's the way we teach 'em," grinned their teacher, somewhat warily, when he confronted the rector. "They act out the stories, see? That way, they're not likely to ever forget them."

Passing the kindergarten, Gideon glanced in the open door to see Donna lifting into her arms a screaming baby. In this one area, she was effective, and seemed to enjoy helping. Westwind was standing by, scowling with disdain at children his own age, whom he deemed infantile. They were singing about a little candle, but Westwind, seeing no candle to sing about, maintained his own individual silence. Funny little boy, thought Gideon fondly, as he entered his study to prepare for the service. However, he had no time to compose himself for, with hardly a knock, in burst Josie, white-faced and panting.

"Oh, Dad, Dad!" she cried.

"What is it?"

"Florrie!" gasped his daughter.

"Sit down," ordered Gideon, "and tell me what about Florrie."

"Well, you know I don't see her much any more, because —well, I don't like the way she and Marcus act, you know—"

"I know," said Gideon.

"But, Dad, Marcus just called up and, you know, she's—pregnant!"

Gideon nodded noncommittally.

276

"And, oh Dad, Marcus is just awful! He says it's her fault. She got careless—about the pill, you know—and he's not about to marry her—"

"No great loss," muttered Gideon grimly.

"But, Dad, she went off somewhere and had an abortion, and—I guess it wasn't a proper doctor, or anything. They can't stop her bleeding, and Marcus says she's dying!"

"And why did he call you?" asked Gideon, with uneasy presentiment.

"Well, I guess I'm the only friend Florrie has, and also, he knows you—you help people like that. Oh, Dad, can you please go to the hospital right away? She's at St. Luke's."

"Josie, you know I can't go right now," objected Gideon. "Church is in ten minutes!"

"But, Dad, this is more important!"

"Look!" said Gideon, standing and pointing out the study window to the people streaming into church. "What would I tell them?"

"Let Leslie do it."

"He's out of town."

"So you'd just let Florrie die—"

Gideon stood at the window for a moment. "Lord, what shall I do?" he prayed, and the answer came to him.

"Now listen to me," said he to Josie with authority. "The one that heals is Jesus, not us. All we do is channel His love, His energy. Anyone can learn to channel it. Now *you* go to the hospital and put your hands on Florrie, and—"

"But I don't know how!" wailed Josie. "You said anybody can learn, but I haven't learned!"

"You might have, if you'd been at my class," said Gideon. "But you can learn fast, right now! Just get in there. Tell them who you are, and that you're acting for me, and they'll let you in. They know me pretty well by now. Then put your hands on Florrie's middle, and let the healing power of Jesus flow through you—"

"But I'm not—"

"You're not connected," said Gideon, as she paused. "I know, but you can connect right now. I'll help. I'll ask the congregation to hold Florrie up in prayer in the communion service— Oh, not by name," he reassured her, reading the objection in his daughter's mind. "And I'll be praying myself for the life of Christ to enter into Florrie and stop the issue of blood, just as He did for the woman in the Bible."

"Can He really do it nowadays?" asked Josie.

"Of course He can!" shouted Gideon, as he hurried out to church.

"But she—shouldn't have done it! She's—"

"Guilty," finished Gideon over his shoulder. "The Lord can attend to that afterward."

Was that right? he wondered briefly. Was that theologically sound? Never mind! It felt right when he said it. That was all he knew.

Church ended at last, and the congregation streamed into the patio for the coffee hour. Gideon was at the door shaking hands.

Before Gideon left the patio, Josie was back, her eyes shining, her brown curls tossed back. "Daddy!" she cried. "It worked! She wasn't in emergency, she was in intensive care, and the nurse who knew you was on duty so she let me in. And Florrie was asleep or something, so I didn't have to explain anything. I just put my hands on her the way you said, under the sheet, sort of, and she didn't even know I was praying. And, Dad, I did all that you told me, but it seemed I could still feel her blood flowing out, so I said, real low, you know, 'Stop it! In the name of Jesus!' Was that awful, Dad?" Josie asked her father. The last two parishioners still present had put down their coffeecups and were listening intently.

Gideon threw back his head and laughed. "No, it was great!" he exclaimed. "You took authority, that's what you did! Come on, we'll finish this in my study." And he took her by the arm.

"Well, I guess it stopped," Josie went on, once they were settled, "because pretty soon Florrie sighed and opened her eyes, and—but, Dad, she's so sad it kind of broke me up. Nobody was there to see her but me—nobody. I asked her if her mother doesn't come, and she said, 'She's mad with me,' kind of shaking her head. Oh, Dad, maybe it would be better if she *had* died!"

"No, God can rebuild her life, if she'll let Him," said Gideon after a pause.

"She wants me to come and see her again," said Josie hesitantly.

Gideon replied, "You will, won't you?"

"I guess so," sighed Josie. "I had about decided not to bother with her any more, she's been such a pain in the neck, but—"

"When people are in trouble, we have to bother, don't we?" Gideon said as they started home. "But now, when you see her, you'll have some help, the best kind of help."

His feelings were mixed as he re-entered the family scene. He rejoiced in Josie's venture in prayer, but his concern for Donna was heavy on his heart. He knew he had to tell Susan something that he had begun to suspect about Donna, something he had refused to even consider, until the thought grew so insistent that he had to accept it. Donna was on drugs.

"I've been wondering, too," Susan said, when he told her. "But I couldn't bring myself to say anything."

"We should have known," sighed Gideon. "Do you suppose Bob is, too?"

Susan shook her head vigorously. "No, I don't think so. He's really working hard on his job, and he wouldn't be alert enough if he were taking anything."

"Well, I'll have to ask him," said Gideon, "about Donna, I mean."

This Gideon did while Donna was putting Westwind to bed that evening. "Dad, I can't be sure, but I don't think she is," Bob responded unhesitatingly to his father's question. "Seems like it, I know, but—no."

"And you—were you, ever—?" Gideon inquired, as he and Bob sat together before the open fire, for the night was chilly.

Bob shook his head. "Not really," he said. "Oh, I smoked grass, but it didn't seem to get much hold on me, and after I came home and got to know God, I never missed it. Look, Dad," Bob reflected aloud, "if she can be healed by prayer, why—?"

"I know," said Gideon, aware of his son's thoughts, "but I don't believe she'd let me pray for her. And to tell the truth, I just don't feel that I could break through to her."

"You've got the power of the Holy Spirit," Bob grinned at his father affectionately. "Didn't you take me down to that garage, and didn't you and Stan and Tom pray for me to receive Jesus and the Holy Spirit, and didn't I speak with tongues as big as life? I sure did."

"Do you still pray in the Spirit?" inquired Gideon.

"Sure," said Bob, "every now and then I do, while I'm driving to work. Makes me feel good! But, gee, Dad, that

280

garage is a funny place for a prayer meeting. Why don't you have 'em in the church?"

"Someday, I hope I will," replied Gideon, adding, "if I don't get kicked out first." He also thought of his confirmation class, in which the young people were learning about the redemptive work of Jesus Christ and the power of His Holy Spirit. "One of these days—" he said again.

Before going to work next morning, Bob knocked at his parents' bedroom door. "Yes?" said Gideon, his tousled head in the doorway.

"Don't try to talk to Donna," said Bob. "Trouble is, she doesn't want to change. She was furious—that is, about as mad as she can get—when I told her that you'd like to pray for her. You can't change people," Bob added wisely, "if they don't want to be changed."

"I guess you're right," said Gideon, remembering how Jesus Himself first asked a sick man, "Wilt thou be made whole?"

"You see," said Bob earnestly, standing with his lunch box in his hand, "it's Donna's religion, kind of."

"What exactly is her religion?" asked Gideon.

"It's hard to explain." Bob's young brow was furrowed in thought. "She thinks she's—kind of seeking the infinite, you know."

Gideon started to say something, and changed his mind. "Okay, Bob, good luck! We won't talk to Donna, unless the Lord opens the way."

The Lord did not seem to open the way. After lunch, Donna suggested to Westwind that he take a nap. Of course Westwind did not feel the need of a nap; he knew best when he required sleep, and he slept wherever he chose. However, for the sake of peace, he lay down, and his mother lowered the shades against the brilliant sunshine and left him. At this time, she usually went into the backyard, sat in the sun, and meditated, so deep in thought that one could speak her name and she would not hear.

This day, however, she had in her hand a little satchel when she gently closed the bedroom door and slipped away. Susan had gone marketing, leaving the house quiet—Josie and David in school, and Donna keeping watch over her little boy. When Susan returned from the store, however, she found Westwind stark naked and alone. He looked at Susan with his direct blue gaze, and said, "Mama gone."

"What?" asked Susan, startled in spite of herself.

The little boy made no move, but simply repeated in his serious voice, "Mama gone."

She can't be gone, thought Susan—ridiculous! She dashed to the backyard, expecting to see the gentle figure sitting in the sun, but no, she was not there, nor was she in the kitchen nor any bedroom, nor could Susan see her on the street. Maybe she needed something at the drugstore. Yet Susan knew deep in her heart that Donna would have stayed until her son woke up, and then wherever she went, he would go, too. From the time he was born, she had hardly moved without him—first in her arms; later tied with a shawl upon her back; later yet, trotting beside her. Where was she? Susan knew a moment of panic, and her voice broke as she turned, as she always did, to Gideon.

"Gideon, she isn't here!" she said, as soon as he answered the phone.

"Who isn't there?"

"Donna! She's—she's gone!"

"Oh, she'll come back. She's just thought of an errand or something."

"Gideon, you know she doesn't go on errands. While Westy naps, she sits in that chair, and she doesn't move until he gets up. Gideon, where do you suppose she's gone?"

"I—I don't know. I'll be right home." said Gideon, understanding more from Susan's tone, than what was said, that he was needed.

He disentangled himself from his office and went home, to find Westwind sitting disconsolately on the front steps. "Mama gone!" said the tiny boy, looking at him with big, wondering eyes.

"Oh, she'll be back, Westy," said Gideon, rumpling the child's hair. It was funny hair, very blond and very straight, and it tended to stick out in every direction. In fact, when the child first came to them, Gideon had the impression that his hair had never been combed, and this was true.

"She'll come back, Westy," said Gideon again. "Don't worry." He strode into the house to his wife, unreasonable alarm hidden in his heart. "Did she—take anything with her?" he asked Susan, when he joined her in Bob and Donna's bedroom.

"Yes, I think she did," said Susan. "You know that little sort of handbag that she used to keep on the closet shelf—it's gone. She couldn't have taken much. I—I've looked through her clothes, and I can't be sure, but it looks as though she took some things. I can't find her hairbrush, and her bureau drawers aren't as full as they used to be." She turned and looked at him. "Gideon, she's gone!"

Gideon sat down heavily on the double bed that they had crowded into Bob's room so that Westy could have the little bed that had once been Bob's. "Do you suppose," he mused, "that Bob told her we suspected her of taking drugs? Could that be it?"

"Who knows?" said Susan. "But surely, Gideon, surely she'll come back. She can't just go off and leave her child!"

"How do you know?" said Gideon somberly. "She never says anything; she just looks vague."

"She does try to help once in a while," Susan defended her, "but she's so absentminded, she'll pick up a dirty dish and put it in the bedroom, or anywhere, and it's really easier to do things myself. She wanders around in a dream."

"All this meditating," growled Gideon.

"Well, what'll we do?" asked Susan. "I called Bob, but he was out delivering lumber and couldn't be reached."

"I don't know of anything else to do right now, except pray," Gideon said. "After all, Donna is a grown woman, and she wouldn't have taken the little bag if she meant to jump off a bridge, or anything like that. Susan—let's pray about it, and I'll call up a few others to pray, too. Tonight I have my confirmation class," he went on, "and they're really getting the idea of prayer. Not long ago the papers reported a little boy who was lost, and somebody in the class suggested we pray for him. So we did, and two or three promised to keep it up, and in a day or so he came safely home."

"Well," Susan agreed, "I guess the only thing we can do is pray, until Bob comes anyway. So let's get at it!"

Their prayer, however, did not last long. "I can't stand it!" Susan burst out. "Gideon, let's go looking for her!"

"But where?"

"In the street, to start with. If she's walking, she can't have gone far."

"She's probably bummed a ride by now," muttered Gideon. "Wait, I'll call Ellie, and get that gang praying."

"Okay," said Susan, "and call your friend, Stan, too, and Tom. Get all the riffraff—oh, excuse me, Gideon! I'm just upset."

Gideon made his telephone calls, picked up Westwind, ushered Susan into the car, and churned down the street looking for his daughter-in-law. It was a fruitless search, and he knew it, but somehow it was easier to move than to sit still and wait.

"Should we—call the police?" faltered Susan.

Tight-lipped, Gideon replied, "I don't—think so. Oh, no, Susan! After all, Donna's only been gone a couple of hours. We might as well go home now, and just wait."

Disconsolately, they returned home. "Where's Donna?" asked David as he hurled himself into the house, banged the door, and flung his books on the hall chair.

For once his mother failed to remonstrate. "We don't know," said she.

"Gee, it's funny not to see her sitting in the backyard," said David.

"Well, she isn't," said Susan shortly.

"Gosh, Mom, you scared?"

"There's nothing to be scared about," Susan replied, trying to speak steadily. "Donna's a grown woman, and if a grown woman can't go for a walk or to the store, or something like that, it's just too bad."

"Yeah, but you *are* scared," said David.

Westwind, meanwhile, made a firm decision, and set off himself to look for his mother. Slipping out the still open front door, he sturdily trudged down the street in the hot midafternoon sun, neatly clad in tiny shirt and rolled-up pants, all pants being too long for his spindly legs. After a while, these garments chafed him; they were heavy and uncomfortable. Therefore he decided that since he had a definite objective which might take some time, he had best be relieved of impediments. Westwind had learned by now that grown people, for obscure reasons, took unkindly to such a simple matter as removing garments, the better to walk. He therefore chose an unoccupied front yard, sneaked behind a blossoming hibiscus, struggled out of his shirt, stepped lightly out of his trousers and his sandals, and went his way on his little bare feet. "Find Mama," he said to himself, and off he went with a complete independence and poised purpose that stunned the casual passerby.

It was not long before Westwind's absence became noticed in the Bruce household. "Hey, Westy!" called David. "Westy, come here, I've got something to show you!" Westy did not appear. David darted from room to room, and searched the yard and garage, but there was no sign of his nephew. "Hey, Mom!" cried David, running again. "Westy's gone! He's not anywhere!"

"He was here just a minute ago," said Susan, hurrying to the living room and looking at the empty place where the little boy had perched, as though her looking could bring him there.

"He's not here now," said David, stating the obvious.

"Oh, my God!" cried Susan, in her extreme distress remembering briefly her wandering ancestors.

"He's looking for his mother, that's what he's doing," said Gideon, coming in behind Susan. "Well, we surely ought to be able to find him! Come on!"

Once more they climbed into the car and cruised slowly up and down the streets. "He can't have bummed a ride, that's for sure," said Gideon, perplexed, as they saw no sign of a tiny boy gone to find his mother.

"Oh, Gideon," said Susan, her voice quavering, "you don't suppose somebody's picked him up? Maybe he's been kidnapped. Oh, Gideon!"

"Let's not get excited," Gideon replied, adding, "but after all, we might call the police. That's what they're for—" He drew up at the next telephone booth and dialed the neighborhood police station.

"You mean a tiny boy without a stitch on?" asked the officer, when Gideon had stated his question. "Yeah, he's here, all right," he chuckled.

"Thank God!" breathed Gideon. "We'll be right down."

"Oh, hurry, Gideon," gasped Susan, quite undone for once. "The poor little thing—he's probably scared to death!"

They went with all speed to the police station, and found Westwind sitting on top of a high desk, a towel hitched about his middle. With both hands he held a pink ice cream cone which he was devouring, lick by lick. Most of his head was hidden by a huge policeman's hat, and two delighted officers were hovering over him.

"Nice man, find Mama," said Westwind, reaching one hand for a lollipop held in a policeman's vast paw.

"Yeah, we told him we'd find his mama," said the grinning officer. That's what we're for."

Westwind waved the lollipop toward an ancient tricycle standing in a corner, and proclaimed, "Westwind wide twicycle!"

"Yeah, we picked it up a year ago," muttered a grinning cop. "Nobody's ever claimed it, so—say, is his name really Westwind?"

"It is," said Gideon feebly, while Susan, overcome with relief, put her arms around the little boy, ice cream and all.

"Let me see if I have this straight: this young man came to report his mother's disappearance and to ask for our assistance," explained the desk sergeant, grinning broadly. "Is that the true situation?"

"I'm afraid so," admitted Gideon, giving him a few more facts.

"As for his clothes—" began the second officer, but Westwind explained their absence quite simply, airing a new word.

"Clothes iwwitate Westwind," he said.

Chapter Twenty-One

It was necessary during the next days to watch Westwind continually. The tiny boy did not cry, but his small, set countenance showed that he had every intention of going forth again and searching for his mother.

Bob, meanwhile, did all he could to cuddle his little boy, reading him stories, singing him songs, and making him feel cherished and cared for. "Mama come back," he would say again and again, "Mama come back."

Westwind only looked at him with a long, contemplative stare and murmured in a small voice, "Westwind want Mama."

Bob would say again, "Mama come back!" To his parents, he said, "She will, you know," as the three of them prayed about it. Josie, meanwhile, tossed back her dark curls and disappeared into her room. She thought little of their manner of praying. They would put in a petition, go into a long silence, and often speak quietly in languages that none of them understood. This had been explained to Josie, but she wanted none of it.

"Nuts!" she would murmur under her breath, finding a reason to evade the prayer-time. Josie secretly wondered whether Donna would ever come back, indeed whether it would be good for her to return to a world in which she did not fit.

The third evening after Donna's disappearance, the telephone rang, and Gideon answered. Josie and David were at the kitchen table, homework spread out between them. Susan was putting away the dishes, and Bob had taken Westwind for a drive.

"Hi," said the soft voice at the other end of the line. "It's Ellie. One of our people was out to the Rock this afternoon —you know, the Jesus commune out in the desert? Well, I've got good news. Donna's out there and has been for three days!"

"Oh, thank God," exclaimed Gideon with relief. "How did she get there?"

"Well, when you called us, we called them. They wouldn't tell me where they found her, but it wasn't much of a place."

"How did they get her to come with them?"

"The way they get everybody," said Ellie. "They told her Jesus loves her. You did tell her that, didn't you?"

Gideon's mind whirled. "Sure!" he said with false heartiness, "in a different way, you know. Our prayer book—"

"Gideon," Ellie said in a gentle reproof, "lots of folks just don't dig it out of the prayer book. They asked Donna if she wanted Jesus to take care of her, and you know, if she would kind of belong to Him. She began to cry, and she said yes, she would. So they had her get down on her knees, right there on the street, and she accepted Jesus as

Lord and Savior. They said she was so happy, she was really something to see. Then they brought her home."

Gideon did not know what to say to this extraordinary recital of the prowess of these peculiar lost young ones who were somehow not so lost. "When can we come and get her?" he asked.

"Well, they want to wait on that, if it's all right. You see, she—hasn't come through yet."

"Come through what?"

"It's kind of hard to explain, but it's sort of like being born, you know—born all over again, kind of."

Gideon sat down. "Besides," Ellie was going on, "they couldn't be sure right now that she wouldn't go back on drugs. She was on them, you know. Downers—tranquilizers. Instant meditation. She may not be completely healed yet. But she soon will be," she added confidently.

Gideon thought—of all the amazing things! Hospitals and outfits of every description try to heal people of drug addiction, taking months or years, and maybe never succeeding. And here were these ignorant, rough youths concerned that a cure might not be made perfect in three days!

"This is beyond me," said Gideon.

"Gideon, we've got to trust them, and trust God that He's in charge. They said they would call again in a day or so and let us know how she is, and when it's okay to come. In the meantime, they ask that you don't tell anyone but your family where she is."

"All right," said Gideon, "we'll keep praying. Thanks, Ellie, very much."

How appalling, he thought, turning away from the telephone, that he should owe such a huge debt of thanks to a

291

group of unconventional young people who were apparently doing for his daughter-in-law what he, his family, and church had not been able to do! "Mama coming soon," he said to Westwind who looked at him wonderingly, and then brightened, as though he believed.

"What is it?" asked Susan eagerly, and calling her and Bob into the living room, Gideon told them.

"I kind of figured on something like that," said Bob.

"What made you figure it?" Gideon asked curiously.

"I don't know, but I've seen kids like those. There were some in the islands, but not many. Most of the kids there were dopers. But when I prayed about Donna," he added, his voice softening, "I seemed to get a picture of her with a bunch of these kids."

"But why," demanded Susan, "why in the name of sense can they do for her what we couldn't?"

"You're just in a different world," explained Bob. "Or maybe yours is the real world and we're in a different one, but anyway, the language isn't the same."

For two days, as inquiries came from the members of his confirmation class, from those attending his course on the Holy Spirit, and even from the bishop, Gideon only replied, "She hasn't come back yet—but I'm sure she's all right."

However, in Gideon's garage prayer group, such gentle remarks fell utterly to the ground.

"Don't give us that," said Stan. "You know something. Come on, where is she?"

"I'm not supposed to say," Gideon confessed.

"Huh," said Stan, glaring, "if you're not supposed to tell, then I know darn well where she is. She's out at that Jesus commune, that's where. Okay, so you're not supposed to tell," he added. "All I want to know is, why doesn't she come home?"

"They say she's not ready," blurted Gideon, before he could stop himself.

"They do, huh?" said Stan furiously. "Look, is Ellie in on this?"

"Well," admitted Gideon, "you see, I called up Ellie and asked them to pray, and—"

"Yeah?" said Stan. "So Ellie is in on it! Honest, Rev, what's with that girl? You know—"

"I know," said Gideon gently, "you really love her."

Stan swallowed hard. "And what's more," he said bitterly, "she loves me too. I know she does, but—well, I just don't know what to make of her."

"I don't either," admitted Gideon, "but look, Stan, at the risk of sounding stuffy, we've got to leave her—and Donna—in God's hands."

"Well, we'll see," said Stan, more to himself than aloud.

That night, Gideon received a call from Ellie, who said that the Jesus commune had reported that Donna still wasn't ready to come home.

"Well, I have an idea," said Gideon. "Their meetings are open to the public, aren't they?"

"Yes," said Ellie. "You mean—"

"Let's go, you and I, Susan and Bob. I don't know about Josie and David. We'd better leave them at home."

"Josie'd probably blow a fuse," smiled Ellie. "Or else," she added, meditating, "she'd go to answer the altar call."

"Maybe," commented Gideon, "but I doubt it. No, we'll leave her at home with David. I imagine Bob will take Westwind. Okay, we'll go!"

"Okay," agreed Ellie timorously.

That very evening they went, and Westwind determined that he would go with them. "Find Mama," said he, utterly refusing to stay at home, sleep, or in any way act like a baby. "Find Mama," he repeated firmly.

"Okay, big boy," smiled Gideon, picking him up and carrying him on one arm to the car. "Maybe this is just the way to bring her home."

When they reached the old roadhouse used as the commune's meeting place, the crowd was gathering, and the band was tuning up. Westwind clung around his grandfather's neck, hiding his face, for the blare of trumpets terrified him. Perhaps the young people pressing all around also made him feel shy, though they quickly found seats and settled down to read their Bibles until the meeting began.

Westwind suddenly spoke up loud and clear. "Where Mama?" said he, in the silence. There was a gasp and a small outcry from a far corner, and Donna herself arose and started toward them, but was interrupted by two other girls, who apparently were urging her to stay where she was. Donna therefore sank back into her seat, tears in her eyes, but gazed across the crowded room at her little boy.

This, however, did not suit Westwind, and when she did not come, he scrambled down from Gideon's arms and started weaving his way through long legs to her. One of the hairy young men picked him up, hesitated a moment, and then carried him to his mother and put him in her lap. Donna clutched him, hiding her face against his, and Westwind twisted himself about to wind his little arms around her neck, patting her cheek contentedly.

The service began with a thunderous burst of music, startling to newcomers, but Gideon and his family entered

294

in with all the rest of the enthusiastic congregation as best they could. Across the room, Westwind stayed snuggled in his mother's arms, tiny hands pressed over his ears, even though she was standing now, and singing with the rest.

During the testimonies which followed the singing, Gideon studied the faces of the young people who arose to tell of their experiences. They were amazingly, heart-shakingly happy! Some beamed and smiled, others remained seriously composed, but in every face—brown, black, or white—there was peace and a dignified, shiny joy such as Gideon had never seen. God help us, he thought! If only I could look upon my congregation and see such love. For it was love, a special kind and quality of love, without self-consciousness. It was, as Josie would have said, weird—but it was a real, all-enveloping, all-encompassing, love, high-shining within every one of them.

Tonight, the commune's leader and founder was the speaker, and Gideon was amazed to hear in his words as much wrath as love. He commanded and exhorted everyone to come to Jesus and be saved, quickly, lest they go down into hell forever, and he went on to describe, with what seemed to Gideon glee, the sufferings of that region. Gideon sat aghast, but noticed that the young people around him seemed not at all disturbed. Presumably, thought Gideon, to those who have already lived in hell there is no terror in such a message—only joy in knowing from what they have been saved, and zeal that everyone else should also be lifted into new life and love. As the preacher expressed it, they would soon be caught up to meet Jesus in the air. Looking with wonder at their faces, Gideon thought, perhaps so—or were they already meeting Him? Who could tell?

The service ended at last, with eight or ten converts kneeling at the altar rail, the leader and youthful elders laying on hands and praying for their salvation and the infilling of the Holy Spirit, and others standing behind and joining in the prayer. The rest of the group stirred about, and some went to the kitchen across the hall, bringing paper plates of food which they graciously offered first to Gideon and his family and to the other outsiders.

Bob seized the opportunity to weave his way through the crowd and reached Donna's side. "Hi, Donna," he said, while she only looked at him with shining eyes. Westwind, still in her arms, patted her on the head and said to his father, "Mama!" as though introducing them.

"Boy, has he missed you!" said Bob.

"Has he cried?" asked Donna.

Bob shook his head. "That little fellow, I've never heard him cry," he said proudly, "except when Grandma first tried to comb his hair. That wasn't exactly crying; he just kind of yelled! No, he did better than cry for you, honey. He went looking for you!"

"Oh!" exclaimed Donna. "Did he get lost?"

"Well, no," grinned Bob. "He landed in the police station and," he added, "naturally without a stitch on."

"Oh, baby!" cried Donna, laughter and tears mixed as she held Westwind tight in her arms. "Bob," she said, looking directly at him, "I've found Jesus! I'm saved! Don't you see I'm different?"

"Yes, I do," said Bob, for no one could fail to see that she was different. "Gee, you look so happy, Donna! And so alive! I've never seen you look like this—gee!"

"Oh, Bob, it's wonderful!"

"Yeah, I can see that it is," he nodded. "But look, honey.

Come on back home with us. We need you!"

"Oh, I can't," said Donna, holding the little boy tight, as though someone would snatch him away. Her eyes were wide. "Oh, Bob, I can't. I'm afraid to go home. What if—I should lose it? Bob, look, why don't you and Westwind come and live here?"

"What?" cried Bob, looking around at a totally foreign world. "You know I couldn't live here!"

"But you'd really find Jesus. You don't know how wonderful it would be, Bob!"

"Oh, no," said her husband, shaking his head regretfully. "No, I couldn't do that. Besides, I've got to work, you know. Somebody's got to earn our living!"

"Oh, Bob," Donna pleaded, "Come and live here for a while, won't you?"

By this time Gideon and Susan had worked their way through the crowd and were standing by. "That's asking too much," said Gideon, supporting his son.

"And why?" inquired Donna, wide-eyed. "Why would it be too much—to just belong to Jesus, and do what He wants you to do? Why?"

"Well, first," said Gideon seriously, "we've got to make sure we know what Jesus wants us to do."

Chapter Twenty-Two

When the Bruce family prepared to leave for home, it proved impossible to disentangle Westwind from his mother. He clung tightly to her neck, and refused to let go. Finally, after consultation, it was agreed that he might stay overnight with her, giving Bob time to decide whether or not he would come back and throw in his lot with the commune.

This was agreed to in spite of Bob's steadfast refusal to go to the altar and be saved, explaining that he was already saved. Then, they persisted, did he have the Baptism in the Spirit? Yes, said Bob, he did. Did he speak in tongues? Looking them straight in the eye, Bob again said yes, he did.

Thus encouraged, or discouraged, as the case might be, they agreed that Bob was to return home and seek the Lord's guidance as to whether or not he should come back and join up with them.

Westwind, therefore, crawled with his mother into a

sleeping bag laid on the floor of an old farmhouse, where five or six young women of the commune shared a room. The sleeping bag had been inhabited before, and its aroma was strong. Westwind, however, did not object to anything as long as he could cling tightly to his mother, and thus he fell asleep.

Next morning, trouble arose, as the few small children resident at the commune were required to stay in the nursery—a room set apart in a shabby bungalow—while their mothers went about their work. Donna was to go with a carful of young people into the city, seeking and saving the lost in the name of Jesus Christ. One young woman's duty that day was to stay in the nursery and take care of the tots. When Westwind found himself abandoned to the unfamiliar and unwelcome company of four other little ones, he dissolved into lamentable and inconsolable sobs. Donna by this time was jouncing over the desert highway on her way to Hollywood, terrified both at the new work assigned to her, and at the necessity of leaving her child for a whole day in the charge of a stranger.

When Gideon stopped at the garage that morning, ostensibly for gas, and reported on the evening, including the fact that Westwind had remained with his mother, Stan took a dim view of this arrangement.

"But Donna can't take care of him there," he expostulated. "You know, they send 'em out to convert the heathen."

"They have a nursery—" Gideon started to explain.

"Nursery, my foot!" exclaimed Stan. "Why, this garage is more Westy's speed than a nursery."

After Gideon had driven off, Stan yelled to Tom, "Get the boy to take over. I gotta go!"

"Where?"

299

"Never mind—just something I've got to do. Ought to be back this afternoon."

Tom shrugged, spread out his hands, and jerked his thumb, indicating to the boy that he was to tend the pumps. "Don't know what bee he's got in his bonnet," Tom muttered to himself, "but like as not it's the Lord. You never can tell these days!"

Without delay, Stan headed over freeways and then the twisting desert highway until he reached the dilapidated set of buildings which were the commune's headquarters. No meeting was in progress, and no one was in sight, so Stan wandered about until he found a girl whose face looked amenable, and asked the way to the nursery.

"Why, over there," she said, waving to a low frame building. "Alice is in charge."

Stan mumbled thanks and went into the big, bare room inhabited by five children. One or two were gravely playing with toys, their solemn little faces immobile. Two others were engaged in some sort of altercation. The fifth, Westwind, was sitting in the middle of the floor, giving himself over, for the first time in his life, to sobs and screams. At first Stan hardly recognized him, never having seen him cry. Vainly did the girl acting as nurse tempt him with toys and cookies, and with false promises that he would soon see Mama. Nothing availed.

"Hey, Westwind!" said Stan. At first the child did not hear him, and Stan knelt on the floor in front of him and said louder, "Hey, Westy! Look, it's me!"

Recognizing through his screams a familiar voice, Westwind opened his eyes, saw Stan, got up and leaped into his arms, and clung around his neck like a limpet, sobbing into his collar, "Go home—home!"

300

"Okay," said Stan, "okay, Westy!" He patted him soothingly on the back. "Shut up. We're going home!" And he stared at Alice as if challenging her to say something. Holding Westwind, he arose from the floor, and simply walked out. Nobody paid any attention as he strode through the yard and into the car. Everyone who saw naturally thought that someone else had given permission, assuming that this was his own child whom he was so competently carrying.

When Donna returned to the commune that evening, she was informed that her husband had come for Westwind and taken him home. She called Bob immediately.

"But honey," Bob said, bewildered. "He's not here. I didn't take him."

"Oh, my God!" said Donna, bursting into tears.

"Yes, Lord, help us, right now!" Bob said, turning her exclamation into a prayer. Then calmly, "Donna, go and get a description of the man who came for Westwind. I'll hold on here."

When she returned to the phone and relayed the information, Bob shouted, "It's Stan! He'll be at the garage. Don't worry, I'll get him. And then I'm coming out to get you. See you later." And Bob darted for his car. With all speed, he drove back to town and into the garage lot. Sure enough, there was tiny Westwind, smudged and contented, polishing a car with all his might. "Oh, thank God!" sighed Bob, as he strode forward and swept Westwind into his arms.

The child looked at him sternly. "Westwind shine car!" he proclaimed. Then he squirmed away from his father, to continue work. Stan stood by, grinning sheepishly.

"Yup, I took him," he said. "I tried to call, but no one was home. Figured I'd get you this evening when you got home from work."

"They—think he was kidnapped," said Bob, laughing but almost weeping with relief.

"Guess he was," said Stan gruffly. "I just marched in, and found him sitting on the floor crying and screaming. You never heard such a racket. So I just took him! After all," and he tousled the little boy's hair as he spoke, "Uncle Stan needs him around here. He's a big help!"

Westwind looked at his father with a lowering expression and said decisively, "No go back!"

"Westwind go home right now," said Bob, waving to Stan as he got in his car and headed for home.

Bob deposited Westwind with minimal explanation, and headed out to the Jesus commune with fire in his eye. When he got there, Donna was waiting for him, all smiles.

"We prayed, and it's in His will for me to go home and be a good Christian wife and mother."

"Well, hallelujah!" Bob shouted. "Come on, honey, let's go."

Thus Donna had returned to the family, to everybody's delight excepting possibly Josie's. She looked at Donna askance, as though she could not believe what she saw, and indeed it was almost incredible, because Donna was a new person. She was alert; she smiled; she took an in-interest in everything; she laughed or sang gospel songs as she helped Susan wash dishes. She went eagerly with Bob to the garage apartment which Angela Pritchard had offered them, and planned what they needed to set up housekeeping there. "We can do it now," she said. "We really can do it now!"

Chapter Twenty-Three

"Hey, what's the idea of this confirmation deal you've been talking about?" asked Stan as he and Gideon chatted one afternoon in the garage workshop.

"Talking about—where?"

"You know, in that class about the Holy Spirit you had me coming to."

"Well, you see," began Gideon, struggling with the difficulties of explaining to an outsider the intricacies of church rituals, "when our babies are baptized, their sponsors promise for them that they will accept Jesus Christ as their Lord and Savior, and fight manfully under His banner against the world, the flesh, and the devil—"

"You mean, without asking them?"

"You can't very well ask them when they're babies," said Gideon, laughing.

"Lousy trick, if you ask me," observed Stan.

"So in the confirmation service we ask the Holy Spirit to come into them and make it all come true—you know, what their sponsors promised for them at their baptism."

"I still say it's a lousy trick."

"Oh no, it's not," proclaimed Gideon with extra emphasis, because he had sometimes furtively thought somewhat along Stan's lines. "Now, you see, they have a chance to decide whether they want to go through with it or not."

"And does the Holy Spirit come?" asked Stan dubiously.

"Oh, yes!"

"How do you know? Do they speak in tongues?"

"Good heavens, no!" cried Gideon hastily, bowled over by a mental picture of the class bursting forth in tongues at the confirmation service, and the bishop fainting in the chancel.

"Why not?"

"Stan, I taught you in the class—the gift of tongues isn't the only gift of the Spirit! Don't you remember? There's prophecy, faith, miracles—"

"Okay, do they prophesy? Do they do miracles?"

Gideon could only shake his head.

"Wouldn't it be something if they did?" said Stan wistfully. "You know, if people on crutches could jump up and walk—like when Jesus was here."

"Yes, it would be something," agreed Gideon.

"Well then, why doesn't it happen? What are you praying for anyway? When you talk about the promises made at their baptism coming true, what do you mean? Are you really praying for the Holy Spirit to come into those people?"

Gideon shifted uneasily. "Well, yes," he replied. "This is what the bishop prays when he puts his hands on each one: 'Defend, oh Lord, this thy child with thy heavenly grace, that he may continue thine forever; and daily increase in thy Holy Spirit more and more, until he come into thy everlasting kingdom.' "

"But he doesn't exactly say to pour out the Holy Spirit upon them. He talks about grace, but nobody knows what grace means—right?"

"Look it up in the dictionary," replied Gideon dryly. "One definition is that grace is a free gift of God to man for his regeneration or sanctification. Isn't that just about how Jesus described the Holy Spirit?"

"Maybe, but then why doesn't anything happen? You know, when the kids pray out at the coffeehouse, things happen!"

"I know," admitted Gideon, remembering those same kids singing high and sweet upon the mountaintops. Gideon mopped his brow. "Well, what would you do if you were in my place?" he asked in all humility.

"I'd teach that class to expect a miracle," said Stan, adding, "I mean, right when they're confirmed."

"But what if the bishop doesn't approve?"

"Ask him ahead of time," said Stan. "Don't spring it on him—ask him!"

"And if he says no—?"

"He can't say no! Didn't you tell me it's all written down in that prayer book of yours? I don't know why you wise guys make a thing so complicated when it's really simple! And, just to make sure you don't cop out," Stan went on, "Ellie and I will be there to check you out."

"You mean, you and Ellie—"

"Well, don't look so surprised. I mean, we both love Jesus and have the Holy Spirit, don't we?" Gideon nodded. "Well, it was only a matter of stopping arguing long enough to pray together, with each one being ready and willing to be wrong. So guess what?"

"Tell me," laughed Gideon.

"Well, we're going to wait for Him to come, all right, but He wants us to wait together. So pretty soon, you're going to have yourself another wedding to perform, Rev!"

"Amen!" said Gideon.

As things worked out, Gideon did not ask the bishop quite according to that plan. The next Sunday after church, he took Susan and David—Josie preferring to remain at home with Donna and Bob—and drove to Lancaster for a few days' rest in the desert. David spent happy hours in the swimming pool, but awoke on Monday feverish and hoarse, so Susan decreed that they must return home at once. That evening, Gideon betook himself to his study at the church, looking forward to some quiet reading since no one knew he was back in town. Sighing a bit, for he had really looked forward to the little vacation, he entered the parish house. But before he reached his study, he paused, hearing voices from the sacristy just beyond his study where the vestry were wont to meet to transact the affairs of the church.

"If we were any other kind of church," said a deep male voice, "there'd be no problem. We'd just call a congregational meeting and vote him out."

Gideon paused in his stride. "Yes," responded another voice which Gideon recognized as the junior warden's, "but in our church no one but the bishop has authority to get rid of a rector."

Gideon froze where he stood. He was not intentionally eavesdropping. He was simply too stunned for the moment to move.

"You'd hardly know now that this was an Episcopal church," growled another voice. "Jews all over the place. Why, they not only use the building on Saturdays, but some of them even sneak into church!"

306

"And the rector's so thick with them, he went to a Bar Mitzvah!" So spoke Reginald Crabtree. "However, technically the use of the buildings is his concern, so we have no leg to stand on there. But all this Holy Spirit business— We're supposed to be Episcopalians, not Pentecostals!"

"May I ask," inquired a milder voice, "on what grounds you accuse him of trying to make us Pentecostals?"

"That class of his," replied Mr. Crabtree. "He's teaching about the gifts of the Spirit. First thing you know, he'll have us all speaking in tongues."

Loud laughter followed this remark, in the midst of which Gideon stole away to his car and drove off. He might have thrown open the door and burst in upon them crying, "Aha!" like a scene in a bad opera, but this he simply could not do. Nevertheless, slow anger rose in him as he reflected that he had stumbled onto a vestry meeting deliberately called when they expected the rector to be out of town. They had no right to do this, for the authority to summon a vestry meeting was the rector's alone. Gideon drove aimlessly up one street and down another being too angry to go home and face his family.

About this, he could not pray the prayer of faith, thought Gideon. Some other time, maybe, he would open the doors so wide that the Holy Spirit might come in, but not now. The situation was loaded against him, since apparently the congregation wanted everything just as it had always been. No eruption of an unknown power must disturb the gentle flow of their contentment with themselves, with God, and with the world.

"No!" exploded Gideon aloud, driving down the freeway at a speed that somehow quieted the whirling of his mind. Even so, he would pray with all his heart for the Holy

Spirit to come into the confirmation service and show forth any signs of His presence that the Lord desired. "Let those kids speak in tongues at the top of their lungs," he muttered somewhat less than devotionally. "See if I care! After all, there are plenty of groups who worship the Lord in their own way. Maybe I'm supposed to leave the church and set myself up as some sort of new prophet—"

"Slow down!" said a voice near his right shoulder.

Startled, Gideon seemed to hear the voice so clearly that he turned to the empty seat beside him and said, "Okay." Then he took the next turnoff and headed toward home, resolved to go on praying for the Holy Spirit to be manifest at the confirmation service, and to implement the prayer by believing that it would be so, and giving thanks and praise to God for it.

"Thank You, Lord," he said aloud. "Lord, I thank You and praise Your name for the glory of Your Holy Spirit coming upon us. Oh Lord, I praise and thank You!"

The joy of the Lord came upon him increasingly as he murmured these words of praise, so much so that he was almost shouting as he drove along, praising the Lord in whatever words came into his mind, whether he understood them or not. There must be power in the very act of praise, thought Gideon, for little by little, as he continued to speak aloud in praise of God, a great peace filled his mind, until he knew that the whole confirmation service was in God's hands, and that the Holy Spirit would do exactly what God knew to be best. "All right, Lord," he said aloud as he got near home. "You know what is best, so just tell me what You want me to do now."

The Lord told him, by reminding him of his conversation with Stan, who had said, "Don't spring it on the bishop; ask him."

Gideon, therefore, taking that as God's answer to his question, made an appointment and went to see the bishop. "I want to consult you about the confirmation service next week," he began.

Bishop Updyke raised his eyebrows in mild surprise. "It will follow the regular order of confirmation services, won't it?" he asked from the depths of his big leather chair.

"Well, I'm not so sure," said Gideon, leaning forward. "You see, I've been praying for the Holy Spirit to really come upon the people as you lay on hands, and—"

The bishop raised his bushy eyebrows and gazed at the rector. "Isn't that the general idea of confirmation?" he inquired.

Gideon finally blurted out, "Yes, but what would you do, Bishop, if someone were to speak in tongues?"

"I would consider it unfortunate," said the bishop slowly, "and I do hope you are not planning to turn your congregation into Pentecostals. Some of them," he added, "are already wondering whether you are just a little—" and he touched his own head significantly.

"Do you think so?" asked Gideon abruptly.

"No, and I tell them so."

"You've been a real father in God to me," said Gideon warmly.

"Gideon," said Bishop Updyke softly, "I love you in the Lord, and I don't want to see you bringing any more trouble on yourself."

"You've been more than good to me," said Gideon. "You stood up for me at a time of deep trouble, and I certainly don't want to make problems for you or the church. I assure you I'm only praying that the Holy Spirit will really come at that confirmation service, but of course, if He does—"

The bishop smiled somewhat hesitantly. "Well," he said slowly, "I certainly can't object to that, can I?"

"The whole class is praying the same way," confessed Gideon.

"Are you warning me that anything may happen?"

"Well—yes!"

"Then we'll just have to see what happens when the time comes," smiled the bishop, rising to conclude the interview.

The day of the bishop's visit to Trinity Church dawned bright and clear, and as the time came for the service, the sun was still bright in the sky while afternoon shadows began to creep over the hills. Gideon stood on the walk outside the church with his bishop, at the end of the long procession led by an acolyte carrying the cross and including all the choirs, from little children to bearded men who rolled forth the bass of the glorious processional hymn, "Hail, Festal Day!" Its intricate melodies were sung partly in unison and partly by a black woman soloist whose voice was wonderfully rich and mellow. Up the main aisle they went, parted at the chancel steps, went down the side aisles, and again up the main aisle until the whole church was permeated with the glory of the music, and somehow also with the majestic presence of the Lord.

The choir took their places and the service began, a service neither brief nor simple, for the church fathers who put it together, thought Gideon grimly, apparently sought to buttress the faith with a strong wall of circumlocution. This was a bit discouraging, yet Gideon persisted in praying with all his heart for the power of the Holy Spirit to come overwhelmingly upon them all.

And then, most gently, the Holy Spirit of the Lord entered, not in sound but in light! The lights in the church began to change, to take on another quality, but in no ordinary way controlled by switches. An elusive brightness filled the church, alive, fluctuating, as though God were breathing in and out of His temple in the same way as at the beginning of creation when He said, "Let there be light!" No tongues of fire were visible upon the heads of those being confirmed as the bishop laid on hands and prayed for each one, but as they returned to their places in the front pews, the lantern of a new joy was lit in their eyes, not fading but rather increasing as the service continued.

When all of the class had gone back to their seats, the bishop faced the congregation but spoke directly to those whom he had just confirmed. "You are entering upon a new life," he said slowly, and Gideon sensed the words were unplanned. "But don't be afraid, because a new power which is part of your holy inheritance has now come into you. It has been yours since the beginning, because God made you both a child of man, and also a child of God. Now you will discover what it means to be not only a human being but also a spiritual being, eternal in the heavens. That's what immortality means—" So the bishop continued, as Gideon listened in amazement. He had never heard Bishop Updyke talk like this. He tried to compose his face, so that it would not break into an unseemly smile as the bishop went on.

"So now, this new one of you, your spiritual being, has just been born. This is the birthday of the real person you are meant to be. You know, when a human baby is born, we look at it, tiny and yet whole and complete, and wonder what it will be when it is fully grown. So I am looking at you now, newborn souls in Christ's heavenly kingdom, and I wonder what you are going to be as you grow in grace and power. You will each serve Him differently to bring the Kingdom of Heaven on earth—some of you in ways that people will call holy, and others that are just as holy, though people may not recognize them as such—bringing forth the beauty of the earth, bringing forth sound industry and honest prosperity, raising children to grow in the worship and love of God. So I look at you now, wondering with great joy, and as I wonder, I praise His name!"

The bishop concluded and turned to the altar, remaining there silently for several minutes while echoes of his words continued, with other words which sounded softly—little murmurings, some understood by those close at hand, some not understood save possibly by a great company of angels, filling every corner of the church.

Indeed, some said afterward that they could almost see, and certainly could feel, the presence of angels, while others detected a holy fragrance, more subtle than incense. Gideon himself sensed this holy fragrance, and a verse from Revelation flashed into his mind: "And I beheld an angel holding in his hands a vial full of odors which are the prayers of the saints." Throughout the church was felt a surge of power, life, and joy, and as the choirs processed down the aisle singing the final hymn, "Now thank we all our God, with hearts and soul and voices—" the people raised their voices and sang with all their hearts.

As the congregation filed out, shaking hands with both the bishop and rector, many overwhelmed with emotion, there came among them a small, swarthy man who grasped Gideon's hand eagerly, tears of joy in his eyes. "Mr. Bernstein!" exclaimed Gideon. "We are so happy to have you with us!"

312

"And our rabbi, he came also," beamed Mr. Bernstein, and with him, too, Gideon shook hands, rejoicing that he could come to a Christian church, joining his praise with theirs to the God who made them all.

"I like the special lighting you have on the altar—around the cross," the rabbi commented.

"I don't know what you mean," said Gideon. "We have no special lighting."

"But I saw a light, coming and going. Sometimes the whole end of the church was filled with light, so that I could hardly see the cross at all."

"What you saw," said Gideon gently, "was directly from God."

"Ah!" breathed the old rabbi, comprehending. "The shekinah glory! To think that I should see it here with my own eyes!"

"Maybe your presence with us had a part in its shining—upon this altar," murmured Gideon.

Ellie and Stan came next, each taking one of his hands, and asking for a wedding service as much like this service they'd just witnessed as possible. Even Josie beamed upon her father in passing, and whispered, "Hey, Dad, you needn't worry about me any more. I got it, too!"

Following her came the senior warden. "Gideon!" he said. He took Gideon's hand, and simply held it tightly in both of his. "Gideon, do you know what happened in there?"

"I know that the Lord was there in great majesty," said Gideon, "and what He chose to do is beyond me—"

"Well—" tears filled Reginald Crabtree's eyes, "I'll just say this, Gideon. Don't leave us! Don't ever leave us, do you hear?"

Gideon nodded, tears filling his own eyes.

When the last lingering parishioner had gone, the bishop and rector entered the sacristy to disrobe.

"You know, a funny thing happened," said the bishop.

"What was that?" asked Gideon, pulling his surplice over his head and hanging it neatly in the closet, lest Angela scold him for untidiness.

"Well," said the bishop, folding his own vestments and packing them to take home, "first of all, what I said to that class, I've never said before, in seventeen years. Something just came over me. And then, just as I finished, I had a queer feeling around my lips, sort of a drawing, as though they wanted to talk. But—the words that came into my mind weren't out of the prayer book. In fact, they didn't seem to be English at all. They might have been Hebrew that I learned in seminary. You don't suppose—?"

"Yes, I do!" cried Gideon.